Gerber knew th

He was the Chinese officer they had been chasing for a year. The one who had marked them for death more than once. The man who had failed each time he ran into Gerber's Special Forces squad.

He was shorter than Gerber had expected. In his mind the officer had taken on gigantic proportions. The man stepped into the room and pointed the pistol at the American's head.

"If I had any intelligence at all," the Oriental said, "I would shoot you dead this minute."

For a moment everything seemed to stand still. Gerber was afraid to move. He felt closer to death than he ever had before because he knew that the officer was right. The quickest, smartest thing to do was shoot him. If the situation was reversed, Gerber doubted he would hesitate.

Instead of shooting him, the officer walked toward the desk. He sat behind it, then placed his pistol on the top. Indicating the chairs opposite, he spoke again.

"Sit down, Captain Gerber, and let us talk about Vietnam, the war and your death."

Also available by Eric Helm:

VIETNAM: GROUND ZERO
P.O.W.

VIETNAM: GROUND ZERO
UNCONFIRMED KILL

ERIC HELM

A GOLD EAGLE BOOK FROM
WORLDWIDE

TORONTO • NEW YORK • LONDON • PARIS
AMSTERDAM • STOCKHOLM • HAMBURG
ATHENS • MILAN • TOKYO • SYDNEY

First edition December 1986

ISBN 0-373-62703-3

Printed in Canada

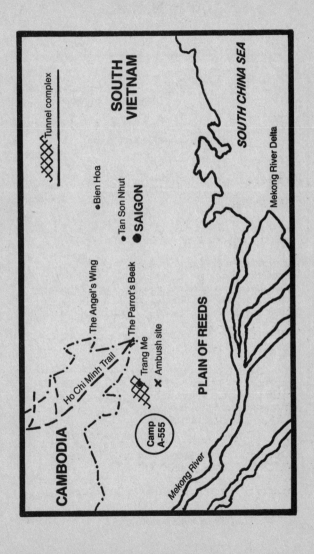

U.S. Special Forces Camp A-555
(Triple Nickel)

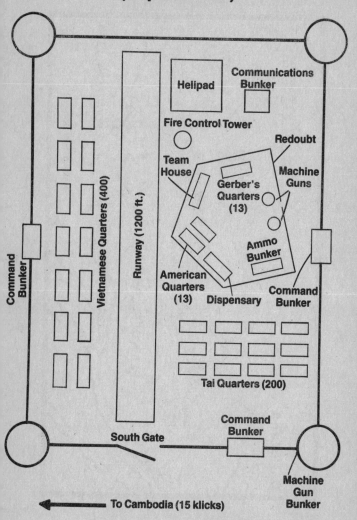

VIETNAM: GROUND ZERO

UNCONFIRMED KILL

PROLOGUE

THE VILLAGE OF TRANG ME, SOUTH OF THE ANGEL'S WING, WEST OF THE CAMBODIAN BORDER

U.S. Army Special Forces Sergeant First Class Ian McMillan crouched in a stand of bamboo and watched. He was looking for movement among the collection of mud hootches, fences of woven branches and broken-down water buffalo pens that made up the darkened village. Since he had scattered his patrol of twelve Vietnamese strikers in a loose defensive ring an hour earlier, a little after dusk, he had seen no movement and heard nothing unusual except for the rustle of leaves and symphony of sound from nocturnal creatures.

The village, only a hundred meters ahead of him, was quiet as the few residents slept. There shouldn't be any activity until almost dawn, he thought. Then the mama-sans would awaken, light the cooking fires and begin to prepare the traditional breakfast of rice cakes and fish heads.

McMillan rose slowly, taking the weight off his left leg, which had gone to sleep. He flexed his knee, trying to restore the circulation in his leg, and as he drew a crooked index finger across his forehead to wipe away the sweat, his palm grazed the three-day growth on his face. Then he slipped back down and relaxed, keeping his eyes focused on the Vietnamese hootches.

But he wasn't really seeing anything. His mind had glided back to his four-day, in-country R and R taken at the Special Forces compound in Nha Trang. He had had a choice of a couple of places, but Louise Denton had been in Nha Trang and she had been excited about the chance to see him again.

In fact, she had been so happy about the opportunity that she had promoted a jeep and met him at the airfield, anxious for the C-130 to land and taxi. Even before it had stopped moving, she drove out on the field while a master sergeant stood near the tower and screamed at her.

The spinning propellers threw swirls of red dust that blew toward the terminal building; then the troop doors opened and the passengers began deplaning. Denton positioned her jeep so that McMillan could not miss it, but when he failed to appear among the disembarking crowd, she was afraid, she had told him later, that she had misunderstood his instructions. He was the last one out.

As his feet hit the blistering PSP, he turned and yelled something up to the flight crew. Then, carrying his duffel bag in his left hand and with his M-14 slung over his shoulder, he held up his right hand to his eyes to shade them from the bright, early-afternoon sun.

Denton roared up, skidded to a stop in a tiny cloud of dust and yelled, "Hey, soldier, want a ride?"

McMillan looked around, pretending that she was talking to someone behind him. Seeing no one there, he pointed to himself and said, "You talking to me?"

"Yeah. I'm talking to you. You want a ride or not?"

He tossed his bag into the back of the jeep, shrugged his rifle from his shoulder to place it beside his duffel, climbed in the passenger's side and put a foot up on the dash. He turned to look at her and said, "Yeah. I want a ride."

Without another word she slammed the jeep into gear, missing first once and then grinding the gears loudly before she roared off the field. As she sped past the master sergeant, who tried to yell at her again, she flipped him the finger.

"You got to watch out for these sergeants," she shouted over the whine of the jeep's engine and the rush of the wind. "Think they run the army."

"Yeah," agreed McMillan.

Denton drove off the base and after a few minutes they approached a run-down building. "I took the liberty of getting you a room in the Jockey Club." She indicated the hotel with a nod of her head. "Lots of Green Berets hang out around here. I don't like it much, but it'll give us some privacy, and I figured we could put up with it for a few days."

Before he got out of the jeep, McMillan stared at the place. It was a relatively small building with a decided French flavor. The facade was flat with dozens of ornate windows, many of them without screens and nearly all of them open. The old stone was weathered to a dirty brown that contrasted with the rich tans of the beach behind the building. Dark streaks ran down the front where the monsoons had washed pitch from the roof. On the ground floor a porch led into the building.

McMillan could see a couple of Vietnamese girls in exceptionally short skirts lounging around in what passed for a lobby. He could tell from their attire that they were hookers. He shifted his gaze to Denton, whose fatigue shirt had its sleeves and a couple of buttons missing. She was wearing shorts cut off from fatigue pants and scuffed, gray combat boots. McMillan found her much more sexy in her ragged, sweat-stained clothes than he did the Vietnamese in their short skirts and skintight blouses.

"This may not be such a great idea," he said.

She turned off the engine. "Why not? We won't be bothered here."

"Looks like a pretty seedy joint."

"Well, I understand that it has hot and cold running water and electric lights that work most of the time. And you can get a passable meal."

McMillan looked at the hotel again and said, "Okay, if you don't have a problem with it, I guess I don't, either."

"Why don't you get checked in officially and meet me on the beach?"

It took McMillan fifteen minutes to get a key, retrieve his luggage and rifle from the jeep, then climb the stairs to the room. It was small, and made even more so by a double bed that occupied its center. Four large posts rose from each corner of the bed, stopping just short of the ceiling; they had been designed to hold the thick OD mosquito netting. An oak wardrobe with a hole punched in one of the doors, maybe by some drunken GI,

McMillan figured, was jammed between the shaded windows, which were closed and made the room extremely hot and dark. A fan suspended from the ceiling turned lazily but did little to dissipate the heat. McMillan wondered why the Jockey Club's operators kept these windows closed, since there wasn't anything worth stealing. The bathroom contained a toilet with its tank resting on top of a pipe that traveled up the wall. From the right side of the reservoir hung a pull chain with a large ring attached to it. Along another wall stood a rust-stained tub on clawed feet, and there was no sign of towels or toilet paper.

McMillan dumped his duffel on the bed and set his M-14 in a corner so that it was almost out of sight. Then he moved back to the bed and opened the bag. He rummaged through it until he found some of his civilian clothes and changed into his beach wear. Finally he shut the bag and stored it on the bottom shelf of the wardrobe. McMillan had thought about taking a quick shower, but he wanted to see Louise too badly to wait any longer. He left the hotel wearing some swimming trunks he had bought during one of his trips to Saigon, a boonie hat to keep the sun out of his eyes and rubber shower shoes to protect his feet from the hot sand.

Denton was sitting on an OD towel on the beach, watching the surf. Wordlessly McMillan dropped beside her and began to study her carefully.

Her tan had darkened a little since he had seen her before Nha Trang. Her red hair, damp and slightly curly from sweat, now hung below her shoulders, and beads of perspiration glistened on her upper lip. She had kicked off her boots, which she had obviously worn because she had to drive a jeep.

Squinting, McMillan shifted his gaze to the calm waters of the South China Sea and the azure sky above it. There were some storm clouds building to the east, but they would probably stay out to sea. A couple of birds windmilled about high overhead.

"When do you have to go back on duty?" he asked.

"Not until after you leave," she said without looking at him.

"How in the hell did you manage that?"

She turned and smiled. "Major Acalotto seemed sympathetic to my needs. Said to take a few days off and have a good time. Now how long are you going to keep me on this beach?"

McMillan reached over and took her hand. "I've seen enough water to last me for a couple of days. Let's go inside."

"I thought you'd never ask," she said, getting to her feet.

Once in the room, Denton moved to the window, pulled up the shades and then the window itself. She turned and began unbuttoning her shirt. "We should get a little breeze off the ocean."

McMillan was still near the door. He leaned against the wall and watched as she slowly stripped. She did it casually, but managed to put a lot of suggestion into it. When she was down to brief panties, he felt like applauding.

"Well," she said, moving to the bed, "You going to stand there all day?" She raised an eyebrow in question and then, watching his face, slowly rolled the panties down her thighs.

McMillan moved across the floor and took her in his arms. She had straightened with her panties still at her knees. She moved her legs, and they fell to the floor. McMillan lifted her and deposited her on the bed. As he crawled on with her, she reached up and slipped her thumbs into the waistband of his trunks. When he was free of them, he moved closer to her, leaned down and fiercely kissed her hungry mouth.

"I'm sorry about this," she whispered, "but I've missed you. I've wanted you."

"Nothing to be sorry about," he said, moving closer. "Nothing at all."

A sudden crashing in the bush nearby, as if some small night animal had sensed a human presence, brought McMillan out his reverie. He blinked a couple of times to clear the perspiration from his eyes, then removed the canvas flap that covered the luminescent dial of his watch to check the time.

It was twenty minutes before sunup, and McMillan was beginning to worry. He felt that something was wrong in the village but didn't know exactly what it was. It seemed as if the settlement were deserted, that the residents had abandoned it during the night, although that couldn't be true. He had seen the villagers the night before, and no one had stirred since sunset.

He was loathe to dismiss his thoughts about Louise and his leave in Nha Trang but knew that he had better concentrate on his surroundings. It wasn't a good idea to let thoughts of women or home or anything else intrude while on patrol. In fact, he shouldn't have let his mind wander as far as it had.

Still, something gnawed at his gut. Without thinking about it, he slipped his combat knife from its sheath. He couldn't explain that move, either, because the M-16 he held was the deadlier of the two weapons. But it was also noisier.

He turned his head slowly so that he could scan the jungle around him. He strained his eyes as he peered between the broad leaves of the bushes and among the teak, mahogany and palm trees, trying to see anything as the sky began to brighten and the ground changed from black to light grays enshrouded by early-morning mists. He thought he detected a slight movement, but with a steady breeze stirring the bush, he couldn't be sure. Suddenly he was uncomfortable. Not with the humidity of the Vietnamese jungle or the heat of the early morning, but the feeling that there were enemy soldiers nearby.

Without warning, a VC dropped onto McMillan's back and struggled to shove a knife into his chest, but the Special Forces sergeant was faster. He released his M-16, shrugged his shoulder, grabbing the man's wrist and flipping him to the ground. In the same motion McMillan's knife flashed, nearly severing the enemy's head in a splash of blood that stained his sleeve. Mc-Millan paused then, breathing hard, his heart hammering in his chest and the breath rasping in his throat.

A second VC leaped, but McMillan caught the movement out of the corner of his eye. He spun to meet his adversary, scrambling to his feet as he turned. He grabbed the man behind the neck and jerked him forward. The Vietcong's arms shot out straight, elbows locked and braced against McMillan's shoulders. The sergeant dropped to his knees, snagging his attacker's belt and yanking him forward.

The enemy soldier lost his balance and fell forward, impaling himself on McMillan's knife. He twisted the blade and forced it upward, slicing through his opponent's abdomen almost to the breastbone. The man shrieked, an errie sound in the morning stillness, and fell to his knees, grabbing at his stomach, trying to hold in his guts as they spilled out of the open wound. He pawed at them, his face turning pale as blood gushed from his belt to his thighs. He groaned low in his throat and fell forward onto the pile of steaming intestines.

McMillan sprang to his feet, staring at the back of the dead man's head, noticing the telltale stubble where the razor had cut the hair on his neck, which identified him as a VC soldier. He glanced at his blood-covered hand as a third VC came at him. The soldier leaped, slamming into McMillan and knocking him to his side.

A fourth VC, who had been crouched near the edge of the fight, slashed at McMillan when he fell. The swipe missed everything vital but cut McMillan on the upper arm, and the sudden pain, dulled by the adrenaline pumping through him, seemed to slow the action to a snail's pace. McMillan reached out with one hand to stop his fall and lost his knife as he hit the ground. As he tried to roll, he grabbed his M-16 and swung it up. But the VC stepped to the side of the barrel, snatching it and trying to wrench it free as he kicked at McMillan's crotch.

McMillan turned and took the blow on the thigh. He twisted and tried to rise so that he could get a clean shot at the enemy; but he felt a pressure in his back that blossomed into pain as a hot liquid splashed down his side. Ignoring the searing agony, he jerked the rifle to free it from the grasp of the VC, realizing that the weapon was his only chance of survival; however, the lightweight barrel bent under the strain. McMillan struggled to his feet, aware now that he was bleeding profusely. Light-headed, he swung the rifle around and pulled the trigger. Nothing happened.

Hearing movement behind him, McMillan whirled to face a new threat. He clubbed the man there with the useless rifle. The VC dropped to his knees, but before McMillan could turn again, he heard a shot. He was aware of fire in his side as if a white-hot poker had been jammed against his bare skin. There was a buzzing in his head, and he thought that his heart was going to burst.

Something hit him in the back again, the blow like a sledgehammer in the spine, and everything began to fade. He didn't realize that he was falling forward and didn't put out his hands to break the fall.

His last thought was of Louise and how upset she would be not to get another letter from him. He wanted her to know that it wasn't his fault. He wanted to shout something, a warning to the men with him, but didn't have the strength. As the blood pumped from his wound, he didn't know that he was dying.

1

**U.S. ARMY SPECIAL
FORCES CAMP A-555,
SOUTH OF THE
PARROT'S BEAK REGION
OF SOUTH VIETNAM**

The party being held in the team house at the Special Forces camp was rather subdued. The team house, a hootch that served as dayroom, mess hall and briefing room, was made of plywood, screen and sandbags, and topped by a corrugated tin roof. Tables with four chairs each were scattered around the dirty plywood floor. An old, unreliable refrigerator stood next to the hootch's entrance, and a bar that separated the kitchen from the rest of the hootch dominated one side of the room.

Each of the men not on duty held a can of beer, and there were empties already stacked high on one of the tables. No one talked much and no one laughed at all. It was too soon after they had freed their friends from a POW camp, recovered the body of another of their friends after he had been forced to call artillery in on himself, and too soon after a series of ambushes had been directed at them.

Robin Morrow, the journalist that a press-loving general in Saigon had saddled them with, sat by herself, one can in her hand and another on the table in front of her. Blond hair hung to her shoulder blades and was brushed into bangs that tickled her eyebrows. She was tall and slender with green eyes, straight even teeth and an infectious grin. But right now she was as solemn as the others because she had been on the camp long enough to get to know each of the men.

Captain MacKenzie K. Gerber, wearing his last clean set of jungle fatigues, the sweat stains just beginning to appear under his arms and in the center of his back, sat across the room, as far away from her as possible. He cast an occasional glance in her direction, marveling at her resilience. On the whole she seemed to be almost untroubled by the experiences of the past month or so. He, on the other hand, felt responsible for everything that had happened. It had been his decision that had put the plans in motion and had caused the deaths and the captures of some of the team members.

As Gerber watched, Lieutenant Jonathan Bromhead, the team's executive officer, entered. Bromhead was a tall, thin kid who still retained his freckle-faced look of innocence, even after completing nearly a year's tour in Vietnam. He studied the silent group briefly, then moved directly to the beer tub. He fished one out of the cold water and then ambled toward Robin Morrow. He crouched in front of her so that he could look up into her eyes.

"How's it going?"

She smiled and shrugged. "Kind of a dead party."

"Yeah, I see what you mean," he answered, looking around. He reached out and touched her bare knee. "You okay?"

"Johnny, you don't have to be so concerned. I'm not going to break," she nearly snapped. "Okay?"

Without a word he reached for the church key that she wore on a chain around her neck. She bowed her head slightly so that he could open his beer.

"Okay, so what are we going to do to liven up this group?"

Robin was trying to watch Gerber without his knowing it. She let her eyes drop back to Bromhead. "I don't know. Maybe some music?"

"Yeah! Music. I'll go get my radio and see if AFVN is still on the air. Who knows what we might hear."

"Good idea." She watched the young Green Beret officer almost run from the team house in his enthusiasm. She thought he was a good-looking young man and could tell that he liked her. She wished that she could return his affection, but there was something about him. Maybe it was just his youth. He seemed to exude self-confidence, sure that he had the answers to everything but that no one would listen to him. There were only two sides to an issue in Bromhead's mind. He saw no shades of gray.

As Bromhead disappeared, Morrow got up and slowly walked across the floor. She stopped and said something to Fetterman, the diminutive team sergeant who alternately claimed an Aztec heritage and a Blackfoot Sioux ancestry, then continued until she was standing in front of Gerber. Her bare midriff, where the tails of her khaki shirt were knotted, was right in front of his face. He pretended that he hadn't seen her coming.

Without looking up, Gerber said, "When did you want to go back to Saigon?"

Her immediate impulse was to dump the beer on his head, but she reined in her anger. She jerked a chair away from the table and flopped into it.

"How long are you going to act like this?" she demanded.

"Act like what?" he said, genuinely confused.

"Oh, never mind. I suppose you all will eventually learn that you can still talk to me. I don't hold any of you responsible for what happened. I'm the one who demanded that I be allowed to ride with the convoy. I'm the one who wanted to watch as the villagers built the school. If it hadn't been for that, I would never have been in the middle of that ambush. Hell, if it's anyone's fault, it's mine. I wouldn't leave when I had the chance and then insisted on riding with the trucks rather than fly in with the helicopters."

Before Gerber had a chance to reply, Bocker entered. He was the team's communications sergeant and spent most of his time in the heavily sandbagged commo bunker that held the radios, field phones that tied into the network out of Saigon, and the tactical situation maps. He held up an envelope so that Gerber could see it and dodged around the others.

"Got the rest of the mail over at the commo bunker," Bocker said. "Afternoon chopper brought it in a while ago. This one looked official. I think it's the one you've been waiting for."

"Where'd Johnny go?" Gerber directed the question to Morrow.

"Went to find his radio to see if we couldn't liven up this group. God, I've never seen a deader bunch. Everyone just sitting around swilling beer as fast as they can." She added, "Well, I'll get even. As soon as the music starts, Mack, I expect you to dance with me."

He was about to tell her that he couldn't and then had a better idea. "You'll owe the first dance to Captain Bromhead." Gerber nodded and raised his voice to include the others. "I've just received confirmation of Johnny's promotion to captain."

"He doesn't know?" asked Morrow.

"He knows it's coming, but he doesn't know when."

"All right." She clapped her hands and rubbed them together. "Now we've got something to celebrate."

Gerber suddenly saw the advantage. The party had seemed like a good idea, but no one was really in a festive mood. Too much had happened. But now, with everyone trying to make Bromhead feel good about his promotion, they would loosen up. Maybe with luck they would be so busy trying to make sure Bromhead had a good time that they would forget everything themselves. Maybe it would work out.

"No one say anything when he returns. We'll kind of spring it on him," ordered Gerber.

Fetterman nodded his approval of the announcement. "The lieutenant's a good man. He deserves it."

"Make that the captain," Gerber reminded him.

"Of course," said Fetterman, grinning. "And of course, now has to pay for all this."

"Sully," said Gerber, addressing his senior demolitions expert, Staff Sergeant Sully Smith, "hotfoot it over to my hootch and see if you can find that bottle of Beam's I have stashed away. This seems like a good time to break it open."

"Right, Captain." Smith slid to a halt near the door. "Say, you wouldn't want some fireworks for the celebration, would you?"

At first Gerber was going to point out that a series of explosions on a military base in Vietnam might confuse some of those not in on the celebration but then decided that he had to let the reins go. Anything to break the mood.

"Just what do you have in mind, Sully?"

"Nothing too spectacular, sir. Maybe a couple of star cluster flares, a parachute flare or two, some tracers and three or four willie petes from the mortars."

"Arrange it," Gerber said. He smiled and added, "But don't use too much of the camp's ordnance. And as a courtesy let Captain Minh in on the gag."

For a spontaneous celebration, it was coordinated beautifully. Smith got back with the Beam's before Bromhead returned with the radio. As soon as the sergeant dropped off the booze, he ran out again.

Bromhead noticed that something had changed during the few minutes he had been gone. The moment he entered, he help up a package that had arrived on the mail chopper. He shouted over the noise that was bubbling around him, "You're not going to believe this." When no one noticed him, he yelled again, "You're not going to believe this!"

Bromhead held up a plastic bag, waving it like a banner. "My folks finally came through. I got the spark plugs for the boat."

"What boat?" asked Fetterman, momentarily forgetting the speedboat they had stolen a couple of months earlier, which now rested at the bottom of the Mekong River.

"Our patrol boat. It would be great, if we still had it."

He tossed the bag of spark plugs onto the table and crouched to plug in the radio, then turn it on. Almost before he could get back to his feet, Morrow was beside him asking if he wanted to dance.

The last thing he wanted was to be the center of attention. But he wanted an excuse to hold Morrow so he pretended that they were alone.

As the music ended, Gerber walked up to him and said, "Let's step outside for a minute."

Bromhead didn't know what to make of the order but followed anyway. He noticed that the rest of the Special Forces men were also leaving the team house. When the last of them was standing in the fading light of the evening sun, there was a pop to the right followed by six others. Overhead, a green star cluster flare exploded. Even before it burned out, a red one burst, followed closely by more red and green so that it seemed that the heavens had broken into plumes of color.

Then a single M-60 opened fire, the red tracers stitching the sky. It was joined by a second and a third, the rounds crisscrossing upward. M-16s, apparently loaded only with tracers, joined in until it looked as if the whole east section of the camp was shooting, a crimson waterfall climbing upward instead of cascading to the ground. From the corners came the hammering of the .50-caliber machine guns, their tracers defining the edges of the waterfall.

From the mortar pits came the unmistakable pop of the weapons firing. Moments later white phosphorus explosions dotted the horizon, the brilliant flashes of fire splintering into flaming debris that rained into the rice fields.

When the parachute flares, followed by more red tracers from the .50-cals, exploded, Bromhead said, "What's all this?"

"You haven't figured it out?"

"No, sir."

Gerber unfolded the paper he had received earlier. "Got this in the mail, *Captain*."

"Cap— It came? It really came?"

Fetterman, who had had the presence of mind to carry the bottle of Beam's outside, opened it and said, "A celebration drink?"

Bromhead grasped the bottle, drank from it, then handed it to Gerber, who followed suit. When everyone, including Morrow, had taken a swig, the bottle was returned to Bromhead, who took a final swallow, emptying it.

"God, that's smooth," he said.

At that moment the heavens seemed to open up again. Gerber knew that Sully had given the order to start the fireworks, which were purchased in Saigon weeks earlier. Giant bursts of color ranging from deep red to golden yellow to emerald green exploded over the camp, lighting it in flickering, multihued, dancing glows. For nearly five minutes the sky exploded into a riot of color.

"Now for the bad news." Gerber turned to watch more of the flares and tracers leap skyward as the last of the fireworks burned out. "With your promotion will come a new duty assignment. You'll probably receive orders within the next few days to a week."

"Well, sir—" Bromhead grinned despite himself "—I was afraid of that, but I guess I must continue upward."

"Hardly a speech about missing old friends and mixed emotions," said Fetterman.

"Yeah, don't get all mushy on us, Lieuten—ah, Captain," said Anderson.

Morrow edged closer to Bromhead and took his hand. "Congratulations, Captain. You deserve it."

"Don't I get a kiss?"

"Of course." She got up on her tiptoes and kissed him, forcing her tongue into his mouth.

Bromhead was pleasantly surprised and responded with enthusiasm while the team stood around, at first watching in silence and then with wild cheers.

Before the shouts ended, Smith ran over. "That about exhausts the show," he reported.

Gerber, ignoring both Morrow and Bromhead, said, "Let's get back inside."

"Ah, in a moment, Captain," said Sully. "I said it about exhausts the show. I've got one more surprise."

"Let's have it," growled Gerber.

Taken aback at Gerber's new tone, Smith shot him a quick glance. "You okay, Captain?" he asked quietly.

Gerber turned his gaze on the NCO. He nodded almost imperceptibly. "Sorry, Sully. I'm just a little depressed about losing my exec, and I'm more than a little worried about Ian's patrol."

"You ready?"

"Okay, do it, Sully. Do it."

Smith picked up the tiny generator that would detonate the explosives he had rigged. He turned the handle three times to ensure a powerful current, then swiveled his head to watch. The first explosion wasn't too impressive, but it detonated a willie pete round that threw brightly burning magnesium high into the sky. At the same time several barrels of foogas erupted into gigantic orange fireballs, illuminating the ground almost to the horizon. This fiery panorama was punctuated with the flat bangs of detonating C-4, the shock and heat waves hitting about the same time.

Gerber took an involuntary step backward. "Wow!"

"Yes, sir. Wow."

"Come on, let's go inside," Gerber said.

The party was finally in full swing, with everyone now chattering animatedly and having a good time. Morrow had given up dancing with the men and was alone in the corner, swaying to the music and clutching a beer in each hand. Foam ran down her arms, and she tried to lick it off without losing the beat of the music. Bromhead sat nearby, watching her.

Bocker had to miss the party because it was his turn for radio watch. He hesitated at the door, saw Gerber and walked over to him.

"Sorry to bother you, sir. Thought you'd want to know that McMillan has missed another radio check."

"You think there's a problem?"

"Well, sir, McMillan is pretty good about sticking to the schedule. I don't think he'd let a broken radio keep him from calling in. I mean, he'd get word to us somehow."

"Well, I'm not worried yet. We've had this happen before, and nine times out of ten it's because the radio broke."

"Yes, sir. Just thought I'd let you know that McMillan was out of touch."

"Thank you, Galvin. If you hear anything, please let me know."

Across the room Bromhead was trying to convince Morrow that they should leave. He could see that she was nearly soaking wet from the exertion of her dancing. Her hair hung damply, and she had unbuttoned her shirt all the way. She had even rolled her shorts higher, trying to cool herself.

"At least there is a breeze outside," Bromhead told her.

Morrow picked up a new can of beer and said, "Let's go see how Mack is doing. He's been sitting there by himself long enough."

Bromhead didn't really like the idea but agreed.

As they approached the table, Captain Minh, the Vietnamese camp commander and Gerber's counterpart, entered. He stopped at the door only long enough to spot Gerber.

"I say," said Minh, his British accent sounding completely out of place in the American camp, "some of our chaps are returning, saying they were ambushed. Thought you might want to meet them at the gate."

"You mean McMillan's patrol."

"That's right."

"Oh, shit." He looked at Bromhead. "We're going to the gate. You stay here and keep the party rolling for a couple of minutes. I think it's going to be bad news."

"I'll go with you, Captain," said Morrow.

Gerber shook his head. "Why don't you wait here, Robin. It'll be for the best."

2

THE SOUTH GATE OF
U.S. ARMY SPECIAL
FORCES CAMP A-555

As Gerber approached the gate, an opening in the south wall flanked by sandbagged bunkers containing .50-caliber and M-60 machine guns, he could see the men of the patrol as they stood waiting for their officers and NCOs. Five feet inside the gate a couple of them sat on the sandbagged wall, which was a second line of defense. They were clutching their weapons with the butts resting on the ground between their feet.

One soldier was rummaging through his rucksack, which lay in the red dust of the compound. Bags of rice and fish rations, a clean shirt and dry socks were scattered on the ground near him.

The men were all carefully looking at the six strands of concertina wire that surrounded the camp or the bunkers near the gate or their own equipment. Even though it was now dark, the full moon threw a dim light over the whole camp, and Gerber could see the Vietnamese strikers trying to ignore a poncho-wrapped body lying in the dirt. What he couldn't see scared him more. There was obviously no American standing with the Vietnamese.

Minh, walking beside Gerber, knew what he was thinking. "Not to worry, Captain. Your chap is probably heading for the team house, old boy," he said.

Gerber glanced out the corner of his eye at the shorter officer and knew he didn't believe it, either. Instead, Minh hurried forward, looking for one of his sergeants.

Before they had gotten very close, one of the strikers said in poor English, "I sorry about this."

Then Minh was there, speaking rapidly in Vietnamese, asking questions, but the speech was too fast for Gerber to follow. He could pick up a couple of words but couldn't really understand what was being said. Instead, Gerber moved to the body and crouched beside it. Without having to look, he could tell that it would be McMillan. There was a stained green beret lying next to it.

Carefully Gerber lifted the corner of the poncho so that he could see the face of the dead man. McMillan looked amazingly peaceful, as if he didn't have a care in the world. There was a dark smudge on his chin, but in the dim light from the moon, Gerber couldn't tell if it was dirt or blood.

Gerber opened the poncho farther looking for the wounds, but he couldn't find them. There was a large stain on the side of McMillan's fatigue jacket, and Gerber thought that it was blood. Finally he looked up at Minh, who had stopped talking.

"What the hell happened?"

Minh shrugged as if he didn't know what to say. In a quiet voice he said, "I believe the VC jumped them just before sunup. No one heard anything until Sergeant McMillan fell. By the time anyone could do anything, the VC were gone."

Gerber didn't speak. He just stared.

"I know what you're thinking, old boy. But these chaps didn't let it happen. They heard nothing. They're good boys."

Gerber closed the poncho and then stood. "I know it, Captain. I wasn't really thinking that they could have saved him. I know they would do everything they could."

As they turned to head back to the team house, Gerber stooped long enough to pick up McMillan's beret. "We better tell the others," Gerber said, trying to mask his emotions. But there was a slight tremor in his voice.

It was strange. He kept losing men, but he never got used to it. Maybe it was because the unit was so small that they got to know each other too well. A general commanding a division couldn't possibly know each of the twelve to fourteen thousand men in his unit. If some of them or a thousand of them or even five thousand of them died, the general would see it only as numbers on a chart or names listed on the casualty reports. Gerber knew each of his men very well.

Somehow it seemed worse now because they were so close to rotating home. It was only a couple of weeks until they would all be back in the World and the heat and misery of Vietnam would be unpleasant memories. If only Gerber hadn't felt the need to send McMillan out on patrol, then things would be different.

Gerber checked himself, realizing that he shouldn't accept any blame. Just because they were close to DEROS didn't mean, as Kepler had reminded him not long ago, that they should stop being soldiers. They had to patrol. They had to search for the enemy. It was too bad that McMillan . . .

He stopped that line of thought also because it was more than too bad. It was tragic, but nothing could be done about it.

They stopped outside the team house, yellow light leaking from the open door and from the screen that was wrapped around the top half of the building to let the air circulate but keep the insects out. Sandbags hid part of the lower wall. "Are you going to be all right, old boy?" Minh said.

It was the second or third time that night that someone had commented on his emotional state. He realized he was doing a poor job of masking his emotions, not that it mattered that much.

"I'm fine," he said, wiping a cold sweat from his forehead. He could feel it under his arms and trickling down his back. He hesitated before saying, "As fine as I can be. Let me tell the team about this alone. Okay?"

"I understand, Captain," Minh said. "I shall check the perimeter and see that the guard is properly mounted."

Inside, Gerber could see that the party had slowed quite a bit. Everyone had sensed that something was wrong, and the moment Gerber entered the room, they knew it was going to be bad news. Without a word from him, they fell silent. Kepler leaned over and turned off the blaring radio.

Fetterman took a single step forward, stopped and said, "Ian?"

Without realizing it, Gerber was twisting the beret he held in his hands. He didn't remember picking it up. This was the first time he had to announce to the team that someone had died. In the other cases, everyone had known that one of them had died because it had been in heavy combat or on patrols into enemy territory. This time it was a routine patrol that wasn't supposed to run into the VC. It was an attempt to provide some medical assistance to the villagers who never saw anyone with medical training.

"I'm sorry," said Gerber, unsure of what he should say. "Sergeant McMillan was killed earlier today. I don't have all the details, but apparently it was some kind of ambush."

"The Viets?" asked Tyme. "What about the Viets?"

"They're all okay."

"That's not what I meant," said Tyme. "Where the hell were they while Ian was getting killed?"

"I don't have all the details. Captain Minh is still trying to find out exactly what happened, but he doesn't think they ran and left him."

"What are we going to do now, Captain?" asked Fetterman.

Gerber moved to the table and sat down, pushing a couple of beer cans out of his way. He set the beret in front of him and turned it so that he could stare at the flash. "First thing in the morning we begin a patrol."

He stopped for a moment to look around him. The others stood staring at him. One or two held forgotten cans of beer. Morrow was leaning against the far wall. There were only Americans in the room.

"First patrol," said Gerber, "will be squad-sized. It will be poorly run with no noise discipline and will follow the path Ian took."

"And?" asked Fetterman.

"The second, a company-sized patrol, will follow about an hour later under the tightest discipline. It will be in position to offer assistance if the first gets into trouble. Maybe we can draw the enemy out. If we can, then we'll have a unit of sufficient size to stop anything sent after us."

"Is there a reason for this?" asked Fetterman.

"We do have to explore the area where Ian was killed. I believe the minor deception might give us a chance to hit the VC who attacked Ian, if they're still around. I can't see any reason for them to have faded away."

"Captain," said Bromhead, "I would like to lead the small patrol."

"No, Johnny. I want you to take the company. It'll be good experience for you, especially now that you're a captain. I'll take the small unit."

"And both American officers will be off the camp at the same time," said Fetterman.

Gerber shot a glance at him and said, "It won't be the first time we've had that situation." He then looked at Morrow, wondering what he should do about her because she was the only American woman there.

She shrugged. "I could go with you," she said hopefully.

"No, Robin. You stay here." Gerber turned his attention back to Fetterman. "Besides, we're not taking all the Americans out. Just a few of them. This is something we have to do."

Fetterman nodded. "Fucking A, Captain. Something we've got to do."

GERBER SAT IN THE MAKESHIFT OFFICE that also served as his living quarters. A map was spread out on the desk that he had built from old ammo crates and bamboo scrounged from the trash pile. Behind him was a metal cot with a paper-thin mattress, and next to the cot stood a nightstand made from an ammo crate. A Coleman lantern and a nearly empty bottle of Beam's rested on the makeshift table. In front of the desk were two lawn chairs that Gerber had bought in Saigon. On one corner of the desk, out of the way, sat a half-finished can of beer that was rapidly growing warm. He reached for the can and took a swig from it, setting it back down as he studied the map.

He heard a shuffling sound at the door and looked up to see Morrow standing there. She was dressed as she had been in the team house earlier but her face had that well-scrubbed look, as if she had just stepped from the shower.

She waited at the door for a moment but didn't step in. "Can we talk?" she asked.

Gerber pointed at one of the chairs opposite his desk, then leaned back, lacing his fingers behind his head. "What do you want to talk about?"

Morrow slipped into the chair and then leaned forward to pick up his beer. As she reached, Gerber could see the tops of her breasts. He wondered if she knew that he could see them and decided that she must.

"I think I would like to talk about the mission tomorrow," she said.

"I don't think there is anything about it that we need to discuss. Unless there is something that I'm not aware of."

Morrow stood and turned her back. She drained the beer and tossed the can out the door. "Mack? I don't want you . . . I think that you . . ." She stopped talking and then faced him. Her eyes searched his, but all she said was "Why do they call you Mack?"

"It's the army," said Gerber, trying to avoid her stare. "Anyone with a name like mine is going to be called Mack. When I was a kid, I went by my middle name. Used my first initial. I guess I thought it sounded more mature to be known as M. Kirk Gerber."

"M. Kirk, huh? I think I like that." She moved back to the chair and sat down again, crossing her legs slowly.

"I don't think you came here to discuss my name," said Gerber quietly.

"Well, you're right there." She laughed self-consciously. "It's that damned patrol tomorrow. I don't think you should go." She stared at him and then added as an afterthought, "Any of you."

"Why not?" Gerber didn't really care why because he knew that he had to go, had to see if he could find out what happened to McMillan. But he wanted to hear what she said.

"Why?" she repeated. "You've done your part here. You're almost ready to rotate home. All of you. You shouldn't be taking risks now that you're so close to being out of this. I don't want to see you, ah, any of you get hurt now."

Gerber let his hands fall to the desktop. He let his eyes wander to her shirt where he could see the rise of one of her breasts only partially hidden by the khaki fabric. He then studied her legs, trying to see them without her realizing that he was looking at them. Suddenly he realized that he had forgotten about the map, the patrol and what might happen in the morning. She had forced herself into his thoughts in a way that he had believed could not happen for quite a while. It was the last thing he wanted, especially when he remembered what her sister, Karen, had done to him.

"We haven't stopped being soldiers, and our job demands that we make contact with the enemy if we can."

"Mack. Kirk. It's just that . . ."

Gerber stood and moved to her. He reached out and took her hand, pulling her to her feet. "Robin, don't make this any harder than it is. If you're worried about being left on the camp, we can get a chopper here for you in the morning."

She pulled her hand free. "That won't be necessary. I'll wait here for your return. Might make a good story." Her voice was harsh and slightly strained. Without another word she stormed out.

For a moment Gerber thought of following her, to try to explain why he had acted as if he hadn't understood what she was trying to say. He wanted to tell her that it was wrong for the two of them to feel anything for one another as his men went into the field to die; for he and Robin to find pleasure together while his men sweated, fought and died in the jungle. He remembered their night in a Saigon hotel when he had no longer worried about such things, had forgotten about Karen for a few hours. He recalled the bliss he had found with Robin. But that had been a momentary aberration, one that he was determined not to repeat. It complicated his life too much to have a woman on the camp, one to whom he had an emotional attachment. Maybe he should go and tell her why he had seemed to become so cold and distant. But the longer he sat contemplating the action, the dumber he thought it was. If he let her go, she would quickly get over her hurt; but if he followed, she would interpret it as a positive response on his part, that there was something more to their relationship than the army officer-journalist one that existed now. Existed at his insistence.

GERBER WAS AWAKE AT DAWN. He hadn't slept well and had spent most of the time with his hands behind his head staring into the darkness at the ceiling. He had heard the occasional pop of the artillery from one of the new fire support bases now surrounding his camp. Once or twice he had heard aircraft fly over. With the coming of the sun, he had gotten up, found his weapon, opting to take one of the new M-16s that had finally been issued to his unit, and headed outside.

At the south gate he found the patrol waiting. Fetterman had already finished making a weapons and equipment check. Bromhead, his new captain bars pinned to his collar, stood to one side, watching as Tyme and Anderson checked each other.

As Gerber approached, Bromhead said, "You sure you want to take this one? I can handle it."

"Johnny," said Gerber, "this is something I have to do. You have your assignment. In a couple of weeks you'll be able to tell others how to run their unit, or rather your unit, but right now this is mine. I'll lead this."

"Just thought I'd mention it," said Bromhead.

"No problem. You seen Bocker or Smith this morning?"

"Galvin was in the common bunker playing with his radios and complaining about being left behind while we got to have all the fun."

Gerber glanced at his watch and then at the horizon where the sun was just making its presence known. "Listen, I don't have time to run him down. I want you to tell him and Sully to make sure that one of them keeps an eye on Morrow all the time."

"Of course."

"And remember, the timetable isn't all that strict. You follow in about an hour."

Bromhead grinned and said, "Don't worry, Mack, I can handle it."

For an instant Gerber was taken aback by Bromhead's use of his first name and then grinned back at him. "Feeling the first power of your new bars, Captain?"

"Thought I would see how they work."

"Don't let it go to your head, Johnny. You're still my exec."

Fetterman appeared then with one of the Vietnamese in tow. "Captains, this will be our guide. He'll try to re-create the route followed by McMillan. He was on the patrol."

Gerber studied the small man. He looked like so many of the other Vietnamese: short, a slight build, black hair chopped off raggedly and very dark eyes. There was nothing to distinguish him from any of the others.

"You know the route?" asked Gerber, first in English and, when there was no immediate reply, in Vietnamese.

The man nodded rapidly and pointed to the west. "I know the way," he replied.

"Okay—" Gerber slapped the Vietnamese on the shoulder "—let's do it. Johnny, tell Minh we're off and we'll see him in a couple of days."

"Yes, sir."

The patrol wormed its way through the six strands of concertina wire surrounding the camp, broke to the west away from the river and entered the high elephant grass. Although the sun was still low on the horizon, the humidity was already making itself felt. They were sweating heavily before they had gone more than a hundred meters. Gerber knew that by midday it would be unbearably hot. The humidity was bad enough, but then they would have the sun to contend with, as well, and even if they were into the jungle, the shade would provide little relief.

After only an hour and a half Gerber called a halt to let the men rest. He had filled four canteens before he left the camp and wondered if he had enough water. The moment security was established, Gerber opened a canteen and took out a couple of salt tablets. He didn't like taking them, but he was already sweating so heavily that he was afraid the heat was going to get to him. He couldn't remember it being so hot and humid before.

It seemed as if they had just sat down, but by his watch Gerber knew that fifteen minutes had passed. He hoped Bromhead would keep the pace slow, trying not to wear the men out before they got into the ambush area. Besides, he didn't want the new captain to catch up. His job was to stay a klick or so behind the squad in case the VC were watching.

Trying to ignore the heat, Gerber signaled the men back to their feet, and they started forward again. The point slid off to the right, and Gerber was forced to chase him back to the proper course. When the pace slowed to something that approximated a crawl, Gerber passed word to the point man to speed it up.

An hour before noon there was a sudden crash in the jungle as if a grenade had detonated. Through breaks in the trees and gaps in the brush, Gerber saw a cloud of black smoke and reddish-brown dust. He dived to one side, his weapon ready, but there was no firing. Only the single explosion.

Without waiting, Gerber leaped to his feet and had to consciously suppress the urge to run forward. Instead, he carefully worked his way in the direction of the explosion, his eyes searching the ground and the jungle around him, looking for other booby traps. Finally he could see Fetterman crouched on the ground, a large bandage in his hand as he worked on one of the Vietnamese strikers.

As he approached, Gerber asked, "Status?"

Fetterman kept working and spoke over his shoulder, his eyes on the wounded man. "Tripped a grenade booby trap. Charlie didn't rig it quite right so the grenade went off with a tree absorbing most of the shrapnel. It should have killed the point man, but it detonated too soon. He's got some pretty bad wounds but nothing really serious, if you know what I mean."

"He need a medevac?"

"No, sir. I would think we can give him a shot or two and let someone take him back to the camp. I've got most of the bleeding stopped already."

"Tony," said Gerber quietly, "if he was an American, would you medevac him now?"

Fetterman turned his head so that he could stare up at Gerber. "I'm not sure I like the implication of that question, Captain."

"Sorry. I wasn't thinking. Listen, let's have our guys take a lunch break and wait for Johnny's group to catch up. He can dispatch the stretcher team and an escort back to the camp, and then they can eat their lunch while we carry on."

"Yes, sir. Aren't you worried about both units being together? Might tip our hand."

"I'm not totally convinced that Charlie doesn't already know what we're up to. He may have had spies in the area who saw both patrols leave the camp. Anyway, I don't think it will hurt."

"Fine, sir, I'll pass the word."

As Fetterman stood, giving some quick instructions in Vietnamese to one of the other strikers, Gerber said, "Tony, I'm sorry about that remark. I should have know better."

IT WAS MORE THAN AN HOUR before they got moving again, into the sweatbox that the jungle had become. Before long, Gerber's shirt was soaked. His hands had become slippery, and it was difficult to hang on to anything. The men were tiring fast, the heat rapidly sapping their strength, and by midafternoon most of the Vietnamese had finished their water. One of them drank from a paddy field they passed, leaving the tree line for a moment. Gerber knew it would make the Americans sick to drink that water but wasn't sure that the strikers couldn't. They hadn't grown up in the germ-free environments that were the pride of American mothers.

By late afternoon they had slowed to a crawl with the men ignoring some of the fundamentals of patrol. They had been trying to follow the trails that Gerber was certain would be booby-trapped. He instructed Fetterman, along with the guide, to take the point. He told Fetterman that he wanted the rest of them to arrive safely, not to take any chances but to speed it up.

Just when Gerber decided to call a halt for the night, the patrol stopped. As the strikers automatically took up defensive positions, Gerber slipped forward to find out why Fetterman had halted. As he approached the hiding spot of the master sergeant, Gerber could hear voices speaking Vietnamese in the distance. There was the unmistakable odor from a fire and the slight breeze carried the obnoxious smell of nouc-mam to him.

Gerber crouched beside his team sergeant. "Is this it?"

Nodding at the Vietnamese soldier who was the guide, Fetterman said, "This is the village. Nuyen here says that McMillan had come out a little farther to the north and set up his perimeter there."

"He's sure about this?"

"Yes, sir. I thought I'd see what's happening in the ville and then Nuyen and I could swing north. We've got an hour or so of light left. Nuyen should be able to pinpoint the ambush site pretty closely, and it shouldn't take us that long to find some physical evidence."

"Okay, Tony. Go to it. We'll stay here."

"Sure, sir. You and the boys rest while the old master sergeant goes off and does your job for you."

"And snap it up, Tony," said Gerber, smiling as he dropped his pack.

3

OUTSIDE THE VILLAGE OF TRANG ME NEAR THE CAMBODIAN BORDER

It took Fetterman and the guide less than ten minutes to find the ambush site. The evidence that he had mentioned to Gerber was obvious in the trampled vegetation gouges in the soft, moist earth and the traces of blood that the hot, damp weather and jungle creatures had failed to conceal. Slowly Fetterman examined the site, aware that the VC often booby-trapped such areas because they knew the Americans would come back to try to learn what had happened.

McMillan's position in the jungle was obvious because he had been the only one attacked.

Fetterman shed his pack at the edge of the ambush site. He stripped his web gear, dropping it on top of the pack and then took a deep, long drink of the warm water from one of his canteens. He kept his weapon with him as he got to his hands and knees and began to inspect the site, trying to piece together the fight.

The jungle around the village wasn't the thick triple-canopy type that was found farther north but a thin, almost landscaped, forest. Short grass and bare ground surrounded the tall teak, mahogany and palm trees that threw a spotty shade. Fetterman crawled around, using his left hand to pat the grass as if searching for a dropped coin. He advanced toward an area of crushed grass that was stained a rusty color. He knew it was dried blood.

Nearby were a couple of smaller patches of blood and part of a trail that pointed into the jungle. He could find nothing to tell him why only McMillan had been attacked or how the VC had stumbled upon him and not the rest of his patrol. Nor could he figure out how the enemy soldiers had escaped without any of the strikers actually seeing them. The strikers had reported hearing a scream, and they had fired a few random, unaimed shots into the trees, but the attack on McMillan had been so swift, they hadn't had time to react.

His search completed, he picked up his equipment and worked his way back to Gerber through the light forest, keeping to the shadows so that the villagers wouldn't be aware that he was near.

Gerber was sitting deep in the trees, his back against a palm, his pack in front of him. He was staring at it as if it would somehow provide him with answers. To one side, Fetterman could see a couple of the Vietnamese smoking American cigarettes, but he could hear no talking from them. They, too, were well back, using the broadleafed bushes, the trunks of coconut palms and the shadows to conceal themselves.

"I've found it, Captain," he whispered.

"And?" asked Gerber.

"And nothing. I can't tell what happened. Some evidence of a struggle. Looks like Ian might have killed or wounded a couple of them, given the blood smears. But I don't know how the VC got there or how they got away."

Gerber turned so that his pack was now at his back. He struggled into the straps and stood up, taking a hasty step to the right to maintain his balance. To Fetterman he said, "Let's set up our night location near the ambush site. Tomorrow we can move into the ville and see if they can shed any light on this."

They spent a quiet evening cautiously watching the villagers, almost all old or very young, go about their chores. The women circulated among the mud hootches, stopping to talk briefly or to pick up some food or leave some. All were dressed in rough blouses, which were the tan of undyed cotton, and black pajama bottoms. Some wore sandals made from old tires, and some were barefoot. The old men were dressed in the same fashion, except that one of them wore an old U.S. Army fatigue shirt with the sleeves hacked off at the elbows.

The cooking fires were extinguished as the sunlight faded, and although there was noise from the ville after sunset, it quickly faded. They heard the discordant music of a stringed instrument for a few moments, but that ended almost as soon as it started. Gerber made the rounds at dusk, telling his men that they would be on half alert throughout the night: they were to pair up, and every other man was to stay awake.

At midnight, in keeping with the standard operating procedures, Gerber used his radio to contact the camp and tell them that all was well. He heard Bromhead check in, too, and, from the strength of the signal, knew that he was close. But Bromhead had done a good job of moving into position because Gerber had seen nothing to indicate that a large unit was nearby. When it was dark, he could see no lights from Bromhead's men, which meant that they had eaten unheated C-rations and that Bromhead was not letting them smoke. Extraordinary discipline to expect from the Vietnamese strikers and even more extraordinary that the new captain was getting it. Gerber was pleased. It demonstrated how much Bromhead deserved his promotion and command of an A-team.

In the moments before dawn, Gerber came awake suddenly, sensing that something had changed, as if a kind of warning had alerted his subconscious mind. He lay with his eyes closed, concentrating on the sounds surrounding him, but could hear nothing other than the noises of the jungle creatures as they moved through the bushes or in the tops of the trees, and the rapid breathing of one of the strikers asleep near him.

For a moment, Gerber berated himself for his paranoia. He wondered if he was doing the same things that McMillan had done in the last minutes of his life. Listening to the surroundings, trying to hear the enemy slipping up on him or feeling, with an almost extrasensory ability, the VC sneaking up on his position. He knew that the sweat coating his body was not from the humidity of the jungle but from the fear that had crept up on him. Without thinking about it, Gerber pulled his weapon closer and took the safety off. He could feel the flesh at the back of his neck crawl as he waited for someone to grab him from behind. And then he realized that his fears were unfounded. All the sounds around him were the natural activity of the jungle creatures, the monkeys calling to each other, the birds screaming and the rustling of the night predators as they raced for their lairs. Gerber knew that he was keyed up because this was the same time of day when McMillan had died.

After a quick cold breakfast of C-ration scrambled eggs that looked pale and tasted plain, a hint of egg flavor in the cardboard mess, Gerber broke camp. He stood for a moment looking at the light mist, which hung close to the ground near the palms and coconuts and signified the coolness of the morning. Overhead, through breaks in the light green canopy, Gerber could see a deep blue sky with only a few high, wispy clouds. The day would get hot quickly, and the humidity would climb rapidly. He would have to watch the pace to make sure that they didn't overexert themselves.

He left half the squad with Sergeant Tyme to search the ambush site again, looking for anything that Fetterman might have missed. But Gerber doubted that the master sergeant would miss anything of importance. He planned to enter the village with the rest of the men and question the people there. Gerber had already coordinated the effort with Bromhead on the radio so that the newly minted captain would keep his men out of sight nearby.

As the six men entered the tiny ville, coming from the north and moving between two mud hootches with rusting tin roofs, the mama-sans working at the cooking fires suddenly disappeared into their hootches. This was not a reaction that Gerber expected, and suddenly he was worried.

The villagers usually ignored the Americans and their Vietnamese counterparts, taking great pains to pretend they couldn't see the soldiers. These women had leaped up the moment they spotted the Americans.

Without a word Fetterman took half of the squad and drifted to the right so that he could cover Gerber and the point element. As they sought the little cover available to them in the village— near the corner of a hootch with a thick thatched roof, behind a fence of woven branches cut from thorn bushes or at the base of a palm tree—Fetterman took the safety off his weapon. He crouched behind the remnants of a mud wall, near the corner of a deserted hootch.

Gerber waved a hand behind his back, signaling the men with him to spread out and prepare to withdraw. He continued walking forward, angling toward the corner of a hootch, thinking that he could use it for cover if they were forced to fight. He didn't plan a retreat because he knew that Bromhead would attack the instant he heard shooting.

For ten long minutes the situation remained static. Fetterman and a couple of the men behind Gerber and the rest waited for something, anything, to happen. When the villagers didn't reappear, when no old men came out to learn what was happening, Gerber moved toward the one hootch where he knew there were some people hiding. Rather than enter uninvited, he stood outside it and called in Vietnamese, "We mean you no harm."

From the left Gerber heard, "Won't do you any good, Captain. They're afraid of us. We'll have to go in and get them."

Gerber turned and saw Fetterman standing there. He hadn't heard the master sergeant walk up. To him, Gerber said, "I hate to violate their homes like that. Probably why they ran in the first place."

"I don't know, sir. I don't like this at all. Usually they just stand around and let us do what we want. They rarely flee unless they're VC."

"All right. Take a couple of men and bring the villagers out. We've got to talk to them, but treat them kindly. We don't want them joining the VC because of our actions."

"You beginning a new career of telling me my job, sir?" asked Fetterman, grinning.

"No, Tony. I'm just making sure that you'll instruct the men to treat the villagers with some dignity. It'll pay off for us."

It didn't take Fetterman long to get the people into the center of the village. Then, rather than have all the villagers stand around being interrogated, the Americans let some of them go back to the cooking fires, and when one of the old men complained that his fields were being neglected, Gerber ordered that he be allowed to leave, wondering if he was making a tactical mistake. The man could flee into the jungle in search of the VC.

As the man disappeared into the trees, Fetterman asked, "You sure that was a good idea?"

Gerber shrugged. "I doubt that he'll cause any trouble, and besides, we've got Bromhead around here with a company. Also, there's no evidence of any VC force. Thought maybe a little kindness would win us some friends. It's worked for us before."

Slowly and carefully they moved among the villagers asking questions about what had happened. After an hour Fetterman had pieced together a story. He reported to Gerber that it appeared as if the VC had entered the village about an hour before Mc-Millan's patrol had settled in for the night. They had been shadowing McMillan and his strikers for most of the afternoon and had been looking for an ambush site but hadn't found anything that would allow them to set up the way they wanted to.

Gerber raised an eyebrow at this and said, "The VC let all that slip to the villagers?"

"I gather they were pretty talkative," said Fetterman. "Felt omnipotent and were discussing the afternoon among themselves as they forced some of the women to cook them an evening meal."

"Ian didn't see all the extra people?"

"He wouldn't know if there were extra people. Besides, the VC stayed out of sight. I haven't gotten to the best part."

"Sorry. Go ahead."

"Seems that this place was once a VC stronghold. The villagers were rabid sympathizers. Government airplanes bombing them all the time. Shooting the water buffalo for target practice and that sort of thing. Then one night the VC came and demanded some young men and young women for recruits. Said that the village owed it to them. The head man refused, saying they needed the young people to harvest the crop for the next few days and the recruiting would have to wait. The VC said no, it had to be right then, and somehow a fight broke out. When it was over, about half the villagers were dead and the rest were marched off into the jungle."

"Then who in the hell are these people?"

Fetterman shrugged. "I think they were moving from another area, found the empty hootches and just moved in. Learned later what had happened."

"The point of all this, Tony. The point?" Gerber wiped a sleeve across his forehead to mop up the sweat.

"Tunnels. The area is crisscrossed with them. They lead from the hootches into the jungle. From the bunkers hidden around into the jungle. From the jungle back to here. The whole village. Dug by the old villagers and the VC over a period of years. These people have kept them in repair because we brought the war back into this zone.''

"I see," said Gerber, nodding. "The tunnels lead into jungle and right into the middle of the area where McMillan's patrol was."

"Yes, sir. Dead into the middle."

While Fetterman continued to question the villagers, Gerber took the rest of the men and entered one of the hootches. There was little inside except a wooden chest, obviously made by the owner because of the rough construction, and some woven bamboo sleeping mats in the corner. By moving one of the mats, they found an entrance to the tunnel system. It looked like an ordinary hole in the ground, but from a different angle they could see that it turned. There was a wooden door covering the entrance.

Gerber wanted to drop down and explore the inside, but he was too big. Instead, he pointed to one of the Vietnamese strikers and watched as the frightened man, clutching a pistol in one hand and a flashlight in the other, climbed into the hole. He pushed on the wooden door, which swung out of the way. The man looked back, sweat covering his face, his eyes wide with fear, but when Gerber nodded, the man disappeared into the tunnel.

Fifteen minutes later the striker, covered with red dust, reappeared shaking his head and chattering rapidly. Gerber didn't understand much of it but thought he was being told that there was nothing of interest down there.

Gerber wasn't satisfied with the answer. He didn't think that the tunnel system would be as barren as the striker indicated and suspected that the man had learned from past experience that, if he found anything, the Americans would require him to search for hours. The only solution was to send one of the team down. Fetterman was the only one whose size didn't make it dangerous. He was only slightly bigger and stockier than the Vietnamese. Gerber decided to wait until Fetterman finished with the questions.

Outside the hootch Gerber saw the master sergeant standing to one side, alone, clutching his weapon in both hands. He was covered with sweat, ragged stains down the front of his shirt and under his arms. There was something peculiar about his posture, and as Gerber approached, he saw the look on Fetterman's face. It was one of disbelief.

"Tony," said Gerber. "What is it?"

Fetterman turned and saw Gerber, and in an instant his face became as passive as if he had just completed a Sunday stroll through the park. "Nothing at all, Captain. Picked up an interesting bit of intelligence."

"And?"

"Brief you on it just as soon as the possibility for real security presents itself."

Gerber was going to demand to be told but decided that Fetterman knew what he was doing. If it was something that would affect the mission, Fetterman would tell him right away, and if Fetterman wanted to wait, it was something that could wait. Still, the captain was more than a bit curious.

Changing the subject, Gerber said, "I'd like you to explore the tunnels a little. See if there is anything down there of interest, and see if there is a way to destroy them without blowing up the whole damned village."

Fetterman dropped his pack outside the hootch. He took the Randall combat knife that was taped upside down to the harness. Carefully he slipped it into his boot where he could get it quickly. Next he took two grenades, and slipped one into each of the front pockets of his jungle fatigue pants.

Silently Gerber handed him a .45, and Fetterman released the magazine, checking to make sure that it was fully loaded. He slammed it back home and racked the slide once, chambering a fresh round. That done, he dropped the magazine again, replacing the round that was now in the chamber of the pistol. He took three spare magazines, placing one in a front pocket of his jungle fatigue jacket, one in a side pocket and one in the top of his other boot.

"Won't that be uncomfortable?" asked Gerber.

"Damned uncomfortable, but you never know when something like that will come in handy. Now if I have to, I should be able to reach at least one spare mag."

"Anything else?"

"Let me see that flashlight." Fetterman took it and turned it on, looking directly into the beam. He shook it twice and banged it against his hand but didn't see the beam flicker. The batteries seemed to be new

Finally he peeled off his watch and handed it to Gerber. He rolled down his sleeves, buttoning them tightly around his wrists so there would be no excess material to snag on any obstructions in the tunnel. He checked himself one last time. "That should be it."

"I don't suppose I need to tell you to be careful."

"Always am. Wouldn't want to do anything to upset Mrs. Fetterman and the kids. I'll be down there for a while, Captain, so don't get nervous."

"It may not help," said Gerber, "but if you get into trouble and need us, fire three quick shots."

"I'll keep that in mind."

Inside the hootch Fetterman sat on the edge of the tunnel and played the beam along the sides and bottom. He looked at Gerber and said, "You know, Captain, I really am getting too short for this shit."

"We all are, Tony."

"Yes, sir." Fetterman dropped to the tunnel floor, stopping there long enough to study the walls around him. They were smooth, almost as if they had been bored rather than dug. He felt the side, but the earth was packed hard and it took the point of his knife to scrape any dirt free. This was a new experience, one that he hadn't trained for. During his career Fetterman had signed up for the most outlandish Army schools, figuring that someday, somewhere, one of them might come in handy. But no one, nowhere, had ever designed a course on how to explore an enemy tunnel system. One that had literally been clawed out of the ground.

Fetterman did know, from his experience on the surface, that the VC would booby-trap nearly everything. Each of Charlie's own soldiers using the tunnel system would know of the traps, but an enemy penetrating the system would fall victim to them. Fetterman didn't think there would be much to worry about once he got deep enough, but near the surface he would have to be extremely careful, even though a striker had gone in before him.

He had dropped down carefully, gingerly placing his feet on the bottom, waiting for a sudden shift that would tell him that he had stepped on the pressure trigger of a mine, but that didn't happen. He pressed on the wooden door and felt it swing back so that he could crawl forward slowly, at first with the pistol in one hand and his flashlight in the other. He quickly realized that he would need one hand to feel his way. He lowered the hammer of the .45 and slipped it into his belt, then switched the light to his left hand and began moving forward again, feeling for hidden protrusions and trip wires.

The floor of the tunnel was packed hard and smooth to the touch with no loose dirt on it. The walls were of red clay with very little bracing. The roof of the tunnel was also hard-packed clay with wooden supports spaced liberally around it. Fetterman was concerned that it would collapse on him and then reminded himself that the Vietnamese Air Force had bombed the village without destroying the tunnels. The odds were that he would stumble across a booby trap long before the tunnel fell on him.

There was no litter on the floor and no recessed niches that hid papers or weapons. The light from the tunnel entrance dissipated rapidly, and Fetterman was nearly overwhelmed by the musty smell. An odor of freshly dug earth was everywhere. Fetterman took a deep breath of the astonishingly cool air, expanding his chest, but the tunnel was large enough to accommodate him. He was surprised that the air wasn't stale and realized that the system would have to be well ventilated. He continued forward, blinking rapidly as his eyes adjusted to the almost total darkness of the tunnel.

He hadn't gone very far when he came to a ladder that led deeper into the tunnel. It forked off to one side, but Fetterman couldn't see much in that direction and knew that anything interesting would be found lower in the system. Using the slightly enlarged area, he turned around so that he could climb down the ladder. If he was going to run into any booby traps, it would be at that point. He kept his feet next to the rails of the ladder, putting as little pressure as possible on the rungs and carefully avoiding the center of them.

When he reached the bottom, instead of stepping to the floor, he turned and used his light to examine the earth. He saw no trip wires, no glints of metal suggesting the firing mechanisms of mines and no slight depressions showing where a pressure plate might be buried. He stepped off the ladder to the side, then crouched so that he could examine the new tunnel.

This one was larger, the roof being nearly five feet above the floor. And it was wider, almost six feet across, and cut into the sides were niches. Fetterman moved to his left and looked into the niche nearest him. There was a wooden platform in it covered with straw. A human stink to the place overpowered the odor of moist earth that he was becoming used to. He couldn't identify what was human about the smell. It seemed to be sweat mingled with urine.

"I'll be damned," he mumbled to himself. "A goddamned barracks."

He worked his way through the barracks and had to stoop to enter the next phase of the tunnel. Crawling along it, still looking for trip wires and booby traps, he felt his way with the fingers of his right hand as he swept the flashlight beam back and forth. He was now finding more evidence of human occupation. An old can from stolen American C-rations. Two almost new rounds for an AK-47. A loop of copper wire that didn't seem to have any function because it was so short. And papers, many of them Chieu Hoi leaflets dropped in large numbers from American and South Vietnamese airplanes, some of which had been used as toilet paper.

Again the tunnel opened up so that it was ten feet wide and five feet high, the sides braced with four by fours supporting wooden beams on the ceiling. Lightbulbs were suspended from wires looped along the beams. The floor was covered with a thin wooden veneer, slatted to let water seep into the ground, although the tunnel was extremely dry. The human odor had given way to the musty, dirty smell of a freshly dug grave.

This was not another barracks area. This time he found an arms locker. At first he didn't think much of it, figuring that the VC and NVA had to store their weapons somewhere, then he realized what he had found. There were three .51-caliber machine guns, what the Communists designated as 12.5 mm. One of them had the huge circular sight on top that was used for antiaircraft weapons and stood on a solid metal tripod. There were several mortar tubes, a couple of them of American manufacture. Off to one side was a rack of AK-47s, most of them Chicom but a couple obviously Soviet made because of the Russian lettering on them.

Then at the far end he saw a weapon that nearly bowled him over. He couldn't believe it. A fully assembled ZSU-23. A goddamned 23 mm antiaircraft gun that contained twin barrels, with wheels folded under and which could be erected and used to tow the weapon. There was a seat near two hand cranks for the gunner. It had to have been brought down in pieces and reassembled; to get it out, the VC would have to take it apart again.

Fetterman moved closer and reached out to touch it as if he didn't believe his eyes. He sat in the gunner's seat and twisted the cranks that would move the weapon. It was fully operational. He shook his head in disbelief.

For several minutes Fetterman sat there and stared. It was such a strange thing to find. An antiaircraft gun underground. It was of no use there, other than for the practice of taking it apart and putting it back together. It wasn't like the other weapons that could be carried easily to the surface. Even the .51 cals could be taken to the surface intact, once the tripods were removed.

Finally Fetterman decided that he had seen enough. It was time to get back to the surface. He could leave his grenades behind as booby traps to cause some confusion among the VC when they returned, or he could carefully withdraw and hope that the enemy wouldn't discover that his tunnels had been penetrated.

As carefully as he entered, Fetterman left the tunnel system. He kept his eyes open for anything that he might have missed, but the upper levels were still clean.

When he approached the entrance to the hootch, he shouted up, "I'm coming out."

Gerber answered him with a quick, "It's clear."

As rapidly as he could, he explained that they had found a VC base camp. He didn't think that the villagers had any idea of how extensive it was. He suggested that they had only seen a couple of soldiers at a time use the entrances in the village but was sure that there was access to the system from far outside the ville, hidden in the jungle.

"They could put a regiment down there, and the villagers wouldn't know it, Captain," he said.

"What do you recommend?"

"That we pull out of here as quickly as possible so that we don't tip our hand. Then we should brief Nha Trang about this. Let them put an infantry battalion with engineers in here to blow it all up. Hell, there's so much stuff down there we couldn't carry it all out in a month."

"Maybe we should just blow the entrances," said Gerber.

"We'd never get them all, sir, and then Charlie would move all his stuff out before we could do anything about it. I only had an hour down there and didn't see even a fraction of it. I mean there is a fucking arsenal down there."

"You didn't steal yourself a souvenir?"

"No, sir. As I said, I didn't want them to know that I had been down there and I don't know how good their accounting system is." He grinned. "But those Russian AKs were mighty tempting. You don't see many with Russian lettering on them."

Gerber glanced at his watch and saw that it was nearly two in the afternoon. There was absolutely nothing they could do about it that day. If they headed back to the camp, they wouldn't get there until dark. If they waited until the morning, they could watch the ville from the jungle and see if the VC showed up, then leave at first light. By dusk he or one of his men could be in Saigon or Nha Trang passing along the information.

"Okay, Tony, take a while to catch your breath. We'll pull back to the ambush site and explore it again. Camp for the night and return to base in the morning."

Fetterman dropped to the ground and said, "Sounds good, sir."

Gerber stood and started to move away but stopped. "I wonder if we're not being a little too clever about this."

"Meaning?"

"The villagers know that we've found some of the tunnels, and they're sure to mention it to the VC if they come back soon. Now if we don't try to destroy the system, the VC might abandon it anyway. But if we drop a couple of grenades down the holes we've found, which would only do superficial damage, it might make the bad guys think that we think we've ruined their complex."

"Or we could be outsmarting ourselves."

"I know, but I just don't feel right about leaving this untouched. I know we can't really destroy the entire complex, but we should try."

"Perhaps we should discuss this some more with the rest of the team back at camp," said Fetterman.

Gerber continued to look at the master sergeant without really seeing him. After a few moments the captain nodded.

"Okay," he said.

4

U.S. ARMY SPECIAL FORCES CAMP A-555

Gerber waited for everyone on the team to find a seat. It was the first time in months that they had all been together in a single meeting.

Fetterman and Tyme sat together at the table closest to the refrigerator. Tyme, who was recovering from a wound received during an ambush that had gone wrong, was sipping a beer. He had only recently returned to the camp. He was a tall, sandy-haired man in his mid-twenties. He was normally quiet, except when someone asked a question about weapons, and then he was all too happy to talk to him for hours.

Sam Anderson, the huge, blond demolitions sergeant, stood in the corner closest to the bar, eating a sandwich he had made himself. He kept his hair cut so short that he looked bald, and his eyes were such a light blue they looked gray. He had an open, friendly face with a boyish smile and the whitest, straightest teeth that anyone had ever seen. Next to his sandwich plate stood a glass of milk.

Galvin Bocker sat at a table with Sully Smith and Derek Kepler. Sully Smith, whose real name was Francisco Giovanni Salvatore Smith, had an American father and an Italian mother. He was on his second Vietnam tour because, like Anderson, he loved to watch things explode, especially when he got to wire the charges. Short and stocky with the olive complexion of the Italians, he was from Dayton, Ohio.

Kepler was the strangest of the team. He had once arrived at camp drunk, but with a 90 mm recoilless rifle that Gerber had spent weeks trying to have sent to him through official channels. Kepler would never tell anyone where he got it, except to say that the men who had it didn't need it. He had been dressed in a nurse's uniform complete with a bra and stockings. He hadn't explained that, either. His expertise at supplying equipment that couldn't be found via normal channels had earned him the nickname of Eleven Fingers. Since he was the intelligence specialist for the team, they expected bizarre behavior, but Kepler seemed to have made it into a fine art.

Thomas Jefferson Washington, the twenty-one-year-old medic whom the others called T.J., sat by himself, staring at his beer, drinking it steadily and quietly. Until the day before yesterday, he had been the junior medic, a position he loved because McMillan was teaching him so much. They had operated on wounded strikers, removing bullets that would have killed them had McMillan not ignored regulations preventing medics from performing surgery.

McMillan's death had hit him the hardest because he had worked the closest with him. T.J. was a big black man with the fine features that suggested his ancestors had come from the eastern side of Africa rather than the West Coast.

Once they were all present, seated or standing at the back and quiet, Gerber stood. He drew a hand across his forehead, looked at the sweat in his palm and wiped it on the front of his dirty fatigue jacket. He said, "We've got a couple of things to decide and a few things to discuss prior to me getting on the chopper to Saigon."

Before he could say anything else, the door opened and Robin Morrow stood there, holding a couple of cans of beer. "Anyone interested in something cool to drink?" she asked.

"No," said Fetterman, "but you can come in, anyway."

From the other side of the room, Bromhead said, "Are you sure that's a good idea?"

"Shouldn't matter, Johnny," said Gerber. "You won't tell anyone what's said in here, will you, Robin?"

She pulled a chair out and sat down. "You should know me better than that."

"Then you can stay." Gerber turned his attention back to the rest of his team. "I think the one thing that you all should know is something that Master Sergeant Fetterman said to me only a few minutes ago. Something he discovered, and when put together with some of the other things we know, makes a lot of sense."

He stopped talking and studied the faces of the men of his team. After nearly a year in Vietnam, they were all veterans. They all knew the score now, what combat was like and what men did when faced with death. These were all men who could be trusted to do their jobs, to die doing their jobs if it came to that. These were men whom Gerber would trust with his life.

He turned his eyes momentarily to Morrow. She was the real enigma. Although she was a journalist who had tricked a Saigon general into letting her come out to the camp, she had volunteered to hold back a story to help them. She had even helped get Sergeants Tyme and Fetterman out of trouble. Now she put up with hardships, staying at the camp for some reason that Gerber refused to understand, and which caused him undue distress.

He had spent a night with her in Saigon that involved little talking. Now he avoided her when they were alone, afraid of what might happen. He avoided any eye or body contact, and tried to exclude her from his thoughts. He felt that they had worked out an arrangement that was satisfactory to them both. He believed the one night in Saigon, with her protestations of love, had been just one night in Saigon. She had been lonely, maybe afraid. He had been lonely, hurt by Robin's sister and reluctant to get involved in any lasting relationship. He was attracted to her, of that he had no doubt, but believed the attraction was because of her amazing resemblance to her sister. His feelings for her were a direct result of his rejection by Robin's sister. He didn't want to explore it any further so he avoided the problem as best he could. Because he had once loved Morrow's sister, Gerber was overly obtuse when dealing with Robin.

"While interrogating the villagers," Gerber began, almost physically shaking himself to put the thoughts of Robin Morrow out of his mind, "Sergeant Fetterman learned something that is shocking. First, though, I should explain that, from the evidence we could find on the field, there is no indication that the Vietnamese strikers left Ian to die. He was killed in an ambush that was set to kill him. There is really nothing the strikers could have done. It happened too fast and too quietly. By the time they were alerted to the problem, Ian was dead, and the VC were escaping.''

Again he stopped talking, wondering if he believed what he had been told and deciding for the twentieth time that he did. ''It seems that Ian was the target of the ambush. Just him. Not the patrol or the Vietnamese, but Sergeant McMillan.''

Before anyone could say anything, Gerber continued. ''I know what you're thinking because it's the same thing I thought when I was told. The VC don't know McMillan and, therefore, wouldn't try to kill him. Well, that's right, but McMillan was the target of the ambush.

''If one of us had been with him, we would have been a target, too. The VC are interested in killing us all. Those of us here who ruined their master plan to rid the area of the Saigon government's presence. The ones who built a camp in their backyard and who have been able to maintain that camp no matter what they have thrown at us. We're the ones who have shown that the VC aren't the omnipotent soldiers everyone thought they were.''

Smith interrupted. ''That would mean we're all the targets.''

''Right,'' Gerber nearly yelled to underscore the point. ''We have been singled out for assassination by the enemy. Master Sergeant Fetterman might have something more to say on that point.''

Fetterman stood. ''Before we all go off half-cocked, let met say that what the captain just explained should be no surprise. We have hurt Charlie here. We have pushed him and prodded him and forced him to do things that he didn't want to do. He has tried to take the camp from us and has failed to do it. He has tried to put a propaganda cadre into the area to explain the failure, and we destroyed that. Each time he has moved a force into the region, we have met him and defeated him. Now he wants us all dead. Ian, unfortunately, was the first victim of this new campaign because he was in the wrong place at the wrong time.''

''So who cares?'' yelled Anderson. ''We all rotate out of here in a couple of weeks, anyway. We'll beat Charlie because of the way the war is being run.''

Now Gerber took over from Fetterman. ''The Cat has a point. All we really have to do is sit tight, and our tours will end and we'll go home. We're all extremely short. But that doesn't end the problem."

"What the captain is saying," said Fetterman, "is that we'll pass the problem along to the team that replaces us here. Charlie doesn't care who he kills, just as long as he takes out one of our teams. Kill all the Americans on one of the teams, even if he has to do it one at a time. The people in the villes won't know it was a different team."

"Sounds like you're suggesting that we extend," said Smith, laughing. "Stay for an extra six months."

"Before we get into that," answered Gerber, "there are one or two other things you should know. Tony?"

Fetterman began to address the group again. "I've talked to Eleven Fingers about this, and he's checked with his informants. There is a bounty on us. A thousand bucks apiece for you low-ranking sergeants, fifteen hundred for me because they don't realize how valuable I am and two thousand for each of the officers."

"Say," said Smith, "how do we collect?"

There was a bark of laughter, which Fetterman stared down. "I believe we have to supply the bodies. If they just wanted insignia, we might be able to find a way to tap into it. We can get all the insignia we need."

"I'll check into it," said Kepler seriously. "I know that some VC units are paying for the wings of helicopter pilots. Don't need the bodies, just the wings. And the warrant officer bars. They're paying for those, too."

"We are not selling any insignia to the damned enemy," said Gerber. "Tony. Finish it."

"Yes, sir. Sergeant Kepler and I confirmed through some of his sources that the Chinese officer is behind all this. It was his plan we wrecked. He was trying to get even for our assassination attempt on him, and when that blew up in his face, he decided to put his people into the field to take us out."

"Jesus Christ!" said Bromhead.

Ignoring that, Gerber said, "I plan to meet with Colonel Bates tomorrow and tell him that I want to extend for six months. I know the clerks in Saigon are going to have fits because of the paperwork involved, but I doubt the Army is going to tell someone who is here and who has survived for a year that he cannot continue to fight the war.''

"Come on, Captain," said Anderson. "This is crazy. We can't stay here for an extra six months.''

"He's right, sir," said Bocker.

"I expected you to at least listen, Galvin," replied Gerber. "Of all the men, I thought you would be the one to listen to the plan before rejecting it.''

"I'll listen to anything. You know that. But extend to see if we can't shoot some Chinese guy? Hell, sir, we've never even seen him." Bocker looked at the other men in the hot, sticky team house, trying to gauge their reactions. Nervously, he wiped the sweat from his forehead.

"Not true," said Fetterman. "I've seen him a couple of times. Once real close. He's out there and he's very good. And he'll kill our replacements before they have a chance to do anything. I want that bastard, and I want him badly.''

From the back came a new voice. Everyone turned to see Morrow standing there. "I've listened to enough of this. It's all crazy. You guys have put in your year. You deserve your DEROS. You shouldn't stay because of some perverted view of war. You don't owe anyone anything, except a good briefing on what is going on here.''

"Miss Morrow," said Gerber, "I appreciate your concern, but you really don't have a voice in this. If you want to return to Saigon, just say the word, and we'll have you out of here in an hour.''

"Sorry, Captain," she said. "I don't want anyone making a mistake that they may live to regret. Providing they get a chance to live.''

"I'm staying," said Gerber, "because it is our responsibility to take care of the Chinese officer. We're the ones who have hurt him, and it's us he wants.''

"I'm staying, too," said Fetterman. "For the obvious reason. I want that bastard.''

The debate raged for an hour. Several of the team members, having planned on their homecomings for a year, were reluctant to change their plans on such short notice. Gerber explained that Army regulations provided everyone who extended with a thirty-day leave before the start of the second part of the tour; they could still have their leave but then would be back doing an important job. They wouldn't be garrison troopers in the World, reading about the war or watching it on the six o'clock news.

Bromhead convinced almost all of the holdouts to extend when he volunteered to give up his promotion so that he could stay to help find and kill the Chinese officer. Only Kepler insisted he was going home. He had classes to attend because he wanted to become an officer.

"Derek, my boy," said Fetterman, "I won't argue with a man who has aspirations toward becoming an officer because someday he might be a general and I could find myself in an awkward position serving under him. But I will say this. If Captain Bromhead can offer up his promotion, I would think that you could wait six months. Besides, it would look good on your records. Volunteered for an extension of his tour to help make the world safe for democracy."

"You'd really give up your promotion?" Kepler asked Bromhead.

"It's a moot point," answered Gerber. "We won't let him."

"I would," answered Bromhead, anyway. "This is something that we should all do together."

"All right," said Kepler. "I can put my plans on hold for six months."

"Okay," said Gerber. "Tomorrow I will see Bates and tell him what we have in mind. I'll explain the situation to him. With luck, I can bring the papers back with me."

"I don't believe it," shouted Morrow. "You have all lost your fucking minds. To stay in this godforsaken hole for one extra day because of some abstract belief is insane! And you people want an extra six months?"

"Miss Morrow!" snapped Gerber. "I don't expect you to understand. I don't expect you to stay, either."

"No, I guess you don't, Captain," she said with obvious anger. "Sometimes you are so blind I wonder how you've managed to live this long. You think of this as some great crusade. Some great adventure. Save the world from Communism and make it safe."

"That's enough, Morrow," Gerber ordered.

"Don't take that tone with me," she shouted back. "I'm not one of your Boy Scouts. I live in the adult world."

"The adult world of journalism?" said Gerber sarcastically. "You really think of that as an adult world?"

"I don't have to take that shit from you, Gerber." She whirled and stormed from the team house.

Momentarily embarrassed and a little surprised by her anger, Gerber tried to cover it by saying, "What got into her?"

"I think it's more a case of what didn't," said Fetterman with a straight face. But everyone understood his meaning.

THE FOLLOWING MORNING Gerber hitched a ride to Saigon on the mail chopper. As the aircraft skimmed the jungle and muddy rice fields of Three Corps, he thought about his men. The team had finally decided they would stay in Vietnam an additional six months for the sole purpose of eliminating the Chinese officer. Once that was done, they would take their next rotation home. No one mentioned that they were really staying to avenge the death of McMillan because the Chinese officer was responsible for it. In fact, he was responsible for most of the bad things that had happened to them during their tour in Vietnam.

Gerber tried to tell himself that he was operating on a higher plane, and that his reasons for staying, while influenced by the death of McMillan and the operations conducted by the Chinese officer, were somehow more moral. He was staying to finish their job. In rare moments he knew that the real reason was to make sure the Chinese bastard drew only a limited number of breaths.

Gerber's mind replayed the orders he had left with Minh and Bromhead. The most important of them called for a platoon-sized operation in the area of the VC base at Trang Me. Gerber had been prepared to take a larger role in the surveillance but figured that Minh knew what he was doing and that Bromhead could use the experience. So Gerber just made sure they understood that someone should be watching the enemy camp until he could get to Nha Trang and pass the intelligence along. He expected one of the infantry divisions recently deployed to Vietnam to send in a battalion or two to take out the VC camp within a week.

That off his mind, Gerber had thrown some spare clothes into an overnight bag and had headed for the chopper. It was sitting on the pad on the northern end of the runway, the blades spinning, the cloud of red dust created by the landing slowly dissipating in the light morning breeze. To the west, storm clouds, that threatened rain later in the day, were swirling above Cambodia, but the bright sun overhead was baking the ground, making it hot and miserable in the open. He had no sooner climbed aboard than he saw various members of the team strolling toward him as if they wanted to be sure that he got on and the helicopter took off safely. Conspicuous by her absence was Morrow. As the noise of the chopper engine increased to a steady, earsplitting roar and the blades began to pop rhythmically, Gerber wondered if she was just pissed off about the whole episode of the night before or afraid that, if she was around, he would order her off the camp. Not that he particularly cared one way or the other. He settled back to enjoy the ride.

SINCE HE HADN'T TOLD Bates that he was coming, there was no one to meet him at Hotel Three. Carrying his overnight bag, with only his pistol safely hidden in his shoulder holster beneath his freshly laundered but unstarched fatigues, Gerber walked along the world's largest PX, a post exchange that would rival any of the department stores in the World. To one side, he could see a movie marquee proclaiming that a Paul Newman film was showing. Gerber passed it, thinking that someday he should try to see a movie there. He caught the odor of fresh hot popcorn drifting from the open doors of the cinema. As he neared the door of the PX, guarded by two Air Force MPs, he decided to enter on a whim.

Just inside, there was an eight-by-eight cubicle that passed for an entrance foyer, which was made of unpainted walls and had a dusty concrete floor. He was told that he would have to leave his overnight bag in one of the open lockers. The MP assured Gerber that his gear would be safe. Gerber nodded, not really caring because the bag contained only some clean underwear and a set of jungle fatigues. If somebody wanted to steal them, Gerber figured they could have them.

The first thing he noticed as he left the foyer and entered the PX itself was a large display of fur coats and diamond jewelry. Gerber looked at the coats, thinking that the last thing someone in Vietnam needed was a full-length mink coat. But he knew they were really meant for wives and girlfriends back in the World.

The main part of the PX was like a warehouse divided into sections for different types of merchandise. He saw everything that anyone could possibly want: stereos, color televisions, civilian suits, food, books and magazines, and on and on. In one corner was a lingerie selection that featured little that was practical but a lot that was interesting.

Two Vietnamese girls were modeling some of the more sedate costumes, wandering among the GIs and talking to them before moving on. For a moment Gerber had an urge to buy something for Morrow. In fact, he headed toward the section, seeing a black lace garter belt with black stockings that he liked, but then he realized what he was thinking and detoured away from it.

Finally he decided that he had wasted enough time and started back toward the door. He collected his bag and stepped outside into the early-afternoon sunlight. A wall of heat slammed into him, and it was only then he realized that the PX had been air-conditioned. In seconds he was through the gate that separated Hotel Three from the rest of Tan Son Nhut. It was a short walk from that gate to the Air Force Officers' Club where Gerber called the Army motor pool and got a jeep and driver to take him over the Bates's new office.

There was only a slight delay in Bates's outer office. Gerber stood in front of the clerk's desk, taking in the metal chairs that lined the room's perimeter, the potted plant stuck into a corner and the low table that held tattered copies of *Stars and Stripes* and *Army Times*. The clerk, newly promoted to Spec Four, waved Gerber into an inner area where Bates was only mildly surprised to see him.

"What can I do for you, Mack?" he asked, waving Gerber into one of the two blue armchairs that sat in front of his wooden desk. There was a matching blue couch against one wall and blue blinds on the window, which killed the rays of the afternoon sun. A bamboo mat was spread between the chairs and the desk. On the wall, paneled in plywood and painted a dull gray, was a single Army picture labeled *The Wagon Box Fight*. There was a quiet hum from an air conditioner in a corner that did little to cool the office.

"I want to extend," said Gerber.

"Oh, you do not," said Bates, grinning. Bates was a stocky man of medium height with graying blond hair, which he wore in a flattop. Laugh lines bracketed brown eyes in a round, tanned face. He was wearing starched, pressed jungle fatigues that held his jump wings and a combat infantryman's badge with two stars above the left breast pocket. "Now, what can I really do for you?"

"I said I want to extend. So does the rest of the team. We need more time to finish what we've started."

Bates stood up and came around his desk. He sat on the corner of it, letting one foot dangle. Gerber noticed the new jungle boots with the green nylon panel on the sides that allowed the foot to breathe. The boots had been polished but not spit shined. Bates clasped his hands and said, "Too late, Mack. Can't get the paperwork done in time. Orders have already been cut. Replacements have been slated, and your exec has been given an A-detachment."

"Let's stop dancing around this one, sir," said Gerber. "I want to stay on and so does my team. We've good reason for it, and I can't believe you'll take an experienced man out of the field to replace him with someone new."

Bates passed a hand through his graying hair and said, "What brought all this on?"

"You have some time?" asked Gerber.

"Plenty." Bates walked around his desk and sat down there. He pulled open the bottom drawer, propped his feet up on it and then laced his fingers behind his head and looked at the ceiling. "Tell me all about it."

For the next hour Gerber explained everything that had happened in the past few weeks, including the speculations about the assassination of McMillan. Gerber talked about his belief that the whole thing was being orchestrated by a Chinese officer, the same one they had discussed time and again. Now it had become more than a conflict of geopolitical ideologies. It had become a personal war between the Special Forces men from Camp A-555 and the Chinese officer who worked with the VC and NVA stationed just across the Cambodian border from them.

When Gerber stopped talking, Bates said, "And you now want to go after this man?"

"Wouldn't be the first time," Gerber smiled. "But, no, all we really want to do is destroy his unit."

"You have a plan?"

"No. But with six months to play with, we can plan some way to get him."

"Without operating in Cambodia again?"

"Listen, Alan," said Gerber, violating military protocol and presuming on friendship, "this man has targeted my team for extinction. He has now started the game, hell, he might have started it a month or more ago, and I don't want to be pulled in the final quarter because of some bureaucratic rule. If I don't destroy him, he is going to destroy my replacement. And that's a fact."

"Okay, Mack, let me ask you one question. Did your team volunteer to stay without any coercion from you?"

"We discussed it for several hours, but after that we were all in agreement. Even Captain Bromhead."

"Say, that's right. Bromhead finally got his orders. I'll have to hit him up to buy me a drink or ten at the club next chance I get."

"He's so happy about the promotion, I think if he was here he would have gone broke buying drinks for everyone."

"Okay," said Bates. "I'll get my clerk to type up the papers for you to sign. You can take the ones for the rest of the team back when you go."

"One other thing," said Gerber. "McMillan had a friend in Nha Trang. I need to go tell her that he was killed."

"The Army will notify his family."

"She's not family. She's just a friend, but I think they were quite close. I would like to tell her."

"I don't know. You're asking for an awful lot here, Mack. An extension this late and now a trip to Nha Trang."

"Well," said Gerber, "there *is* something else. I told you about the VC base at Trang Me. I need to go to Nha Trang to let the SFOB know about it so that they can get something in there to destroy it."

Bates stood. "That information can be forwarded from here."

"Of course it could. I could be debriefed by one of the Intelligence officers here, but I would really appreciate it if I could go to Nha Trang. Louise deserves it."

"Louise?"

"Sergeant McMillan's friend. She deserves better than hearing about his death via the grapevine. We're supposed to take care of our own, and she is one of ours."

"I'll get you on the afternoon flight and have the papers dispatched to your camp as soon as they're typed. You'll need to get them back as soon as you can."

Now Gerber stood. For a second he hesitated, studying the older man. Gerber had caused him a dozen problems in the past few months, but Bates had always been there when he needed help. He had protected Gerber and the team from Crinshaw and the other brass hats stationed in Saigon.

"Thanks, Colonel," said Gerber. "I knew I could count on you. You've been a big help."

"Sure," said Bates. "Get out of here before I change my mind."

5

ABOARD AN AIR FORCE C-130 EN ROUTE TO NHA TRANG, RVN

Gerber sat in the red webbing that formed the seats along both sides of the C-130's fuselage and wondered exactly what to say to Louise Denton. With the roar from the four Allison T56 turbo-props and the lack of soundproofing inside the aircraft, it was almost impossible to carry on a conversation with any of the other passengers. As they were boarding, the flight engineer or the loadmaster had handed out earplugs. That virtually isolated the passengers from one another.

Sitting on the ground in Saigon with the doors open and the ramp down had been hot and miserable. Gerber was belted into his seat between two perspiring, overweight sergeants. They had leaned across him, mumbling apologies, and then carried on a long-winded, extremely loud argument about the relative merits of the hookers they had shared the night before. Gerber tried to ignore them and finally got up to move away from them. Moments later the loadmaster had shut the doors and closed the ramp, and they had bounced down the runway for takeoff.

Once airborne, the air in the cabin had turned so cold that the crew was forced to use the heaters. Now Gerber tried to figure out how to break the news to Denton. And then he wondered where he should tell her. He wasn't sure that the relationship between Denton and McMillan was quite as close as he had led Bates to

believe but thought he owed it to her to tell her in person. Tha
left all the questions that were swirling around.

In case her reaction was bad, he wanted her away from the oth
ers so that she would have time to compose herself. The hospita
would be the wrong place, as would the club or a downtown Nha
Trang restaurant or bar. Everything was wrong because it was al
too public. Maybe he should just find a jeep and tell her there
Tell her quickly, and then let her decide what she wanted to do

Of course, if she wasn't as in love with McMillan as Gerbe
thought, none of it would matter. He could tell her in a hospita
corridor, or call her on the phone or let her learn about it from
others.

And none of it gave him the words he needed to tell her. Tha
was what he really dreaded. How do you break the news to some
one that a person close to them is now dead? It wasn't completely
unexpected because the Special Forces lived on the edge all the
time, but that didn't make the task any easier. Nor did it give him
the words. He didn't want to blurt it out, and then he realized tha
people always drew out telling good news. They tried to make i
seem bad. Tried to make it a joke. But bad news, really bad news
was told in as few words and as quickly as possible.

For a moment Gerber stared at the men across the aisle from
him. They were all young and all looked scared. Three or fou
were Army and the remainder were Air Force, and all were wear
ing new fatigues. He could tell they were new by the bright green
color. They hadn't had time for the sun and repeated washings to
bleach them to a light green. It meant the military was drafting
men younger and sending them to Vietnam quicker.

Gerber realized he was trying to distract himself from the
problem at hand. Where to tell her? How to tell her?

He supposed the best thing was to just say something like
"Louise, I have some very bad news. Ian was killed in action."
There was no way to soften the blow. Let her ask questions if she
wanted more information. Let her take it from there, and he could
react to her. Louise could set the tone.

There was a jeep waiting for him at Nha Trang. It sat in the
shade next to the tower, the windshield down, and as Gerber ap
proached, he saw why. Both sides were badly cracked, the driv
er's side looking as if it had been hit by bullets. The driver, who
was a regular Army sergeant, was leaning back, one foot on the

dashboard, his hat pulled down over his eyes. As the passengers walked down the ramp of the C-130, the sergeant sat up and started the engine, heading for the only person wearing a green beret. He pulled up next to the officer and leaned over to yell, "Captain Gerber?"

"Yes."

"I've been sent over to give you a lift."

Gerber threw his gear in the back.

As soon as he had climbed in, the sergeant gunned the engine, and they roared off in the direction of the Fifth Special Forces Headquarters. Here Gerber spent the rest of the afternoon filling them in on the VC base camp they had found. He talked to Major William Houston, the Intelligence officer, a couple of other staff officers and three NCOs who made copious notes and checked a dozen separate maps. Every few seconds Gerber would remember the real reason he was there and would feel his stomach turn over. As he finished the debriefing, he realized that he would have to call someone at the hospital to make sure Louise was still there. He was not looking forward to the next hour.

Outside the debriefing room Gerber found a clerk's office with a phone and then found the number of the hospital in a mimeographed phone book that had most of the numbers crossed out. New ones had been scribbled in the margins. He had spent weeks trying to forget the number after Karen Morrow had left Vietnam.

After nearly ten minutes someone located Louise Denton and got her on the phone. When she answered, it sounded as if she had run through the ward. "Ian, is that you?"

"No, Louise," said Gerber carefully. "This is Mack Gerber. You remember me, don't you?"

"Of course, Captain. Are you here in Nha Trang?" There was no suspicion in her voice.

"Yes, for the day. I thought we might get together for a while."

Her voice suddenly turned cold. "No, Captain, I don't think that would be a good idea."

"No, wait! I'm afraid you don't understand. I'd like to meet you for a few minutes when it's convenient." Gerber was aware that his own voice sounded strained and unnatural. He tried to lighten the mood slightly by saying, "I'll buy you a drink. Anything you want."

There was a long pause before she said, "I get off at six. There's a small club that the medical people use. Do you know it?"

"Yes, I know it." All too well, Gerber thought. Karen Morrow had taken him there a couple of times when he had been in Nha Trang, and he wasn't sure how he would react to being in it again. It was filled with memories of his affair with Karen, and it was a place that he had planned to avoid. Although she didn't know it Louise was making this harder than necessary.

"I'll meet you there a little after six."

"That'll be fine." Gerber hung up, thinking she had totally misunderstood why he called. She had sounded as if he were trying to date her, and although they had had some interesting discussions while she was at his camp with a medical unit, he had never done anything to suggest that he was interested in her as a woman.

With some time to kill, he decided to head over to the PCOD lounge for a couple of drinks. Something to relax him for the coming ordeal. He didn't want to see Louise because he knew what was going to happen.

SHE WAS SITTING with two other nurses at a table at the rear, out of the way. The club was small, only a couple of tables surrounded by chairs, with a bar stuck in one corner. There were four stools in front of it and a small mirror behind it. Denton had her back to him, but he recognized the red hair piled high on her head to conform to Army regulations. She was wearing jungle fatigues but there was no mistaking the feminine shape. Gerber knew that she had brought the other two nurses so that he couldn't try anything. He wondered how he could separate her from her reinforcements.

He walked up behind her and placed a hand on her shoulder to get her attention. She turned her head, looked up and smiled briefly. Then she saw the look on his face. She stared into his eyes for a moment and then shook her head as if she had seen a ghost. The blood drained from her face, and Gerber realized that she knew.

She looked at the two nurses with her and said, "Would you excuse us?"

Neither moved.

"Please. It's all right."

As the two women left the table and headed for the empty stools at the bar, Gerber slipped into a chair and took Denton's hand. She squeezed in response and said, "Please," without realizing she had spoken again.

"Would you like to get out of here?" asked Gerber.

She bit her bottom lip, gripping it in her teeth, then closed her eyes and shook her head. "When?"

"Two days ago, about dawn."

"I knew it," she breathed. "I felt it. Do you know what happened to him?"

"Louise, I'm very sorry about this. I didn't know how to do this. I haven't had to do it before."

She held herself together as long as she could. The tears that had been burning her eyes spilled over, running down her cheeks. She dropped her head to her arms and rested them on the table.

Gerber stood and reached out, lifting her from the chair and guiding her out of the room. One of the nurses who had been with Denton half rose, and Gerber shook his head, telling her that it was all right. The woman hesitated, saw Denton take Gerber's hand and dropped back to her stool.

Outside, they turned right and walked rapidly to the corner of the building where the shadows would hide them. Gerber twisted her shoulders so that she faced him, then put his arms around her. She clung to him and mumbled something that Gerber couldn't understand. She began to shake as she cried harder. Finally she regained control of herself. She leaned her cheek against his shoulder and said quietly, "We got married, you know. When he was here. Just went downtown and got married. It didn't mean anything to the Army, but it did to us."

Gerber hadn't counted on this. The revelation about the marriage caused him even more distress. He was at a loss for words. Everything he thought of would sound trite, he realized. Everything would sound insincere. He had felt this before and hadn't found an answer to it. He wondered how ministers could talk to the relatives of the recently dead. What could they say that would relieve the pain? Everything seemed so inadequate.

"Is there someone you would like me to call?"

She didn't answer right away. Then she said, "Do you know what happened?"

"We've managed to put some of it together. He was ambushed while on patrol. I know it'll mean nothing to you, but we put him in for a Silver Star."

"It'll make his parents happy," she said. "Now, if you don't mind, I would like to go back into the club and drink heavily for about three hours and then pass out."

"Tell you what," he said, a little too cheerfully. "I'll buy the first one and then leave quietly."

"No. Please. Drink with me. No one here knew Ian, and I want to think about him a lot tonight. No one here will understand."

"Louise, Ian was special to all of us. He had a talent that we're going to sorely miss. I think a little of all of us died with him, and I would be more than happy to drink with you tonight. Anything you want, you've got. We, meaning the team and I, owe him that much. You're one of us, too."

Denton slipped her hand into his and nearly dragged him back into the club. She stopped at the bar long enough to order a bottle of Scotch, but when the bartender set it in front of her, she pushed it away. "Not Scotch," she said. "Beam's. A bottle of Beam's."

"You can drink anything you like," said Gerber.

"And tonight I want to drink Beam's."

"Good choice. You want a mixer?"

"Straight. I want it straight, and I want a lot of it."

Three hours later Denton's eyes were unfocused, and she was weaving back and forth in her chair as if she were having trouble sitting up. She couldn't speak in full sentences, and what she did say made little sense. She had finished most of the bottle herself and had ordered a second.

At midnight Gerber decided that it was time to get her back to her room. He corked the remainder of the bourbon, stuffed the bottle into one of the side pockets of his jungle jacket and stood. Denton looked up and smiled. "What's this?"

"Time to go. You've had enough."

"I don' thin' there's any such thin' as enough."

"Sure there is. You think you can find the way?"

"The way where? To room? You have ta help. You have ta take me."

Gerber led her from the club, keeping her upright with great difficulty. At the door to the nurse's quarters, she stumbled and fell and ended up sitting on the floor, giggling helplessly. She couldn't stand up, and she couldn't stop laughing. Gerber bent and picked her up. She wrapped her arms around him and buried her face in his neck. "Nice," she mumbled. "Real nice." The word sounded like "nahce."

"Where to?"

"Right. Go right and don' fall."

To Gerber's horror, Louise Denton lived in the same building where Karen Morrow had lived, except on a different floor. But each one mirrored all the others, and Gerber had an uncomfortable feeling of déjà vu. The only way he could find Louise's room was by walking up and down the hall, reading the signs on the doors listing the occupants.

To make matters worse, when he found her quarters, he learned that she lived alone in a room that duplicated the one Karen had lived in. Denton's roommate had DEROSed. He was alone with her in her room.

He set her on the bed, a standard Army cot with a thick mattress, and OD blanket and worn cotton sheets. As he moved to the wall switch so that he could turn on the light, Denton stood up and began to undress. She dropped her fatigue jacket to the floor and was struggling with the buttons on her pants.

"Help me!" she demanded. "I canna get them."

"Louise, go to bed."

"Wha's wrong, Cap'n Mack. You don' like me?"

"I like you just fine, but in the morning you wouldn't like yourself. The best thing for you is to go to sleep. You're set for it now."

"I don' wanna sleep. I wanna play." She continued to try to unbutton her pants, weaving around until she lost her balance and fell again, landing on the small area rug that lay on the painted plywood floor. She finally tugged at her pants with all her might and scattered the buttons. Then she wiggled from side to side on her bottom, all the while sliding the pants over her hips. She kicked her legs until the trousers had slipped to her ankles, then sat quietly for a moment. Suddenly she bent forward and pounded the floor with both fists, demanding, "Why?"

Gerber sat beside her and put his arm around her but didn't say anything. He waited for her to do something. Her shoulders shook for a moment, and he heard a broken sob. Denton cried quietly for a while, the tears staining her already dirty face and dropping from her chin to her chest. Finally she leaned her head against his shoulder, and he could hear the sobs diminishing. In a couple of minutes, she was sound asleep.

Carefully he lifted her to the bed and tried to remove her pants, but then realized that he would have to take off her boots to manage it. That finished, he got her pants off and tossed them to the single metal chair in a corner. He was tempted to remove her bra, but it was under her T-shirt, and he figured she would not appreciate his removing it. He then took the dustcover from her bunk and spread it across her inert form, even though it was still fairly hot and the fan turning slowly on the ceiling did little to relieve the heat. He moved to the windows, which were covered by bare venetian blinds. Pulling two of the slats apart, he peered through them. He opened the window to catch the slight breeze from the sea. There were lights visible below, but nothing that was bright enough for him to identify the source. He let the blinds bang back against the plywood wall and window frame.

He walked across the room, stopped at the door for a second and looked at her. She was a very pretty woman who had had a lot to drink. She had red hair that was more auburn than red, a complexion that was tanned to a golden brown by time on the beach and eyes that were like liquid emeralds. He realized that, if the situation had been different, he would have been tempted to take her offer, but it had been the liquor talking.

Gerber felt an overwhelming sadness for the Louise Denton's of this world, for himself and for all those who found themselves in that place called Vietnam.

To himself, he said, "If you want, call me, Louise." He snapped off the light and closed the door.

As he left the quarters, he saw a couple of nurses playing cards in the dayroom at the far end of the hall. He walked toward it, the sound of his footsteps muffled by the dirty plywood of the floor. He leaned in and asked, "Any of you know Louise Denton?"

"Yeah. So?"

"She got some bad news tonight and drank quite a bit. Somebody might want to check on her. Make sure that she's all right."

"Okay, Captain. Sure will."

Gerber then went over to the Playboy Club where the Special Forces people drank when they came off duty. He ignored most of the men inside, not recognizing any of them. The Special Forces had expanded so much recently that it was no longer the elite bunch it had been where everyone knew everyone else. He bought a beer at the makeshift bar opposite the door and took it to a small table hidden in a corner where he could drink it alone. After he finished drinking the beer, he decided he didn't want another. He had had too much for one night, and he didn't want to get drunk. Finally he left, walking to the barracks reserved for transient military personnel where there was a room held for him. He took the bottle that he had saved from Denton's spree, poured himself a final drink and hoped that he wouldn't have to spend another day trying to tell someone that the person she loved had been killed in action. He didn't understand how the officers in the World could do it day after day.

6

**SPECIAL FORCES
OPERATING BASE, NHA
TRANG, RVN**

Unlike the mornings in the bush, Gerber awoke slowly. The sunlight, filtering through the screened window, woke him. He turned over, not wanting to leave the comfort of a real bed with real sheets on it. He didn't want to get up because that would mean returning to his responsibilities at Camp A-555. It would mean a morning of hassles with clerks who had momentary power over him with their manifests and flight rosters. It would mean standing in hot departure lounges waiting for aircraft that might not arrive because no one had printed schedules. Units were tasked to supply aircraft for the ash and trash flights, but mission requirements, not to mention enemy action, sometimes dictated the airplanes be diverted.

Gerber rolled to his back and opened his eyes. He could see a rough ceiling with two wires leading to a lone light bulb. To his left was a folding metal chair where he had put the uniform he had been wearing the night before. To the right was the single open window, the blinds locked to the top and a light, warm breeze blowing through. The walls, made of quarter-inch plywood, had been painted a revolting light green, and a woven bamboo mat rested on the floor. There was a shelf nailed to the wall opposite the window, with a bar under it to hang uniforms and civilian clothes. It was a stark, impersonal room that provided nothing except a convenient resting place for the men whose destination was Nha Trang.

He got out of bed, grabbed his shaving kit from his overnight bag and headed to the shower. Ten minutes later, feeling refreshed, he put on his clean uniform. Unlike those worn by the rear area progues, his uniform was not starched or freshly ironed. He checked out of his room and left the building.

Outside, he headed over to the PCOD lounge to see if he could find some breakfast. Failing there, he wandered toward the hospital, accidentally walked into a mess hall and was offered something to eat. Since they were serving fresh eggs, fresh fried potatoes and fresh fruit, Gerber decided not to argue and grabbed a metal tray, a metal cup and utensils that looked as if they had survived the Second World War. But since the food was better than anything he had at his camp, he was happy.

Two hours later Gerber was on a C-123 heading to Dau Tieng where he could hop on a chopper to take him to the Triple Nickel. He caught a ride about midafternoon and in less than an hour was standing alone on the helipad in a swirling cloud of red dust and debris, watching as a couple of the team members rushed over to see him.

"Colonel Bates is in the team house," Smith informed him before he had a chance to speak.

Gerber smiled at the sergeant and said, "Yes, Sully, I had a fine trip, and it's good to be back."

"Sorry, Captain. Thought you would want to know about the colonel."

"Yes, of course." He held out his overnight bag. "Get this to my hootch, and I'll trot over and see what the colonel wants."

"Orders," said Smith. "He brought our extension papers and orders for leave. Gave us about three days to clear out of town."

Gerber found Bates talking to Fetterman as the two men studied a map spread out on a table. As he entered, Fetterman looked up and said, "I was just showing Colonel Bates where we found that VC base camp."

"Go right ahead," said Gerber. "I'll grab a cup of coffee if any of you thought to leave some for me."

Without a word Fetterman turned back to the map, and as Gerber moved toward them, Bocker entered the team house.

Grinning, he headed straight for Gerber. "Welcome back, Captain."

"You been talking to Sully?"

"Yes, sir. He said that you were in a bad mood and I should welcome you back before I said anything else to you."

"Well, I appreciate the thought even if the motives aren't all that swift," said Gerber, also grinning. He sipped the coffee he had poured. "Something I can do for you, Galvin?"

"Yes, sir. Got a lieutenant colonel on the line from some leg outfit. Claims that he has been detailed for a special mission and wants to coordinate with you. Wonders if tomorrow morning, about 0800 will be convenient."

Gerber shot a glance at Bates, who merely shrugged. To Bocker, Gerber said, "Where does he want to meet?"

"He'll fly in here, if that's all right."

"Tell him I'll be waiting for him."

As Bocker disappeared, Bates said, "Guess your little trip to Nha Trang did some good. I figured it would be a week before anyone moved on it."

LIEUTENANT COLONEL EDWARD THOMPSON looked the part of an Army officer as he stepped off his shiny helicopter at exactly 0800 the next morning. He was a short, barrel-chested man with stubby legs. Under the rim of his helmet, Gerber could see small, dark eyes and thin black eyebrows. The man had a large nose and a small mouth with thin lips. His cheeks looked as if they had been smeared with black shoe polish, but Gerber knew it was the stubble from a beard that he could not shave close enough to hide.

His fatigues were starched to within an inch of their lives, the creases knife sharp and his boots nearly radiating black. The camouflage cover of his steel pot had been washed recently, his flak jacket looked new and he didn't have an Army-issue weapon. He had a pearl-handled revolver in an Old West holster strapped to his hip. Gerber wondered if he could outdraw the VC.

Trying to suppress a smile, Gerber moved across the helipad to shake hands with the new arrival. When he was within speaking distance, Thompson shouted over the roar of the Huey turbine and the popping of the blades, "Don't you remember how to salute?"

Immediately Gerber knew that he was in trouble with this guy. Without saluting, he approached the colonel and said, "We try not to identify each other for the VC here. Saluting only tells Charlie who the officers are."

Thompson nodded once, "It's your base, Captain. Is there somewhere we can talk?"

"Thought we'd wait for your crew to get their aircraft shut down and then all go over to the team house."

"The crew will remain with the aircraft and do their jobs," the colonel said stiffly. "There is a war on, and we all have to make sacrifices. It won't hurt them to stand by here with their equipment." Thompson stepped away from the helipad, heading in the direction of the redoubt. "This the way to your team house?"

"Yes, sir." Gerber thought of a dozen things to say, a half-dozen pieces of advice about how to survive in the field, but decided to remain silent. He knew Thompson's type, the ones who never bent the rules, who went strictly by the book. Gerber knew it wasn't that kind of a war. Thompson would learn fast or be replaced after he was KIA.

In the team house Gerber introduced Thompson to Bates. Although Gerber hadn't been formally introduced to Thompson, he had read his name off the tag sewn to his flak vest. The two colonels shook hands solemnly. Then Gerber, with Fetterman's help, began the unofficial briefing.

After an hour Thompson nodded and said, "I have everything I need. I can begin airlifting my battalion in here this afternoon."

"Whoa, Colonel," said Gerber, waving his hands. "We don't have the facilities to support a battalion. We couldn't even accommodate a regular company."

"Don't worry about it, Captain. My boys are used to roughing it. They can see how well those shelter halves we issue to them work. We'll bring our own food, too. All you'll have to do is supply the ground for them to sleep on. Tomorrow we'll head out into the bush."

"Pardon me, Colonel," insisted Gerber, "but if you have the aviation assets, wouldn't it be easier to insert them closer to the target? Why make them walk fifteen klicks?"

"You let me run my battalion, Captain," said Thompson harshly, folding his map and sticking it into one of the large pockets in his fatigues.

"Glad to, Colonel," said Gerber. "But I don't want to see Charlie get away from the tunnels with all that equipment. There is too much hidden out there that could be used against us. A battalion-sized sweep through here is going to tip our hand and give the VC time to get the stuff out of there."

"From what your Sergeant Fetterman said, I doubt he could get all that much of it out."

"Unless he had a regiment in there and each one of them carries away two rifles. All we would find down there would be that damned antiaircraft artillery and the straw they use in some of the sleeping areas."

Bates, who had been listening to the argument with a great deal of amusement, entered the conversation. "Colonel Thompson, why not throw a company of infantry into the LZ closest to the village as a recon and blocking force? That should prevent the VC from evacuating their equipment."

"Because, Colonel, that would leave a company out in the open with no chance for immediate support if they got hit. Take us hours to march to their relief."

Gerber could contain himself no longer. "Oh, for crying out loud. You're airmobile. If they get hit, you can fly them reinforcements in a few minutes. Especially if you have the majority of your battalion here and the aircraft on standby."

"Don't you go taking that tone with me, Captain. I am fully cognizant of the capabilities of my unit and its aviation assets."

"Yes, sir," said Gerber. "Sorry."

"I'll tell you what, Captain. I will bring the battalion in here, and before we move out, I will dispatch a company as a recon and blocking force. I'll need one of your people to advise that company, and I would like another to guide the ground force."

"Ah, Colonel," interrupted Bates again, "Captain Gerber's team is scheduled for leave."

"All of them?" Thompson asked incredulously. "At once?"

"Yes. A special circumstance."

"Colonel Thompson," said Gerber, "I'll be happy to go with the recon company and delay my departure by a couple of days."

"Mack," said Bates, "the commercial flights are all arranged. You might not be able to get another one for a week or more."

"I'll take that chance."

"That leaves us one man short," said Thompson.

"Oh, no, sir," said Fetterman, speaking for the first time since the briefing had ended. "I'll go with your other force. I'm quite familiar with the terrain and the route."

"Tony?" said Gerber.

"If you can do it, Captain, so can I. That gets everyone else out on time. It's no big deal."

"What about Mrs. Fetterman and the kids?"

"Well, sir, someday I'll let you in on a little secret about Mrs. Fetterman and the kids, but for right now let's just say that they understand that my job sometimes requires a little overtime."

Then Gerber, with sudden insight, said, "Colonel Bates, would you like to accompany us on this operation? You don't get out into the war all that much."

"Why, thank you, Mack. I would be delighted."

THE NEXT MORNING Gerber had to admit that he was impressed. Thompson had gotten his battalion deployed from its staging area in Bien Hoa to the camp by sundown that same night. He saw to it that each of his companies had enough hot food to feed all the combat troops. Each man had some kind of shelter before the sun set. They were not much larger than the Second World War pup tents, made from the shelter halves issued to the men and staked to the ground. Each company had its own area, its own perimeter and its own guards. Thompson and his staff declined the offer of the team house and erected their tents in the center of the battalion. All in all, it was an amazing piece of logistical work.

At dawn Gerber and Bates climbed aboard a helicopter along with six other American soldiers from the 173rd Airborne Brigade. There were fifteen aircraft in the flight so that the force being lifted to an LZ some two klicks from the ville numbered almost a hundred and fifty.

The flight was short, and Gerber expected to be on the ground in minutes. What he hadn't expected was a burst of machine gun fire from the trees on one side of the LZ as the helicopters began the approach. Since it was only one weapon and the location was identified by the muzzle flashes, the flight continued, no one concerned about the single enemy soldier hiding there.

But then the situation changed as a dozen others opened fire, raking the right side of the flight. The gunship escorts rolled in, firing their 2.75-inch rockets into the trees in a futile attempt to suppress the enemy.

The door gunners, each manning an M-60 machine gun, began to fire, raking the trees with their concentrated 7.62 mm ammunition. Gerber, sitting beside an infantryman, yelled over the noise of the engine and the rotor blades and the hammering of the M-60s, "Why don't you fire back?"

"Pilots don't like the new boys shooting out the doors. Some of them tend to shoot holes in the rotors, and they frown on that."

Gerber shot a glance at Bates, who was also sitting beside him, clutching his M-14, knuckles turning white. But there was a grin on his face, and his eyes were sparkling as if he hadn't had so much fun in years.

The volume of fire from the ground seemed to increase, and Gerber could identify AK-47s, .30-caliber machine guns and a couple of 12.5 mm antiaircraft weapons. He watched part of the windshield disintegrate, but neither pilot seemed to notice as they fought to hold their position in the formation. One of the grunts grabbed at his shoulder and slumped to the deck of the helicopter, his blood splashing over the back of the pilot's armored seat.

Then they were on the ground with the crew chief shouting, "Unass the aircraft. Get the fuck off!" More enemy weapons joined in, filling the air with green-and-white tracers. Fountains of black dirt and filthy water geysered as mortars began falling around them.

Gerber leaped from the helicopter, took a single step and dived to the ground to find cover behind a bush. Behind him the choppers lifted as a unit and roared skyward rapidly, the door guns still firing into the trees in front of the grunts now on the ground.

Bates crawled to him and yelled unnecessarily, "Now what?"

"Let's see if the company commander knows what he's doing before we make any moves."

Before Gerber stopped talking, there was a series of pops, like fireworks being shot in sequence, and M-79 grenades began exploding at the edge of the tree line into tiny clouds of black smoke and silver shrapnel. At the same time the gunships, which had been escorting the Slicks off the LZ, returned, their rockets and machine guns strafing the trees where the heaviest of the enemy fire seemed to be located.

When that happened, there was a lull in the enemy firing, then the grunts were on their feet, running forward, some of them firing from their hips. Gerber and Bates joined the assault, and as they all reached the cover of the trees, the gunships broke contact, peeling away to the right and then standing off slightly as if waiting for the VC to try something else.

In the trees Gerber couldn't see much. Directly in front of him, there appeared to be a single enemy soldier sighting an AK. Gerber fired a quick burst, saw it hit the man high and spin him before he dropped to the ground, his weapon flying from his hand. Gerber sprinted forward, leaped a small bush and was crouching over the enemy corpse. One of the bullets had neatly removed the top of his head and another had severed the jugular.

Gerber picked up the enemy weapon, not as a souvenir but to deny it to the VC, and continued into the trees. Behind him he heard an M-14 fire twice and turned to see Bates disappear into the bush a few feet away. Before Gerber could move, a sound to his right caught his attention. He spun to see a VC leaping through the air, a knife clutched in his hand. Without thinking, Gerber moved to parry the attack. But the enemy crashed into him, slamming the flimsy rifle against his stomach. Gerber pulled the trigger once and let the momentum of the impact force them both to the ground.

Rolling clear, Gerber was on his feet, using his M-16 to cover the VC who had both arms clutching his stomach as blood leaked out his back in an ever-decreasing stream.

Gerber looked at the barrel of his rifle and saw that the force of the blow had bent it slightly. He didn't know how the weapon had fired without blowing up but was grateful that it hadn't. He pushed the barrel against a tree, bending it nearly double. He then ejected the magazine and put it in his pocket to keep the ammunition out of the hands of the VC. Throwing away the useless M-16, Gerber unslung the AK he had picked up. He made sure a round was chambered and then checked the two bodies for spare magazines.

Finally, with Bates, also holding an AK, in sight again, Gerber joined the sweep through the trees. There had been a momentary flurry of hand-to-hand combat as the Americans assaulted the enemy positions, surprising them with the ferocity and speed of the attack. But Charlie, realizing that he might not be outnumbered but was being out-soldiered, fled.

As Gerber reached the opposite edge of the tree line, he saw nearly a hundred VC and a dozen or so NVA fleeing across the rice fields, trying to reach safety on the other side where they would probably disappear into what they thought was the haven of their base camp.

Then to the right Gerber heard someone yell "Grenade!" He dropped to the ground and saw a grunt leap for the explosive. Rather than throwing himself on it as the Hollywood heroes often did, the soldier picked it up and threw it at the escaping VC. It detonated far short of the enemy but had been thrown fast enough that it inflicted no American casualties, either.

Getting to his knees, Gerber shouted at the man, "Well done."

Weapons fire from the Americans tapered off as the targets disappeared among the palms, teaks and mahogany trees of a finger of jungle across the paddies. Then the gunships, which had been waiting another turn, rolled in. For a moment Gerber knelt in the protection of the tree line and watched as the rockets, fired in ripples, whooshed overhead, and then miniguns, sounding like a gigantic buzz saw, raked the new enemy position. At first there was some sporadic return fire, but that quickly died as if the enemy had learned that shooting only brought a hostile response.

While the gunships were working out on the enemy, the grunt company commander crawled through the trees until he found both Gerber and Bates. When he was near them both, he asked, "What do you think?"

Without pointing and trying not to gesture, Gerber said, "We need to keep the VC off balance. They weren't really prepared for us, and those choppers are a little more than irritating, but I think Charlie is going to keep on the move. He's running now and won't stop until he's either in Cambodia or in that base we found."

"And we don't want him to get comfortable in that tunnel system," said Bates. "It would take us a month to dig him out of there. We have to keep the pressure on."

"But the colonel can't get here—"

"Captain," said Gerber, "I just saw fifteen choppers take off. He can have another company here in a few minutes. I would get on the horn and tell him to put a company into point X-ray Delta as soon as he can."

The grunt captain pulled his map from a pocket and looked at
. Gerber reached over his arm and pointed. "That's the clear-
ig right there on the other side of the ville. If they sweep out of
iere, they should be able to hit the VC in less than thirty min-
tes. That keeps up the pressure Colonel Bates spoke of."

"And what do we do?"

"Should be obvious. We attack across the rice fields as quickly
s we can."

As the grunt stood to go find his RTO, Gerber grabbed his
leeve. "I assume that your people are all fairly green. Tell them
) step on the rice plants as we sweep through the paddies. It will
eep their feet from sinking deep into the mud."

\T CAMP A-555 Fetterman watched as the rest of the team
limbed aboard the Chinook CH-47 that would take them to Sai-
on so they could catch the Freedom Bird to the World. As Tyme
tarted up the ramp, he stopped long enough to yell over the noise
f the twin engines and popping blades, "You sure you don't need
is?"

Fetterman leaned close to the other man's ear and shouted right
ack. "The captain and I can handle this little recon chore, and
hen we'll be joining you youngsters in the World."

"Then I have only one thing to say. FIIGMO. See you in a
nonth or so."

"Right you are, Boom-Boom. Now get on this thing before I
·hange my mind and go in your place."

Fetterman moved away from the aircraft as the rear ramp closed
.nd the rotors began to pick up speed. Then the helicopter lifted
)ff the ground, hung for a moment over the PSP of the pad, kick-
ng up huge clouds of red dust, and turned to the north to begin
ts climb out. In only a minute it was a speck near the horizon.
When it was out of sight, Fetterman turned toward the commo
)unker where he could see a couple of the grunts waiting.

As he approached, Colonel Thompson came out, saw him and
:aid, "Looks like your captain and my company stepped on their
licks. We're going to put in another airlift. You want to accom-
)any me?"

"Be delighted, sir."

They entered the team house together, but Thompson stopped short. He saw Robin Morrow sitting at one of the tables, a can of beer in front of her as she worked a crossword puzzle.

"What is that civilian doing here?" demanded Thompson.

"That is Miss Morrow, a member of the press."

"Well, get her out of here."

Before Fetterman could move or speak, Morrow had picked up her puzzle and beer and said, "I think I will find somewhere else to sit." She swept by Thompson without so much as a glance in his direction, but as she neared the door, she mumbled, "Asshole."

When she was gone, Thompson spread his map out on the table. "Near as I can figure and from what the pilots have said, they ran into it near the LZ, which was right here."

Fetterman stared at where the colonel's finger tapped the map. The team sergeant nodded. It was the right LZ. He pointed and said, "The ville is here. Now on the other side of it, here, is an open area where we can put thirty helicopters if we have to. It's less than a klick to the village, and if the VC are retreating toward it, we should be able to make contact with them here. That would also take some of the pressure off the captain."

"You've been there, then, I take it."

"To that specific LZ, yes, sir. We passed through it once. There are no obstructions in it. There are bunkers surrounding it, but they were deserted when we swept through."

Outside, there was the sound of more than a dozen Huey helicopters as they approached for landing. Thompson turned to look but couldn't see anything through the side of the building. He grinned at Fetterman and said, "I believe our ride has arrived."

"I'll grab my weapon and meet you at the choppers, sir."

"Snap to it, sergeant," said Thompson unnecessarily.

7

EN ROUTE TO THE LZ
NEAR TRANG ME

Fetterman felt uncomfortable as the flight approached the LZ. Not because of the helicopter with its cloth troop seat or the steel pot on his head and the web gear hanging from his shoulders, but because he didn't know the men he was riding into combat with. He had never seen any of them in action, had no idea what kind of training they had had in the art of jungle fighting and didn't know if they were reliable when the shooting started.

All he could do was hope for the best and that was what had killed his great-great-great-grandfather, William J. Fetterman, who had hoped for the best when he rode out of Fort Phil Kearney with eighty cavalrymen and infantrymen to meet two thousand Sioux Indians led by Crazy Horse.

As the terrain under him changed from paddy fields reflecting the sun to sparse jungle that concealed the ground and possibly the enemy, Fetterman realized they were nearing the LZ. He chambered a round in his M-3 grease gun and fastened the chin strap of his helmet so he wouldn't lose it when he jumped from the helicopter. He noticed that the young men on the chopper with him let theirs dangle free just like John Wayne. It wasn't a good sign.

They began their descent, and Fetterman could see the hardwood teak and mahogany trees rising up until they towered over the chopper. Fetterman expected the shooting to start at any second, but there was none. As the skids of the aircraft touched the ground covered with short grass, Fetterman was out and moving toward the tree line, following the group of men who had been on the ship in front of him. Thompson was leading a charge at the innocuous-looking trees, running across the open ground, like a back on a broken field. Without a sound he entered the jungle and disappeared from sight, and Fetterman fully expected the ambush to spring at that second.

The helicopters lifted off safely and headed back toward the camp. Fetterman, still waiting for the ambush, entered the jungle and saw that the colonel and his men had stopped long enough to explore some of the abandoned bunkers. These were low affairs, a single log concealing the firing port, bushes and dirt spread on top for camouflage and a shallow hole in the back so that the VC could enter and retreat. Fetterman watched a lone man leap into the back of one, as he had probably been taught to do, and before Fetterman could shout a warning, there was a gigantic explosion that shook the ground and filled the air with a cloud of dirt and debris.

Immediately there was a second explosion, and he saw two more troopers fall. Over the noise and screaming, Fetterman ordered, "Don't move! Don't anyone else move!"

When he saw several heads turn toward him, he shouted, "Is there a medic here? Get a medic over here. And an RTO."

"Sergeant Fetterman," yelled Thompson, "we have to move out. There is a schedule to maintain."

"Yes, sir, there is. But let's take care of the wounded first." Fetterman pointed at two men who stood near the smoking remains of a bunker. "You two back up slowly, and try to put your feet into the prints you made moving forward." To the rest of them, he said, "It's probably only the bunkers that have been booby-trapped, but let's all take it easy."

For the next twenty minutes Fetterman directed the operation as the officers and top NCOs from the company stood by and watched, realizing that they were seeing something extraordinary. Fetterman got the men out of immediate danger, formed a defensive ring around the bunkers and then led the medics in to treat the wounded. Seven men had been severly injured in the explosions, and although Fetterman took a little longer than anyone liked, no one else tripped a booby trap. They had been about to question his methods when he found the trip wire that would have detonated a captured two-hundred-and-fifty-pound bomb, which could have killed an entire platoon.

A medevac chopper was called in. It circled, waiting for one of Thompson's men to throw a smoke grenade, and the wounded, along with four dead, were evaced out. That done, Thompson made his way to Fetterman and asked how he thought they should assault the village.

"I don't think we should assault anything, Colonel," Fetterman replied. "What we should do is simply take up a position on this side of it, fanning out in a modified U ambush, and wait for Captain Gerber and your people to push the VC into us."

"What about the tunnels?"

"They are probably already occupied, and our delaying will only show us the locations of some of the entrances if we can see the VC use them. It might also give us a clue as to the size of the force we're going to meet. Where are your X rays?"

For an instant Thompson was puzzled and then said, "Oh, the engineers. Still at your camp. Didn't think we would need them on the first lift."

"Probably right, sir. Once we get the enemy located, we'll need to blow some of the upper tunnels and the entrances to begin boxing in the VC. One thing, though. We'll never find them all, and we'll need to be extremely careful. We'll want to let Charlie know we're here and that we mean business. If he doesn't surrender, we have two choices. Dig him out, or seal him in, though I doubt we'll be able to seal him in. The system is too extensive. The choice will be up to you, as long as you don't let all that ordnance he has hidden down there get out."

"You're mighty concerned about all that, just like your captain."

"Yes, sir, and if they were going to be shooting it at you, you would be concerned too."

Thompson ran off to talk to his company commander on the scene. As Fetterman watched in growing horror, the men began to sweep through the jungle, hacking at the vines and bushes with machetes, chopping their way through the undergrowth, smashing the smaller trees to get them out of the way and shouting orders at one another. They had nearly no noise discipline; not one of them knew how to glide through the undergrowth without disturbing it. Then he noticed that Thompson's men only carried two canteens apiece. He sometimes carried as many as five because water was so much more important than food in a jungle environment. The heat of the sun seemed to drain the strength with a rapidity that was frightening.

They would learn, he decided, and it wasn't his place to try to teach them now. Crawling silently through the jungle would be of no advantage in this operation and maybe they sensed that. Perhaps next time they would know enough not to shout at each other or to hack at the jungle plants and to tape down the equipment that would rattle. When they returned to base, he could mention it to a couple of the older NCOs so that something could be done on the QT.

In twenty minutes they were in position. Fetterman was near the center of the line and watching the now deserted village. Even the water buffalo were gone. It was as if the inhabitants knew that something was going to happen and they had decided to vanish until the threat was over.

Thompson, his RTO close at hand, was mumbling into the handset, telling his company commander with Gerber that they were in position to block the enemy retreat. Fetterman wasn't sure he liked being that close to the RTO because Charlie, sometimes unsure who were officers, shot at everyone near the radio, figuring to get an officer or two that way. The antenna, sticking an extra two or three feet into the air, made the perfect aiming stake for enemy snipers.

As soon as word was passed that the other company was in position, Gerber told the captain with him to move out rapidly. The gunships had stopped hosing down the trees, and there was only sporadic sniping coming from the VC. The grunt captain had wanted to send squads out to deal with the snipers, but Gerber wouldn't let him. Instead, he told him to have the grenadiers lob grenades into the trees near where the snipers were hiding. They may not kill them that way, but they would surely stop the sniping. Besides, once they started the assault, they could deal with the snipers in an efficient manner.

On command from the captain, the whole company left the tree line and began a sweep across the rice fields. Immediately they were taken under fire, the round splashing in the water or kicking up dirt and mud from the dikes. A few of the grunts dropped to the ground, uninjured, but scrambled for protection behind the low dikes around the paddies.

"Keep moving," shouted Gerber as he fired a five-round burst from the hip. He was watching the tracers, using them to aim. "Get up and keep moving. Grenadiers, hit the trees. Let's move it."

"But they're shooting at us," someone mumbled.

Gerber didn't respond. He just reached down and grabbed one of the grunts by the shoulder straps of his pack and lifted him, pushing him forward toward the trees. Gerber was suddenly calm, watching for the telltale muzzle flashes in the shadows of the tree line. Since there were no mortars being fired and the shooting was so poorly directed, Gerber felt almost safe.

"There aren't that many of them. They're trying to hold us up to let their friends get away," Gerber told them.

In seconds they were in the next tree line and the shooting increased momentarily, but the VC could no longer see the Americans easily, and the muzzle flashes were now visible in the shade of the jungle. Each time a VC fired his weapon, a dozen Americans returned the fire, and it was quickly neutralized. Grenadiers were almost fighting one another to drop their rounds on the enemy. They were just getting into the rhythm of the movement when they heard firing in the distance and knew that the enemy had reached the village and the blocking force.

Gerber waved the men forward then, trying to get them to move rapidly through the trees, taking a couple of chances so that they would be in position if the VC tried to force their way back. Gerber figured that Charlie, not knowing the size of the blocking force, might decide to try to overrun his pursuers rather than tangle with the blocking force. Gerber wanted to be ready.

But the counterattack never came. The firing from the other side of the village died out gradually as Gerber and his people moved into position just inside the trees where they could see the mud hootches. When they were set, the company commander used his radio to get instructions from Thompson, and then both units slowly entered the village, leaving some of their men to establish security.

The two forces met near the hootch where they had found the first tunnel entrance. They didn't waste time standing around talking about it but found as much cover as possible near it. Men hid behind part of the fence of woven branches, near the corner of another hootch and among the coconut trees around them. One or two leaned their rifles against the trees and took long, deep drinks from the lukewarm water in their canteens. Others poured water on the go-to-hell rags wrapped around their necks.

"And now?" asked Thompson as he was joined by both Gerber and Fetterman.

"Obviously," said Gerber, shading his eyes and slowly searching the jungle in the distance, "we have Charlie on the run. He has faded into his tunnel system, figuring we have no idea that it's here. The fact that we haven't taken any sniper fire recently is significant. Charlie wants us to assume that he has left the area and is nowhere around. He wants us to move into the jungle chasing shadows and not search in this village. He doesn't know that we know."

"One thing," cautioned Fetterman, "these tunnels honeycomb the whole area so that he can pop up behind us. To lead us off, he may throw a couple of people to the wolves to draw us into the jungle. We don't want to lose anyone because of carelessness. We have to be alert outside the ville. That's where the problem will develop. You might want to get some patrols out, roaming at the edges of the perimeter. Deny Charlie the opportunity to get set."

Thompson turned to one of the company commanders, "You heard that, Jones? You get your people set and tell them to be ready for snipers. And get a couple of twelve-man patrols out there."

"Yes, sir." Jones started to salute, but his hand had frozen halfway and he stared at Thompson, a look of horror on his face. Thompson chose to ignore the mistake.

"I would also suggest," added Gerber, "that we spread this command party out. As the saying goes, 'One grenade can get us all.'"

Thompson pointed at a lieutenant and the other captain and then indicated the trees. Both officers took off into the jungle without acknowledging the order.

"Now?"

"We wait for the engineers," said Gerber.

"Unless we want to put some people into the tunnels to explore them," suggested Fetterman.

"Let's wait," decided Thompson. "I know I wouldn't want to go down there with the enemy hiding there. I couldn't order anyone else to do it."

"I think we should get charges set," said Gerber, "make a sapper attack into the upper levels, leave the explosives and then get out. The concussion of enough high explosives should pretty well scramble Charlie's brains, and then our people could go in and get him."

"If the tunnels don't collapse," offered Fetterman. "Or Charlie hasn't built in blast doors to direct the concussion."

"And if the tunnels collapse, we've got a bunch of VC buried a bit early," said Gerber.

"But we won't have an accurate body count," said Thompson. "We've got to get some kind of body count."

"Yeah," said Fetterman, "it would be a damned shame to kill a VC and not get a chance to count his body. Make everyone look real bad."

The engineers, looking as scared as a kid sitting in the principal's office, arrived fifteen minutes later carrying giant packs of explosives. A platoon of grunts, carrying more equipment, including detonators, det cord, rifles, grenades, flares and their normal packs, followed them into the village. Gerber quickly spread them out so that a clever VC couldn't kill all the engineers and destroy all the equipment with a well-placed bullet.

"Now that we have everything," said Gerber, "we sweep through here carefully, pinpointing as many tunnel entrances as we can. The security people can check their immediate areas because we know there are tunnels in the jungle. Once we have them spotted, we move into them in a coordinated effort, trying to set the explosives so they all go up at once."

Thompson nodded but said nothing.

"Then we check the tunnels themselves. We should put some people into them to try to assess the damage. We want to be sure that we seal the place off."

"How?" asked Thompson because he knew that it was an almost impossible task.

"We'll have to leave people here to watch. We must have patrols throughout this area for the next month so that each time a VC pops up, someone is there to see him and capture him. Failing that, they need to shoot him, but a prisoner can tell us more about the damage and show us tunnels we might have missed. A dead man is just so much cold meat."

"I don't like it," said Thompson.

"You have a better idea?" asked Gerber.

"No, Captain, I don't. That doesn't mean I have to like the plan. I don't like having my people in the field for too long."

"I understand," said Gerber. "But then, they're not that far from our camp and can be resupplied easily. You'll have the ville to use as a base. All you're doing is patrolling this area where you know the VC live."

"Oh, it's a good plan," agreed Thompson. "But I still don't like it."

Without further comment he walked over to one of his company commanders and began issuing instructions. In a few minutes the company stood on line, divided into platoons and given quadrants of the village to explore, with specific instructions about what they were to look for.

With Gerber and Fetterman to lead them, the grunts swept through the village, turning over everything in sight and digging into piles of manure, looking for hidden openings into the tunnel system. But they had little luck. They did find a dozen bunkers that were independent but only two or three tunnels that led deeper into the major system.

The troops positioned outside the ville, at the edge of the jungle, found another six tunnel entrances. And farther away, in the area where McMillan had been ambushed, they found another two. At that point they decided they had found enough.

Coordinating the activity, the engineers, led by grunts or, in the case of the main entrance that Fetterman had found a couple of days earlier, by Fetterman, entered the tunnels. Fetterman prepped his by dropping a grenade down it and then leaping to the tunnel floor before the dust had a chance to settle. But he could see nothing in the billowing cloud created by the grenade.

An engineer followed closely, communicating his nervousness to Fetterman by his rapid breathing and the hiccups he had caught as they entered the tunnel. Fetterman, pistol in hand, scrambled toward the ladder that led to a lower level. When he found it, he dropped another grenade and ducked back. As it detonated and the concussion carrying the dust washed over him like a wave on a beach, he whispered to the engineer, "Throw your satchel charge down there now with the delay fuse set for three minutes."

If the engineer was inclined to argue, he quickly forgot about it. He worked his way past Fetterman so that he could look down the ladder. He set the fusing of the satchel charge and tossed it into the dust that was still swirling in the tunnel. Before the engineer could speak, Fetterman had begun to rapidly crawl back the way he had come. In less than a minute he was out of the tunnel and running across the open ground to the cover of another hootch where Gerber waited. The engineer was right behind him.

As he leaped for cover, Fetterman said, "About a minute, Captain."

Then, almost as Fetterman stopped speaking, the ground began to shake, and there was a rumbling as the satchel charges placed by all the teams began to explode, the concussions reverberating through the underground channels, shaking the walls and floors of the tunnels. It was as if they had created a miniature earthquake that fed on itself, rocking the surface of the land, causing the hootches to sway like small boats on a choppy sea.

From nearly fifty locations dust and smoke came boiling out of the concealed entrances as more of the tunnels collapsed. For a moment it was quiet, and then, as if something underground had caught fire and exploded on its own, there was a violent rumble as the whole village lifted and then fell back, settling three feet lower than it had been.

"I think their arsenal went up then," commented Fetterman.

"Whatever it was," said Thompson, "I don't think we have to worry about anyone getting out of there."

Watching more of the dust pour out of the ground, Fetterman said, "It's too bad. I would have liked to have gotten that antiaircraft gun out of there. Would have made a real nice addition to the camp's weapons.

Gerber wanted to laugh. "Ah, Tony, you're never happy. What in the hell would we do with a 23 mm antiaircraft gun? Even if we could find ammo for it."

"I'm sure that Boom-Boom would have thought of something."

Thompson interrupted. "Well, as I said before, I don't think we have to worry about anyone getting out."

"No, sir," agreed Gerber, "but it wouldn't be a bad idea to leave some people in the area to make sure. And have some people check out the tunnels."

"I'll leave a platoon or two," said Thompson. "I'm going to whistle up the choppers now. I imagine you boys will want to catch a ride back so that you can begin your leave."

"Mrs. Fetterman and the kids appreciate it, sir," said Fetterman.

8

SPECIAL FORCES CAMP
A-555

It didn't take the helicopters long to pick up the teams. The flight back to camp seemed to be much shorter than the one that had brought them out. Gerber sat in the troop seat, leaning against the ripped gray soundproofing that failed to reduce the noise from the turbine, and thought about the nature of the Vietnam War. He had left his hootch early in the morning, spent the day in combat with the enemy, some of it hand-to-hand, and now he was on his way home. He could sit in his hootch, read the afternoon paper— the *Stars and Stripes*—listen to the radio, or even watch TV if he was so inclined. Not exactly the classic view of war, but more of a nine-to-five-type job.

In fact, with the huge influx of American troops in South Vietnam, there was a change in the culture. The Americans were bringing it with them. Instead of small bases in the boonies manned by a few American troops and a couple of hundred locals, the brass was building big base camps. Islands of American culture in the middle of Vietnam.

They were erecting steak houses, discos, television and radio stations, clubs for the enlisted men, NCOs and officers, tailor shops, souvenir shops, and bath houses employing young Vietnamese women. Thousands of troops were arriving, including the newly reorganized 1st Cavalry, which was now airmobile. And each of the troops in the field was supported by seven or eight in the camps. These troops consisted of clerks, cooks, maintenance

men, supply men and people to brief news correspondents and
design recreational programs. There was even talk of building
library.

It wasn't the way to fight a war, especially the Vietnam War, but
the bureaucrats and congressmen—the chairborne commandos
Gerber thought wryly—wanted to be sure that the boys were
comfortable while they were away from home. Gerber shook his
head, wishing that President Johnson and Secretary of Defense
McNamara would leave the fighting of the war to the officers who
knew what they were doing. The whole thing was getting out of
hand, and if they weren't careful, it wouldn't be fun anymore.

Gerber smiled at the thought: men in Washington with no con
cept of this war, or any war, were making policy that affected all
aspects of the war. Of course, no one had asked his opinion, and
maybe that was the problem. The policymakers hadn't bothered
to learn what they needed to know to make intelligent decisions
They seemed to think money would solve a problem, and if tha
didn't work, the obvious answer was more money.

In the distance he could see the buildings of his camp twin
kling in the late-afternoon sun, their tin roofs now rusted so that
they seemed to glow gold. The camp was rectangular with a shor
runway on the western side. Just off the eastern edge of the run
way was an oval redoubt, which was not more than seventy-five
meters across. It was an earthen breastwork that was five feet tal
and had only one tiny entrance on the east side, which was pro
tected by .30-caliber machine guns. Six strands of concertina wire
surrounded the camp. Scattered among the rows of wire were
claymore antipersonnel mines, barrels of foogas, trip flares and
booby traps. The nearest cover for an attacking force was a clump
of trees almost five hundred meters away on the south side of the
camp.

Smoke from one of the fires that was burning trash sent a cloud
of black smoke into the sky from near the center of the Vietnamese hootches. Several rows of the small, eight-man hootches stood
on the west side of the runway. Gerber made a mental note to tell
Minh about it. Charlie could use the smoke as a spotting guide
for his mortars, and he didn't think Minh would like it if the
mortars kept falling among the strikers' hootches.

As the helicopter's skids touched the ground, Thompson
leaped out to run over to the commo bunker so that he could make

radio contact with his people still in the field. Bates, Fetterman and Gerber didn't see any need to follow him and, instead, walked toward the team house. Gerber knew that they should clean their weapons and even make a few notes for the after-action report that the brass hats in Saigon would want, but he was too tired to be worried about the bureaucratic trivia. Besides, he had a leave to get ready for.

As they approached the team house, Gerber said, "Come on, Alan, I'll buy you a beer."

"Just what I had in mind," said Bates. "How about Sergeant Fetterman?"

"He can buy his own. In fact, he has his own supply, and it's even cold. I can't offer you a cold one."

"Well, now, Captain," Fetterman said, "if your party with the colonel isn't private, I might be persuaded to supply the cold beer."

"Then by all means, join us," said Gerber magnanimously. He laughed and said, "And since when did you need an invitation?"

"Just trying to be polite in front of company." Fetterman unbuckled his pistol belt so that it hung open in the front supported by the shoulder harness. There were sweat stains where it had been locked around his waist.

Inside, they found Robin Morrow sitting at one of the tables, her feet propped up and four cans of beer in front of her. She was wearing shorts and a khaki shirt, which was unbuttoned halfway to her belly button and damp under the arms. She had her hair pulled back off a forehead beaded with perspiration. When she saw them, she said, "Welcome back, gentlemen. Would you care for a drink?"

Fetterman said, "No, but you can stay, anyway."

"I'll have one," said Bates.

Morrow let her feet drop to the floor and used her church key to open one of the cans. She pushed it across the table at Bates and said, "There you are, Colonel."

When they were all seated, Morrow asked, "So how did the mission go?"

Without looking at her, Gerber said, "The mission went fine. It was just fine. What do you want to know for?"

"I was assigned to do a story on the Special Forces, and the story isn't finished yet," she snapped. "You're welcome for the beer."

Fetterman leaped into the conversation by saying, "There ar a couple of things we're going to have to do to get ready to tak our leaves."

"I know," said Gerber. He looked at Bates. "I suppose yo have some idea about who you want to send in for our replace ments."

"I thought you said you were staying so that you wouldn't b replaced," said Morrow.

"Yes, but we'll be gone for thirty days, and there has to b someone in here to take over temporarily."

"Don't worry about it," said Bates, setting his beer on the ta ble in front of him. "You've got almost a battalion here right now and they won't be leaving for about a month. Also, I've got Cap tain Bromhead in Saigon organizing a new A-Team. There'r quite a few unattached Special Forces troops running around, an it doesn't hurt to have an extra team. I'll bring him in here to hol things down. Once you've returned, I'll send him home for month."

"That would work," said Gerber, nodding. "Johnny know the area around here quite well. Be a real advantage for him to b working here. Should have thought of that myself. In fact, should have thought about leaving him a couple of my NCOs t help him while he's getting his feet wet."

"I could stay an extra week, if that would help," said Fetter man.

"I don't think that's really necessary, Tony," said Gerber "Hell, Johnny's been here a year and had some of the best train ing available. I guess he won't need the help."

"Besides all that," said Bates, "I plan to stay out here until w get him established. And there's Captain Minh, who will still b here."

"As far as I can see," said Gerber, "that leaves only one prob lem: what to do with Robin."

"Hey," she said, "I'm right here. Why not ask me if I have an plans before you go deciding?"

"Do you have any plans, Robin?"

"Thought I'd just stay here and see how the camp runs with out you people. I might discover you're not the valuable asset tha you claim to be."

Gerber looked to Bates again. "What do you think?"

"She can stay if she wants, though I don't see much point in it. Won't be anything happening. I'll be here to look after her until Captain Bromhead arrives."

"I don't need anyone to look after me."

"With all due respect," said Gerber, "I disagree. Hell, I would want someone out here with you even if you were a male journalist. It's not good policy to have Americans all alone in the field."

"That leaves only one question," said Bates. "What are you two going to do about leave?"

"Hadn't thought that much about it," interjected Fetterman before anyone could speak. "Leave seems to be an unnatural state for the soldier. Sort of like peace. Soldiers have to exist in peace because there is eventually going to be a war and then it's too late to train them, but they are out of place. It would be better if they could be frozen until they are needed."

"Lovely speech, Tony," said Gerber.

"Yeah, I kind of liked it. Anyway, the point is I haven't given it much thought."

"Well, while the master sergeant is trying to figure it out," said Gerber, "I thought I'd go to Hong Kong. Spend my time running from tailors to camera stores and researching the Oriental mind."

"That's a pretty bizarre plan," said Morrow. "Why go to Hong Kong?"

A hundred answers sprang to mind, most of them involving Robin's sister, Karen. Gerber wanted to say that he could go to Hong Kong and still be half a world away from her. He could go to Hong Kong and remain in a fairly alien environment where there wouldn't be constant reminders of Karen Morrow, where he wouldn't have to worry about running into people he knew who would ask complicated questions. It was a place to hide, and it seemed to be better than a dozen other choices that had crossed his mind.

Instead of any of that, he said, "It has an intrigue that attracts me. Besides, it's very close by air to a lot of other places I might want to see. It would be a good base to operate from. If I got tired of Hong Kong, I could go to Manila, Macau, Singapore, even Australia."

Fetterman sat across from Gerber and slowly nodded. "An interesting plan, Captain. I like that. Mind if I tag along?"

Gerber raised an eyebrow in question. "What about Mrs. Fetterman and the kids?"

"You know, Captain, you tend to worry about them more than I do. Mrs. Fetterman and the kids understand about the warrior. There will be no problem from that quarter."

"If you're sure, Tony, then by all means let's go to Hong Kong." Gerber turned his attention to Bates. "Colonel? How about you? You should be getting ready for some leave time. I know you've been here longer than a year."

Bates finished his beer, then set the can on the floor so that he could crush it under his boot. "While it's true that I've been here for about a year, it's also true that I have a leave coming up. I plan to use it to visit my wife and daughters." He smiled and nodded at Fetterman. "Mrs. Bates is not quite as understanding as Mrs. Fetterman seems to be. Cindi wants me to come home and end my career at some comfortable base on the West Coast. I told her I could get my eagle by extending here, so she has agreed. But as soon as I get things organized, I'm on my way home."

He uttered a cheerful laugh, as if at some private memory. "If it wasn't for that, I'd be on that plane with you. We could really tear up Hong Kong."

"I guess that pretty well settles it." Gerber got to his feet. "I'd better go pack if I'm leaving in the morning." He stopped talking and said, "Hey, how exactly does this work? I mean, we won't be screwing anyone up by just showing up to go to Hong Kong?"

"Just go to Tan Son Nhut and take a commercial flight out. Cost you some money, but that won't screw anyone up. If you don't mind sitting around Saigon for a day or two, you can check in with the military people down there and grab a space on an available flight. They don't fill those up until the people arrive and one or two, more or less, won't affect them. Might delay somebody by a couple of hours, but that would be it."

"Sounds like the ticket."

As both Bates and Morrow stood to go, Fetterman said, "Say, Captain, can I talk to you?"

Gerber waved a hand at Bates and Morrow and said, "Catch up with you in a minute." He sat back down and asked, "What's on your mind, Tony?"

"I think I might pass on that trip to Hong Kong, if you don't mind."

The most pulse-pounding, pressure-packed action reading ever published

Razor-edge storytelling. Page-crackling tension. On-target firepower. Hard-punching excitement. Gold Eagle books slam home raw action the way you like it—hard, fast and real!

Gold Eagle Reader Service

901 Fuhrmann Blvd.,
P.O. Box 1394
Buffalo, NY 14240-9963

"Of course, I don't mind. Decide that maybe you ought to visit Mrs. Fetterman and the kids? Especially since you dumped Le Quan Kim on them?"

"I didn't dump him on them. I worked out all the details of the adoption beforehand. I even talked to our embassy and proved to the satisfaction of the Vietnamese government that Le Quan was an orphan. After his village was burned, the Vietnamese were very happy to get rid of him and Mrs. Fetterman was very happy to see him."

"Sorry. I didn't mean that quite the way it sounded. I just meant, did you decide they might want you to come home for a month?"

"No, sir. I want to stay here. On the camp."

"What in the hell for?"

"The reason we discussed before. The reason the whole team is going to come back. To get that Chinese bastard. We talked about this a couple of times, but since Ian got zapped, we haven't done much about it."

"No," said Gerber slowly, "we haven't. But then, we haven't had much of a chance. We've been busy, but I have a feeling he's going to be pretty busy himself for the next month. This is the first time we've had this many Americans on the camp. I don't think there is much he can do now. Not with Thompson's battalion running operations all over our AO. He's going to have to bide his time until a few of the people leave."

"I know that, Captain, but—"

"But nothing, Tony. I'll bet our taking out that base camp has hurt him, too. That was something that took years to build and stock, and now it's gone. Granted, he can operate out of Cambodia, but it's not quite as convenient as having an arsenal in our backyard. It'll be a month or more before he can do anything here."

"Yes, sir."

"We deserve this leave. We should take it. Get some rest, and when we come back, we'll be more than ready to hit him. You know, you can overtrain."

"There are things I could be doing during that month, sir."

"Tony, no one said we *had* to stay away a month. We are *authorized* to stay away for a month."

"Does that mean . . ."

"It means that if I get bored chasing women, drinking heavily and being a civilian, then I plan to come right back here and get into the swing of things. Besides, it's only thirty days."

Fetterman rubbed his chin as he thought about it. "You know, it might be nice to be somewhere you could take a hot bath and not worry about someone dropping a mortar round in there with you."

Now Gerber smiled. "It might be nice to be somewhere you could find a nice lady to wash your back for you."

"I bet I could find you a volunteer around here," said Fetterman.

"Now what does that mean?" asked Gerber, knowing full well what it meant.

"Are you really that blind?" asked Fetterman. "Do you really think there are so many interesting things happening around here that a journalist would hang around waiting for the big story to break?"

Although Gerber knew what was coming, he said, "Maybe you better explain yourself, Master Sergeant."

"I think I may have said more than I should have. Listen, Mack—" he used Gerber's given name for the first time "—it's none of my business and I know all about your trouble with Morrow's sister, but don't let what one bitch did color your thinking, no matter how closely related they are."

Gerber got to his feet. "I think this discussion now borders on territory that you are forbidden to enter."

"Yes, sir. I understand. I just wanted to make sure that you aren't making a mistake by keeping your eyes closed. A terrible mistake."

"Master Sergeant!"

"I've said my piece, and that's all I'll say."

"Then I suggest we go pack so we can take the morning chopper out of here. I'll want to brief Minh about the operation today so he'll know what happened and will be prepared to help Colonel Thompson."

"If I was out of line, sir, I beg your pardon, but I wanted to make sure the situation was under control."

Gerber snorted. "I don't know what I might have said to make you think I had the situation under control. No, seriously, Tony,

I appreciate what you've said, but I think you've read something into the situation that doesn't exist."

"Yes, sir. See you in the morning."

GERBER ATE BREAKFAST alone with a notepad beside his dish of cold powdered eggs and cold cereal covered with lukewarm milk that he had made earlier. He kept adding to the list of things he wanted to leave with Minh, wondering if he was overdoing it. He knew that Minh was as familiar with the camp as he was. In fact, the only thing Minh didn't know about yet was the operation run the day before and that was only because it had been an all-American mission.

Just as he finished eating, Minh wandered in, poured himself a glass of warm orange juice, ignoring the Vietnamese woman who was standing in the kitchen area washing dirty dishes in a large metal tub. Minh flopped into the chair opposite Gerber.

"I say, old boy," said Minh, "I hear you wanted to talk to me."

Gerber pushed his dirty plate aside, stood to make his way to the coffeepot to fill his cup and returned. He picked up his notepad. "This is going to be redundant, I'm sure, but I want to make certain that we've covered all the bases."

"Go ahead, but you had better hurry because the mail chopper will be here soon."

Gerber moved to the bar that separated the kitchen from the rest of the team house. He told the woman she could go for now and finish the dishes later. When she was gone, Gerber moved back to the table and sat down.

For the next twenty minutes they discussed the operation of the camp, the locations where patrols would be the most useful and what to do in the event of a major attack against the facility.

Neither Gerber nor Minh believed such an operation would be mounted now that the VC base had been discovered and eliminated. Both believed that the enemy would spend six or seven weeks recovering from the loss of the base; Gerber and his whole team would be back long before anything happened. Besides, there was a whole new American battalion sitting around the camp so nothing could happen until that battalion redeployed to Bien Hoa.

There might be some mortar attacks or harassment raids, but nothing major. The VC had made a concentrated effort to take the camp when it was first built and had smashed the better part of a reinforced regiment against the camp's defenses. With a brand-new American battalion, five hundred men strong added to those defenses, the VC couldn't mount an attack.

Minh nodded through most of this and commented about some of it, taking it all in. To finish up, Gerber said, "Colonel Bates will be here most of the time, and you can count on him. He's a good soldier and will give you anything you need."

Fetterman entered then and dropped his two suitcases on the floor near the door. He was wearing new jungle fatigues so green they seemed to glow. There were no insignia on them, just metal master sergeant stripes pinned to the collar. His boots gleamed as usual, his hair was combed and he was freshly shaved. He looked as if he had just stepped out of an air-conditioned NCO barracks rather than coming from his own hot hootch. Gerber raised an eyebrow in question at the suitcases.

"Duffel bags are good for carrying equipment and jungle fatigues, but civilian clothes just don't travel well in them," Fetterman said. "Besides, I don't want to look like a soldier on leave because then you're a marked man. Everyone and his brother or sister will be out to separate me from my hard-earned money."

Gerber waved him over as Minh stood up. "I'll take my leave now," said Minh, draining the last of his warm orange juice.

"See you in a month, Dai uy," said Gerber as Minh disappeared through the door.

"As you can see," said Fetterman, pouring himself a cup of coffee, "I'm ready for this."

Before he could take a seat, Morrow appeared carrying a suitcase, which she placed next to Fetterman's. To Gerber, she said, "Do I have your guarantee that I can come back here if I take a couple of weeks off?"

Gerber rocked back in his chair and studied her. It was the first time that she had worn a dress since she had arrived on the camp. It was light yellow with a slightly dipped neckline and short puffed sleeves. The hem brushed her knees. She had washed her hair and trimmed it herself so that she had bangs.

"If I say no, will you go, anyway?"

"No. I'll sit here until I rot," she said with a smile on her lips.

"Well, then," responded Gerber, "I guess we'll let you come back, providing that Crinshaw and the boys in Saigon don't stop you."

Fetterman pulled a chair out and held it for her. "Where are you going, Robin?"

"I haven't decided yet," she said. "Just figured I'd ride into Saigon with you and then catch a flight out. Maybe go home for a visit."

Gerber felt his stomach turn over at that because he thought of Karen Morrow and her husband. He nodded and said, "Sounds like a good idea."

Fetterman eyed Gerber meaningfully but said, "Where are your bags, Captain?"

"In my hootch. As soon as I hear the chopper, I'll hotfoot it over there and pick them up."

"Robin," said Fetterman, "you look beautiful. You should spend more time dressed like this."

For an instant she was going to contradict him, to say that she was here to do a job and that she dressed to do it. Then she realized that Fetterman was not being condescending but trying to be nice.

"Thank you, Sergeant. I appreciate it."

Gerber stood and explained, "I should go find Colonel Bates before the chopper gets here."

From the door a voice said, "Don't bother, he has arrived."

"Tony and I are ready to go, Colonel," said Gerber. "Just as soon as the chopper arrives. Thought I should let you know and see if there was anything else I needed to do."

Bates made the ritualistic trip to the coffeepot and then to the table. He said, "I believe that, between Captain Minh and myself, we can handle anything." He turned his attention to Morrow. "Robin, you look exceptionally nice this morning. Is this a special occasion?"

"No, Colonel, I just decided to take a little vacation while the rest of the team is gone. Kirk promised me that I could come back here later."

"Kirk?" said Bates and Fetterman at the same time.

"My middle name," said Gerber, explaining the whole situation to them. "Sometimes I prefer it because it has no connection with the Army."

From outside came the sound of a helicopter approaching. Gerber said, "That'll be our ride."

Bates stood and held out his hand. "Good luck to you all on this. Have fun and try not to think of the rest of us here fighting to save the world from the evils of Communism."

"Don't worry," said Fetterman, laughing, "I won't."

Gerber took Bates's hand and shook it. "Thanks for everything, Alan. See you in about a month."

As they all approached the chopper, two of the crewmen leaped from the back and came forward to take the bags out of Morrow's and Gerber's hands. The helicopter sat on the pad, its blades stirring up a cloud of red dust. The rotor wash caught the hem of Morrow's dress and flipped it about, revealing her thighs. She tried to hold it down as she ran toward the cargo compartment of the aircraft.

Gerber, relieved of his burden, stepped up so that he could shout into the cockpit window at the pilot. He looked in and smiled as he recognized the man.

"So, Randle, you fly us around again."

Randle nodded and moved the boom of his mike over so that Gerber could speak into it. That way Randle could hear what Gerber said on the intercom.

"Listen, you be careful on this one—we're going on leave so we don't want any trouble."

"Oh," shouted Randle over the noise of the Huey's turbine, "you mean you don't want to hear that we took fire on the way in."

Gerber almost shouted back and then saw the grin on Randle's face and realized that the pilot was kidding him. "Yeah, exactly like that."

"Well, hop in and we'll get you to Saigon in about forty minutes. Then I'll let you buy me lunch."

"You've got a deal."

With that, Gerber climbed into the cargo compartment of the helicopter. He noticed that both the crew chief and door gunner were helping Morrow get settled, and fastening her seat belt. Obviously enjoying it, she simply grinned at them and let them do it. She smiled at Randle when he turned in his seat to make sure that everyone was ready.

They lifted off, turned north and then back to the south as if Randle were circling the camp so that Gerber and Fetterman could take a look at it, but neither was interested in seeing it.

Gerber glanced to his left and saw that the wind whipping through the cargo compartment was toying with the hem of Morrow's skirt, trying to force it up. She sat with both hands holding it tightly around her knees.

The flight took forty-two minutes. They touched down at Hotel Three ten minutes before noon. Almost before the passengers could unbuckle their seat belts, Randle had the engine shut down and was standing outside the aircraft, stretching. He reached up with one hand to help Morrow down.

"I can make it myself, ah, Lieutenant," she snapped.

"Yes, I know you can, but I don't have many opportunities to try out the manners that Congress has graciously given to me. And I'm only a warrant officer."

"In that case, thank you. Can you tell me how to get over to the commercial terminal?"

"I would imagine you can catch a ride if you go over to the building with the tower on it," said Randle, pointing across the helipad. "They'll probably be more than happy to drive you over. I'll have the door gunner carry your luggage."

"That's not necessary."

"Of course it isn't, but he'll kill me if I don't order him to do it. That is, if you don't mind."

"In that case, I'll be delighted to have the help."

As Morrow and the door gunner started across the field, Randle leaned back against the side of the helicopter, his arms folded and said, "She seems to be a nice lady. I wonder why she hangs around with the grungy Green Beret types."

"She has no sense," growled Gerber. "You want food or not?"

"Say, Captain, your way with words amazes me. You ever thought of running for mayor?" Randle shot back.

"Okay, sorry. Let's go over to the O Club and I'll buy you a steak."

"And my Peter Pilot?"

"And your Peter Pilot."

BY THE MIDDLE OF THE AFTERNOON, Gerber and Fetterman had been manifested on a flight to Hong Kong that would leave the next morning. They had been assigned quarters for the night, both of them in a giant barrackslike building where senior NCOs and junior officers waited for flights. It resembled a warehouse in a bunk bed factory. There had to be two hundred bunks in the building, each of them with yards of gauze that served as mosquito netting. The walls climbed only halfway to the ceiling and the rest was enclosed in screen to let in the evening breezes. Sixty-watt light bulbs in funnel-like fixtures hung every twenty or thirty feet. Ceiling fans rotated above them but seemed to have little effect on the heat. Since everyone in the barracks was about to get out of Vietnam and because they were assigned bunks on the basis of which flight they were leaving on, no one was inclined to complain about the arrangement.

9

TAN SON NHUT
INTERNATIONAL
AIRPORT, SAIGON

The next morning Gerber and Fetterman presented themselves at the military counter in the airport. It took almost no time to check their baggage and verify authorization for leave outside of Vietnam. They showed their passports to the civilian customs officer, a Vietnamese man with long, straight black hair and oval brown eyes, who went through their baggage but didn't perform a body search. So he didn't find the .45 automatic that Fetterman had tucked away. Beside the customs man was an American sergeant with the black armband of the military police who wanted to see their orders. He inspected those and their other papers carefully, then handed them back with a bored smile and wished the two men a good trip.

With the customs requirements satisfied, they were led to a waiting room where a hundred other men, all dressed in civilian clothes, sat reading books and magazines or staring out the window, watching the jets take off and land. The room was furnished with mismatched furniture, tattered copies of magazines, mostly *Playboy* and other girlie glossies, newspapers and old paperback novels. The floor was littered with crushed cigarette butts and empty Coke cans. The air was hot and stale, and there was a low murmur from the men waiting for flights out of Vietnam.

After an hour they were led across the tarmac, which radiated heat in shimmering waves. The glare made it hard to see as they approached the ramp leading into a 707. Gerber shivered involuntarily as he entered the air-conditioned comfort of the plane. As he left the heat and humidity of tropical Vietnam, he thought it would be a while before he was that uncomfortable again. He forgot that Hong Kong was also close to the equator and near the ocean. It would be as hot and humid as Vietnam.

The flight took less than two hours. Gerber didn't have time to sample much of the booze stashed away on the aircraft. Since it was a commercial airliner, the stewardesses were allowed to serve limited quantities of alcohol, especially since it was such a short flight.

Fetterman kept his nose buried in a series of brochures about Hong Kong that he had found somewhere, mumbling occasionally that he had discovered something they should be sure to explore.

At those times Gerber merely nodded and said, "Well, put it down and we'll see about it."

Before Gerber could get used to the idea that he was leaving the war zone and that no one would be shooting at him for the next thirty days, the pilot announced their approach into Kai Tak Airport. He suggested that if window passengers looked below, they would be able to see the various islands of Hong Kong, the new territories and, with luck, some of Red China. Gerber didn't really care to see Red China, but Fetterman was interested if only because it was the birthplace of their biggest enemy.

They touched down and rolled to a stop, and just like in Vietnam, they were herded into the terminal where the Army had a small auditorium, which was filled with folding chairs facing a screen, so that the officials could explain the rules and regulations of Hong Kong and R and R. Those soldiers who were on R and R were informed which day they had to report back so they could catch their return flights to Vietnam. Those who were on leave would have to make their own travel arrangements but needed to make them at least three days prior to departure to ensure they got a seat. That done, and the various forms signed, they were told that, if they wanted to take the Army bus into the city proper, they needed to pick up their baggage and get outside.

As the others swarmed from the room, each fighting to be the first out the door, Fetterman said, "You aren't interested in the bus?"

"Thought it would be nice to get away from Army control as quickly as possible. Besides, did you really want to have the Army take us into Hong Kong? We'd end up doing it by the numbers, for Christ's sake."

Fetterman picked up his suitcases and gestured at the door. "Lead the way."

They left the Army's reception room and were back into the main terminal where hundreds of people hurried up and down the concourses looking for their departure gates. Following the signs that were in a dozen languages including English, Gerber and Fetterman found their way to the main exit of the terminal.

"Say, Tony," said Gerber, "I don't suppose you speak Chinese."

"No, sir. But since English is one of the two official languages of Hong Kong, I'll have a chance to practice my English."

"While we're here, how about knocking off that sir and captain shit. You know my name."

"Thought I did."

"Now what the hell does that mean?" asked Gerber.

"Nothing, Mack. Nothing at all."

Just as they reached the tinted glass doors, a voice yelled after them, "Hey, Kirk. Over here, Kirk."

Gerber thought nothing of it as the door swung open and the hot, humid air of Hong Kong rushed in to greet them.

"Hey, Kirk, wait up."

Fetterman said, "Somebody yelling at you?"

Then the voice came again, angry. "Hey, Mack. Will you wait for me?"

Gerber turned and saw Robin Morrow, still wearing her yellow dress, now wrinkled, running across the concourse. People were stopping and staring at her as she waved a hand to catch their attention.

"I think that is for you, Captain."

"Shut up, Master Sergeant. We've only been here for fifteen minutes and already you're a pain in the ass. Maybe that's why they don't want officers and NCOs to fraternize."

There wasn't much choice when Morrow caught them. She tried to grab one of Gerber's suitcases, and failing that, she took one of Fetterman's. Before they could say anything, Morrow began chattering away as she led them down a sidewalk, past the banks of parked taxis, most of which were old American-made automobiles. They hit a parking lot and walked between the cars. Gerber noticed that the day was not as hot as it would have been in Vietnam and wondered if the sea breezes blowing across the harbor were responsible for keeping the temperature in the low eighties.

"I've got a car," said Morrow, struggling with the suitcase she had taken from Fetterman. She set it down, grabbed it in both hands and started off again. "My boss paid for it. Gave me a suite downtown that you can share if you like. It has two bedrooms so there is no problem. I know that neither of you are overpaid, so sharing the room might help. My publisher is paying for it, too. Told him I might have to entertain some people, so he authorized it. I mean, I told him—"

"Stop," ordered Gerber. "Stop."

"Yes, Kirk. Mack?"

Gerber raised an eyebrow at Fetterman, who said, "It's your ball game, Mack-Kirk."

"Well, I don't know anything about this town," said Gerber, "so we'll let you take us to your hotel. Then we'll decide what to do from there."

They reached the car, a bright blue Mustang convertible, which had the top down. Morrow unlocked the trunk and then opened the driver's door so she could leap behind the wheel. "Pile in gentlemen and hang on. These people don't drive all that well, and I'm out of practice."

They filled the trunk with their suitcases, putting one in the backseat. Fetterman got into the back next to it, shaded his eyes with his hand and searched the skyline of Hong Kong, surprised at the number of tall buildings around him. Hong Kong was a large, modern city.

"This is terrific. I survived a year in Vietnam to die in a traffic accident in Hong Kong." Gerber climbed into the passenger's seat and reached for the seat belt.

After a short hair-raising ride through the city, they came to the hotel, a glass and steel high rise called the Regency. When Morrow saw the look on Gerber's face, she said, "I had to stay here. We have some kind of deal with the owners and get a good rate. Otherwise, I would have had to pay for it out of my own pocket."

Fetterman pushed on the back of Gerber's seat. "Come on, Captain. It won't hurt to look at the inside. We've come this far already."

Gerber started to open the door, but a uniformed man swooped out from under the canopied entrance to help him. The bellhop reached for the one bag in the back seat as soon as Fetterman was out of the way, then almost demanded that the trunk be opened so he could get the rest of the luggage.

"Do I let him have it?" asked Morrow.

"Why not?" said Gerber, shrugging.

Upstairs, as soon as the bellhop had been tipped, Gerber turned around. They were standing in the posh living room of the suite. There was a long, low, aqua couch along one wall and over it hung a seascape, which picked up the colors of the couch. End tables flanked the couch, and lamps with off-white shades and large bubblelike ceramic bases stood on them. Across from all that was a large, mahogany secretary that opened into a bar. It was well stocked with beer, Coke and a dozen bottles of Beam's Choice. In one corner of the room was a large TV console and sitting on it was another lamp, a smaller version of the ones on the end tables. In the other corner near the window was a round table surrounded by four armchairs. The window, hidden behind light, wispy sheers and heavier, darker drapes, stretched the length of the outside wall.

Morrow pointed across the room at a door near the couch. "You two can stay in there if you want."

Gerber went to the door and looked in. He was in a tiny foyer that separated the bedroom from the private bath. Between two double beds, covered with spreads of the same aqua color as the couch, was a small table that held a lamp and a bible. There was a massive dresser with nine long drawers against the wall. A chair stood in one corner with a floor lamp next to it. A walk-in closet filled one wall and a window the other. The curtains were open, and he could see Hong Kong Harbor.

His reflection in the giant mirror on the door of the bathroom startled him for a moment. He walked over to it and looked in. There was a huge bathtub inside. He looked back at Fetterman and Morrow and then at the tub. He hadn't had a bath in nearly a year. In fact, he hadn't had a hot shower in that year. There'd been cool or cold showers by the dozen and a couple of baths in the streams and rivers around the camp but not a long, hot bath with nothing to worry about except keeping the water warm.

Then he remembered another room in another hotel where he had found a bathtub. Except that it hadn't been the gleaming porcelain facing him now, but an old ceramic job with Victorian feet on it and rust stains where the water dripped. He put the scene out of his mind because it dredged up too many unpleasant memories of Karen Morrow.

To the others he said, "I think I'll take a bath, if no one has any objections."

"No objections," said Morrow, obviously relieved. "In fact, I was about to suggest the same thing."

"Tony, you can use the bathroom now if you like. Because I'll have it tied up for a while."

"No, sir. I thought I'd hit one of the tailor shops down the street. I'd like to get a new suit to wear in Hong Kong. I have the feeling that my collection of civilian garb is not sufficient for the task at hand."

"Well, don't let me stop you." With that Gerber closed the door, and moments later they could hear water running in the bathroom.

Morrow sat on one of the four chairs near the picture window in the living room. The curtains were closed so they couldn't see out into the city. She crossed her legs and took a deep breath.

"Tony? Can we talk?"

Fetterman studied her carefully and then moved to one of the other chairs. "What can I do for you, Miss Morrow?"

"Oh, for God's sake, call me Robin." She stopped and looked at the liquor cabinet, then rose from her chair to fix herself a drink. "I've noticed, Tony, that you don't miss much of anything. You have a finger on the pulse of everything that's going on around you."

"I thank you for the compliment."

"So," she said slowly and then blurted, "what am I doing wrong?"

Fetterman studied his hand intimately for a moment and then said, "I suppose you're referring to our captain."

Having finally begun the conversation, she decided to stay with it. "You probably figured that I came here because I knew you'd be here."

"And I take that to mean the captain would be here." He held up his hand before she could say anything more. "Sorry. I shouldn't do that. It's just a delaying tactic while I try to figure out what I should tell you and what the captain would like me not to say. It's a fine line that I'm now preparing to walk."

"I appreciate it." She sat down again but found she could not look him in the face.

"Let me say this," said Fetterman. "Mack Gerber is probably the finest officer I've ever met. He's the only expert on small unit tactics fighting the Vietnam War. I would never tell him that I recognize some of them from the Indian Wars, but that's where he got them. I say all this so that you'll know I'm a completely unbiased source." He grinned, but she missed it.

"All right. Your sister seemed to be the right woman for him. They got along well. Hell, they got along beautifully. They could have conversations and hardly exchange a word. They were so in tune with one another they didn't need to talk. It was an incredibly interesting thing to see. I think the captain had planned to ask her to marry him.

"Then suddenly it was over without a very good explanation. She just wanted nothing to do with him, and he couldn't understand it. Now we know the problem. She was preparing to go home to her husband, all of which you should know already."

"But men do it all the time. Have a girl in every port and leave them high and dry when they become a problem."

"Doesn't matter," said Fetterman. "Doesn't matter if a billion men have done it to a billion women. I mean, it doesn't make it right for her to have done it to him."

"That's a damned lousy attitude."

Now Fetterman was uncomfortable. "Let me rephrase that. Makes no difference if a billion men did it to a billion women or a billion women did it to a billion men. Didn't make it right for her to do it to the captain. He'd never do it to anyone."

"Sorry."

"The point of all this is that the captain is trying very hard not to let anyone get to him again. He just isn't in the right frame of mind to let it happen to him. I know he slips up now and then."

Fetterman grinned as he watched the blush start at her neck and work its way up her face to her hairline. "And you have a second strike being Karen's sister."

"So what do I do?"

"If your feelings are real, then hang loose. If things are meant to work out, they will. Don't push it. The captain will realize what you mean to him in time, but you have to give him time, no matter what's happened in the past."

"You mean like coming to Hong Kong and then conning him up to the room?"

"Well, it's a bit late to worry about that, but I think in his frame of mind he won't really notice."

"Okay," she said and finished her drink in one hasty gulp. "Were you serious about buying a suit?"

"Of course. If I'm going to help you, I'll need some good clothes to escort you to the nicer places."

"Then by all means, let's go."

In the hotel lobby they decided to bypass the tailors in the same building and explore the streets nearby. There were signs proclaiming suits in less than twenty-four hours, but Fetterman wasn't sure the quality would be too high. He needed a custommade suit, and he quickly learned that there were good off-the-rack selections available that could be fitted and altered in little more than an hour.

After searching several shops, Fetterman found a dark blue pinstriped, three-piece suit that he liked. The fit through the shoulders and the waist was good. The legs needed to be altered slightly.

They sat in a couple of old chairs arranged against one wall, each with a tiny table next to it, and faced four of the three-position mirrors, which allowed customers to see their new clothes from all angles. Fetterman noticed a smell in the shop that reminded him of cleaning fluid and laundries. The room itself was badly lighted with four spotlights over the four mirrors. There were plate-glass windows in the front, but the streets were narrow, preventing the sunlight from reaching the pavement. They could easily watch the bustling crowds from where they sat.

After a few minutes an old man approached them, smiled as he bowed and asked if they would like something to drink while they waited—no charge, of course. When the drinks arrived, Morrow and Fetterman sat back to observe the pedestrians jostling past the windows of the tailor shop.

Morrow wanted to talk about Gerber some more, to try to learn more about him, but didn't know how to bring up the subject again. And she was afraid that she had already told Fetterman more than she cared to have him know about herself and her feelings. Besides, she wasn't sure that she liked what Fetterman had told her. She cursed her sister under her breath, wishing that Karen had stayed in the World with her husband.

Fetterman sat relaxed, his drink in his left hand, and it seemed as though his eyes were closed, but his head moved occasionally as he watched someone pass the shop. Morrow had never seen anyone look so relaxed.

"I've spent years in the Army waiting," said Fetterman, as if reading her mind. "Waiting for clerks to type papers when they didn't want to, for officers to condescend to see me when they didn't want to, to get into the mess hall when I didn't want to. Waiting on everyone else to do a job that he didn't want to do because he had been drafted or lied to or was just in a bad mood. It does no good to worry about it, so I learned to use the time to rest and relax."

"Wish I could do that," she said.

"It's easy enough. Just remember there's nothing you can do about the waiting. If you appear agitated, then you've let the clerk win, but if you're enjoying yourself, he'll hurry to move you on and irritate you. Either way, you've won."

Morrow laughed. "I'll try to remember that."

"And to make this even nicer, I have the opportunity to spend the time with a very pretty lady."

"Why, thank you, Master Sergeant." She stopped talking for a moment and then asked, "Why do they call you 'master sergeant'?"

"You mean other than the fact that I am one?"

"Yes. They don't call Tyme 'sergeant first class', or Sully 'staff sergeant.' They're just called 'sergeant.'"

"The captain started it. I think it was because I was taking over from the last team sergeant who had been killed. He was trying to establish my authority by reinforcing the fact that I outranked them all. I think it's now come to mean that I'm a master of a lot of military trades. Or maybe master of all I see.''

''I wouldn't think you'd need any help in establishing your authority,'' she said.

''That's the kind of man the captain is. He was taking no chances. Just trying to help the FNG.''

The conversation had naturally evolved back to Gerber, and Morrow was wondering what she should say.

Fetterman, however, didn't give her a chance. He leaped to his feet, tried unsuccessfully to set his drink on the table and said, ''I don't fucking believe it.''

He dashed across the shop to the window and tried to look down the street. He looked back at Morrow and said, ''You wait right here. I'll be back in a moment.''

''What is it?'' demanded Morrow, puzzlement written all over her face. ''What's going on?''

But Fetterman had dashed to the door and raced into the street. In the distance he thought he could see the retreating back of a man he recognized. The sergeant pushed through the crowd, elbowing people out of his way, ignoring their shouts of protest in his hurry to close the gap. But the man's pace never slowed, and he never looked back. He seemed to know exactly where he was going, and Fetterman couldn't close the distance between them.

He could swear he saw the man turn a corner. But when Fetterman got there, he saw another crowded street with a dozen turns and a hundred shop entrances. There were a thousand places to hide if the man had wanted to hide, and Fetterman could no longer see him. For ten minutes he stood on the corner, searching the crowd, staring into hundreds of Oriental faces and thousands of tourist faces, but recognized none of them. Finally realizing that the man had eluded him, he returned to the tailor shop where Morrow stood waiting near the door, the puzzled look still on her face.

''What the hell was that all about?''

''You wouldn't believe me if I told you. I thought I saw someone I recognized, but before I could catch up, he was gone.''

''Another American?'' she asked, not really sure what she thought.

"No. A Chinese of my acquaintance. Well, we haven't really been formally introduced," said Fetterman idly. "Anyway, he got away."

10

THE STREETS OF
HONG KONG

Fetterman, having collected his new suit along with one for Gerber, left the shop and headed back down the street, looking for the man he had seen. With Morrow in tow, not sure what she was supposed to be doing, Fetterman nearly ran along, peering into windows like a shopper gone mad. No sooner did it seem they would stop than Fetterman took off again. He was up and down the side streets, narrow roads flanked by tall buildings and colored by a hundred neon signs, brushing by the hucksters and ignoring the kids trying to sell things.

Morrow, tired and hungry, didn't say a word. She followed, occasionally asking, "Just what are we looking for?"

"Nothing," said Fetterman, never doubting the identity of the man he thought he had seen. He would know the face anywhere, but the man had simply disappeared.

Finally realizing that it was getting late, Fetterman said, "He's probably gotten out of here by now. I won't find him until he's ready to be found. Let's head back."

"Is this all a secret," asked Morrow, "or would you like to explain what the hell you are talking about?"

"Later. I'll tell you it all later."

"I'll accept that," said Morrow.

"Now then," said Fetterman, trying to change the subject. "Do you have something special in mind for dinner? Should we dress for it?"

"I think—" Morrow nodded "—you should dress. I would like to be treated to a fancy restaurant, although I do have an expense account and probably should buy your dinner."

"I'm never one to turn down free food," said Fetterman.

Back at the hotel they rode up the elevator in silence. As Morrow stopped off at the door to her side of the suite, she said, "I'm gong to change. I'll be over when I'm ready."

Fetterman found Gerber sitting in a chair, spinning the dial of the television set. He stopped long enough to say, "Want to see Matt Dillon speaking Chinese?"

"Not really," said Fetterman. He dropped his packages onto the couch and said, "Robin said she wanted to be taken out to dinner and we should dress for it. She said her expense account would pay for it, but I think it'd be a nice gesture if we took her."

"Whatever you decide, Tony."

Fetterman disappeared into the bedroom to clean up. He came back briefly to pick up one of the packages and then went back to the bedroom. He returned after a few minutes. He went to the bar and poured himself a shot of Beam's and sat down. He noticed that Gerber had already poured himself a drink.

"Had a strange experience today, Captain," said Fetterman.

"What was that?"

"Saw the Chinese guy."

"What Chinese guy? There are millions of them out there."

"*The* Chinese guy. That bastard who has been giving us fits in Vietnam. Saw him outside the tailor shop."

Gerber moved to the bar and stood with his back to Fetterman, pouring another shot of Beam's into the crystal glass that had been set to one side of the cabinet. He was also pouring the Beam's over ice, something he had thought he would never do, but it had been so long since he had been able to get ice that he felt obliged to use it.

With the drink in his hand, he turned so that he could look out the window at the contrasting views of Hong Kong. High-rise buildings of glass and steel were surrounded by primitive structures of stone and wood, which had been there for decades, maybe centuries. In the distance Chinese junks sailed in the harbour as 707s flew over them.

Keeping his eyes on the scene outside, Gerber said, "Don't you think it's a little strange that we've been here only a couple of hours and you think you've seen the Chinese guy already?"

"No, sir, I don't."

Reluctantly Gerber took his eyes off the view of Hong Kong and looked at his team sergeant. Fetterman was decidedly out of place, too. The civilian clothes he had bought didn't to seem to fit right, although the tailor insisted that they couldn't be cut any better. Gerber figured it was because he was so used to seeing Fetterman in jungle fatigues, or even a ninja suit, that anything else looked bizarre. Or maybe it was Fetterman's military bearing that made him seem out of place in civilian clothes. Gerber had to admit that the suit was a fine one.

"That's a pretty big coincidence. We take leave in an area with the largest concentration of Chinese outside of China, and in less than a day you claim to have seen one specific man."

"Are you suggesting that I can't tell one Oriental from another? I thought we went through that at the trial."

"Take it easy, Tony. I just can't accept the fact that our man is here. It's too big of a coincidence."

Fetterman stood up and moved across the carpet slowly, as if he were afraid he would leave footprints in the deep pile. "I would agree," he said, "that as a coincidence it's too big. I suggest it's not a coincidence."

"What?" Gerber was thoughtful.

"Think about it logically. There is no way we could be in town for less than a day and run into a man we thought was still in Vietnam, unless he knew we were going to be in Hong Kong and came after us."

Gerber collapsed into one of the chairs. "Go on, Tony."

"I'm suggesting that McMillan was killed not because any American had been targeted. He was killed because he happened to be a member of our team and was out by himself."

"That would take an incredible intelligence system. Hell, they probably don't even know our names."

"But they do. You know, Captain, that there have been VC in the strike companies. That's how our cover was blown when we crossed the Cambodian border after the Chinese guy. I'm sure the embassy offices downtown are loaded with VC sympathizers. Our orders to Hong Kong had to be sent there, as well as circulated in a dozen military command structures, all of which could be riddled with VC.''

"Okay, Tony," agreed Gerber. "Maybe they do know who we are and could get the information."

"Then it follows, sir, that the Chinese guy is going to know exactly who has spoiled all his plans. When we talked to the team about any Americans in our camp being the targets, I think we were wrong. The Chinese bastard is going to want to kill specific men and McMillan was the first."

Gerber drained his glass and sat down. "I can buy that the VC know who we are. I don't buy the fact that they would chase us to Hong Kong. Doesn't make sense."

"Makes the most sense of all. He's got us on foreign territory without the support of our team and without weapons." Fetterman smiled but didn't mention the .45 he had smuggled in. He wouldn't be surprised if Gerber knew about it, though. "He can move freely between here and China, bringing in weapons and men. He has another invisible line on the ground that will protect him. It's even better than the one between Cambodia and Vietnam because it's heavily guarded and there won't be any Occidentals crossing it without seventeen different types of identification and months of negotiation. We are helpless compared to him."

"No," said Gerber, shaking his head. "I just don't buy it. You found him too quickly."

"But that's the point, Captain. I didn't find him. He found us. There are only so many hotels in Hong Kong, and it wouldn't be all that hard to bribe a desk clerk to let him know when we checked in, or rather when Morrow let the desk know we were going to use half her suite."

"I don't buy," repeated Gerber slowly, as if he were considering the possibilities.

"If you want proof, I think you have it." Fetterman waved a hand around the room. "Robin managed to locate us pretty quickly, and all she knew was that we were coming to Hong Kong."

"But that's the point," snapped Gerber. "She knew."

"And I am saying that the Chinese bastard knew we were coming to Hong Kong. The information was lying around for the grabbing. Hell, we didn't try to keep it much of a secret around the camp, and there are still probably VC in the strike companies. The information was out there to be had, for anyone who wanted it. We just never thought the VC would want it.''

Before Gerber could respond, there was a knock at the door. Gerber spun to face it, his right hand reaching for the pistol that he wasn't wearing. Fetterman chuckled. ''I guess you do believe me. But I don't think he would knock. Blow the door in, riddle it with machine gun fire, but not knock.''

Gerber laughed at his own paranoia. ''You're right, of course, Tony. I would imagine it's our date.''

''*Your* date, Captain. I'm just along for the ride, so to speak.''

''If your attitude doesn't change quickly, you're going to be along for a quick trip out the window.''

Since Gerber hadn't moved, Fetterman went to the door and opened it. Morrow stood there wearing a bright red silk dress, which looked as if it had been made just for her. It had long sleeves, a mandarin collar and was tight across the chest, stomach and hips. A slit up the side revealed her thigh each time she moved, and Gerber found it provocative even though he had seen her naked on a couple of occasions.

''Come in, Robin,'' said Fetterman, smiling broadly. ''We were just talking about you.'' He stepped back out of the way and then said, ''It's really your room. You didn't have to knock.''

''I wanted to make sure that you both were dressed before I entered.''

Gerber, still talking about the Chinese officer, whom Fetterman was convinced he had seen, asked, ''What do you intend to do?''

Now Fetterman smiled. ''I intend to offer Robin a drink and then find out where she wants to go for dinner.''

''That's not what I meant.''

''I know, but right now there's nothing to be done. All that has happened has been a recon. There will be no action until much later.''

Morrow dropped onto the couch. ''You guys come all the way from Vietnam so you can talk like you're still in the war?''

''No, of course not. Now,'' said Gerber, ''where did you get that Suzie Wong dress?''

''You don't like it?''

"I think it's marvelous," said Gerber. "So what are we going to do for dinner?"

Fetterman suggested that since they were in Hong Kong, they should eat Chinese food the first night. But Gerber, having watched rice farmers fertilizing their fields, wasn't sure that he wanted to eat anywhere that served rice. Still, he deferred to Fetterman's idea. Morrow didn't care. She was happy to go out to dinner.

Then, they had to decide whether they wanted to take the car or walk. This time Gerber made the decision, saying that he would like the opportunity to see some of the sights without whizzing by them. Besides, he didn't want to ride with Morrow again right away. The experience had been too frightening.

The trio left the hotel and walked to Nathan Road, a wide avenue down the center of the Kowloon Peninsula. They headed north along Nathan, passing dozens of small shops that sold everything from jade and gold to silks and satins. After a while they turned onto a narrow road lined with bars that offered drinks and dancers, each advertised in glowing neons and flashing lights. Finally they found a small restaurant that wouldn't make them wait for dinner. Each of the three decided to order a variety of foods. The idea was to share them with one another so that they would have the chance to taste the different courses and the different sauces. Fetterman used chopsticks with an ability that suggested he had never seen a knife or fork. Morrow gamely tried to copy him but kept dropping her food. Eventually she gave up and decided to use her fork.

The mood was pleasant as they lingered over the meal, savoring every dish. Gerber was glad of the company. He tried not to let anything distract him. There was nothing pressing that any of them had to do the next day. They didn't have to worry about someone dropping a grenade in with them. Although the restaurant was small, it was air-conditioned, which made it as comfortable inside as it was in the hotel. The humidity and the heat were left on the street.

Fetterman summed it all up after they had finished eating. "This is how the rich do it. Spend their time eating big meals because there is nothing to do tomorrow."

"I doubt it's quite that easy," said Gerber, "because somebody has to keep track of the money."

"They hire people to do it. Meet them for lunch to talk about the money and then plan dinner."

Gerber was feeling the best he had in months. He had completely forgotten about Karen Morrow, even though her sister was sitting across the table from him. He was having fun talking with her and Fetterman, discussing things they had lived through during the past months.

Fetterman was particularly lively when telling about his adventures in France during the Second World War. It was great fun, and before the check arrived, Gerber suggested that they find somewhere to dance because the evening was young.

Morrow agreed immediately. Fetterman, sensing that Morrow would be happier if he found something else to do, said he wanted to go back to the hotel. Gerber wouldn't hear of it because it was their first night in town. Finally he agreed, too.

They left the restaurant, stepping into the blazing lights of nighttime Hong Kong. Gerber was surprised by the number of neon signs, the lights in shops and the almost holiday atmosphere of the streets. They followed the crowds for a while, dodging the kids trying to sell them small carvings and the men trying to sell them larger things, moving away from the center of the city where their hotel was located and into one of the more remote districts. They found themselves on the dock for the Star Ferry, saw that it was docked and decided to cross the harbour to Hong Kong Island. They walked south on the Island and then turned to the east, following the crowds there. They turned down one street, heading more or less back toward the waterfront and moving into the area known as the Suzie Wong District.

They strolled along slowly, watching the people around them. The crowds thinned slightly, and the streets were less well lighted. Neither Gerber nor Fetterman thought a thing about it, but Morrow suggested that they should find somewhere else to walk.

Before either Gerber or Fetterman could respond, a fourth voice entered the conversation from slightly behind and to the right of them. It said in accented English, "The lady is right. This is not a safe place to be."

"Well, thank you," offered Fetterman, stopping and turning around.

A man materialized from a shadow near an alley. "You could be robbed. You could be injured."

"We'll watch our step," said Fetterman.

"To show your appreciation," said the man, who was definitely Chinese and looked to be in his twenties, "you should give me money." His voice had become slightly threatening.

Wordlessly both Gerber and Fetterman moved so that Morrow was protected between them. Fetterman was on the alley side and Gerber nearer the street and standing a little behind them.

"I think we'll pass on that," said Fetterman, "but still appreciate the advice."

"You do not understand. It was not a request. I will have your money."

Fetterman flexed his knees and took a small step forward with his left foot. "We don't want trouble but are prepared to give it. Now why don't you just fade away before you get hurt."

Three men emerged from the alley, standing side by side. The one in the middle reached behind him and pulled a knife, its blade gleaming in the little light thrown out by the streetlamps.

"Why don't you just give us all your money before you get hurt," said the one with the knife.

Fetterman shrugged his shoulders and slowly began to reach under his coat as if to find his wallet. His eyes never wavered from those of the guy with the knife. The sergeant, standing lightly on the balls of his feet, suddenly kicked outward and upward as if trying to punt a football. There was a high-pitched scream, and the man with the knife fell to the pavement.

Before his friend on the right could move, Fetterman spun, his foot slashing out again, connecting with the second guy's jaw. He staggered backward, as if trying to keep his balance, but hit the side of the building and slipped down into a sitting position.

The last punk had no chance to see any of it. As Fetterman was taking out the man with the knife, Gerber had leaped forward, his fist flashing. In rapid succession he hit the man in the chest and throat, then kicked his feet out from under him. He fell heavily to his side, landing on his arm with a sickening snap.

Fetterman shot a glance to his side where Gerber stood. He then leaned forward so that he could speak to the barely conscious man lying in front of him. "You just wouldn't listen, would you, asshole? I warned that you'd get hurt. Now if I was real irritated with you, I'd break both your knees. Just remember this next time you plan on ambushing some innocent tourists.''

He straightened, looked at the second man and saw that he would be no problem. He turned and saw Gerber crouched over Morrow, who was sitting on the sidewalk with both arms wrapped around her stomach as if she had been punched.

''She okay?''

''Yeah,'' said Gerber. ''Just a little scared.''

Fetterman reached out to take one of her hands. ''Spends months in Vietnam with us, weathers a dozen mortar attacks, even goes on patrol with us, and she's scared by three street thugs?''

With Gerber's help she got to her feet. She brushed off the back of her skirt, trying to look over her shoulder to see if there was any damage to her new clothes. ''I just wasn't ready for this. I thought we were safe in Hong Kong.''

''So did I,'' said Gerber, glancing at Fetterman. ''So did I.''

Back at the hotel, they all stopped in the main room of the suite to have a drink. Fetterman performed the bartending honors, making Morrow's drink extra strong because she seemed to be more upset by the mugging attempt than she was letting on. He noticed that both knees of her stockings were torn, as if she had fallen to them before landing on her backside.

As she took a deep drink, she exclaimed, ''Hey! I got a question. Why didn't we report that to the police?''

''What for?'' said Gerber. ''They didn't steal a thing from us, and they were punished for trying. They came off a lot worse than we did.''

''Robin,'' said Fetterman, ''you look like you could use a long hot bath. Take some of the sting out of this.''

Gerber, joking all the way, said, ''And if you need someone to wash your back, I think we could find a volunteer.'' After he said it, he wondered if it had been a wise comment. He had spent the majority of the past few weeks trying to avoid just such a situation, but tonight, mellowed by the wine, it seemed like the thing to say.

She smiled at that and stood up. ''I'll give you a shout. I may need a refill on this, too.'' She held up her glass.

''Just let us know,'' said Fetterman.

As soon as Morrow was out of the room, Fetterman spun on Gerber and demanded, "Now do you think I'm seeing things? That was no normal mugging. We were set up."

"Wasn't a very good attempt. You'd have thought they'd have guns."

"Captain, it's nearly impossible to get guns in Hong Kong. They send a couple of martial arts experts with knives at us and figure that they're going to take us. They overlooked the fact that we know the stuff too and can kick the shit out of almost anyone we meet."

Gerber took a sip of his drink before he spoke. "Not exactly the first team. And a stupid move because it alerts us."

"No. Not really. It appears to be a mugging. If they kill us, that's fine, but if they fail, they figure we think it was a mugging. No harm to them."

"I have to admit that I'm much more inclined to believe you now," said Gerber, rubbing his chin. "We haven't been out of Vietnam for twenty-four hours and we run into a street gang. We weren't exactly in the best part of Hong Kong, but still, the co-incidences are adding up too quickly."

"So what are we going to do?"

"Well, I don't plan to spend my whole leave hiding in a hotel room just so the Chinese bastard won't have a chance to kill me. I suppose we could always check out of here and go to Japan or Manila, or even home."

"Captain, let me remind you that we all volunteered to extend so we could kill the son of a bitch. Now that we know he's here, let's get him."

"Tony, I'm not going to start a war in the streets of Hong Kong."

"No one said a word about starting a war, but we do know he's here and he won't have all the protection of the VC around him. He's delivered himself into our hands."

Gerber sat on the couch and kicked off his shoes. He wiggled his feet, watching his toes. "I wouldn't go so far as to say he's de-livered himself into our hands. We don't have him, and we don't know where he is. I would, however, guess that he can move back and forth across the Red Chinese border with ease. Something we can't do."

"So you're going to let this opportunity slip through your fingers because it might be a little bit difficult?"

"I might remind you, Master Sergeant, to whom you are speaking." Gerber grinned. "But I probably don't have to. Okay, let me say this. Right now we don't have enough information to work with. We need some more."

"And then?"

"The son of a bitch targeted us first. He's on my list. If we can manage it, we kill him."

11

HOTEL REGENCY, HONG KONG

The breakfast dishes littered the table as Gerber sat sipping coffee and staring out the window at Victoria Harbour far below him. The junks still sailed next to modern hydrofoils on the deep blue water. Fetterman was finishing his eggs, toast and orange marmalade. As he took the last bite, he said, "How do we go about finding him?"

"I don't think we have to worry about it. He's going to be looking for us. All we have to do is make ourselves available and he's going to turn up."

"Okay, that makes sense." Fetterman pushed his plate away and picked up his coffee. "So we play Joe Tourist. Ride the bus, take the ferry, use the tram, just about anything a tourist would do. We let him come to us."

"Right."

"Then I have only one other question. We aren't normal tourists. Won't that look strange?"

"I wouldn't think so. Even though we're not regular tourists, we would normally do some things that tourists would. I mean, one of the first things you did was go buy a new suit. We went out last night to a Chinese restaurant. Tonight maybe we ought to head over to the Aberdeen area and have dinner on one of the floating restaurants. Those are things that would be expected of us. They are the things we should do."

Fetterman nodded and then added, "We've just come out of a year in Vietnam. Shouldn't we be looking for female companionship?"

"Tony, I'm surprised at you. First, we *have* some female companionship. But if you feel that we need more for protective collaboration, then by all means we should try to obtain it."

"That brings up another question." Fetterman stood so that he could look out the window. "Shouldn't we tell Robin what's going on? She's as big a target as we are when she's with us."

Now it was Gerber's turn to be quiet. He continued to sip his coffee as he pondered the idea. Finally he said, "This is a very delicate area. We're playing fast and loose with a lot of international law and civilized ideals. We've moved the war from the Vietnam mainland into a different part of Asia, not to mention involving nationals from a couple of other countries."

"Yes, sir. Do we tell her?"

"It's a hell of a story."

"Yes, sir, and she has proved that she can hold back a story if it helps her friends."

"Tony, I think the last thing we need to do at this point is tell her. It's not that I don't trust her, I just don't think she needs to know right now. If the situation changes, we can tell her, but right now, I think we should hold our peace."

"So our plan for today is to run around Hong Kong as targets."

Gerber had to laugh. "Not much of a plan." At that moment, Morrow's door opened and she stood in the opening, her gaze moving back and forth between the two men.

"What's not much of a plan?"

Fetterman said, "The travel arrangements the captain made for us. I told him that it wasn't much of a plan, and he was repeating what I said."

"If that's the case," said Morrow, "I can come up with something better if you like."

"We're in your hands," said Gerber.

"Then if you're ready," she said, "let's get going." She ducked back into her bedroom long enough to grab her purse, then followed them into the hallway.

As they rode the elevator down, Morrow said, "If you don't mind, I'd prefer not to take the car. I mean, I have it parked now and I may never find another parking place for it. Nobody told me that you couldn't find parking places in Hong Kong. I thought the boss was doing me a favor by offering me the thing."

Gerber shrugged and said, "I guess it doesn't bother me." He turned to Fetterman. "Tony?"

"Can't see where it will make any difference," he said. "Might make things easier if we don't take it."

"Easier?" asked Morrow.

"Don't have the hassle with traffic and don't have to worry about a place to park. Besides, there's a lot of public transportation available."

Outside, they saw a green Rolls-Royce go by. Morrow pointed and said, "We should have stayed at the Peninsula. Those are the cars they use to haul their guests around. Better than the buses we're going to have to take."

They turned to the right, strolling along the sidewalk, looking into shop windows and trying to ignore the kids who were following everyone. They reached the gates for the Star Ferry and could see the green-and-white vessel as it sailed toward them. At first Gerber was going to suggest that they take a ferry to one of the other islands but then remembered they had been picked up by the muggers in the Suzie Wong district. Although he didn't want to make things too easy for the enemy, he could see no reason to make it too difficult, either. Without a word he steered Morrow toward the ferry.

As they boarded, watching the chairs being turned around for the return trip, she said, "We did this last night."

"But we didn't see much of Hong Kong Island. Besides, the ferry to Macau leaves from there, and we can gamble on Macau."

"If we do this right," said Fetterman, consulting the map he had found in the hotel, "we can get over to Aberdeen to have dinner in one of the floating restaurants."

Morrow looked from one man to the other and then outside as if she had never seen water before. She asked, "What is this fascination you have for the ocean? Ferries to Macau. Eating in floating restaurants. My God."

"Well," said Fetterman slowly as if considering the question carefully, "it limits the number of enemy approaches and greatly decreases the number of men needed for a successful defense."

"Thank you," she said. "I didn't know we were expecting an attack."

"Not a large one." Fetterman smiled.

After the ferry docked on Hong Kong Island, they spent an hour walking around, just watching the crowds and studying the architecture of the old buildings.

Much of the old British architecture of massive tan stone and giant windows with huge arches had given way to flimsy buildings with small windows and balconies that climbed the fronts. Mattresses, sheets, clothing and flags were draped over the railings of most balconies. A riot of sound, from radios tuned to Chinese stations, from televisions, people shouting and even bands playing, flooded the street.

There were cars, the drivers leaning impatiently on the horns although the snarled traffic was clearly going nowhere on the narrow, winding streets. Hucksters stood in front of small shops, demanding that pedestrians enter to purchase something, anything. Gerber and his two companions passed dozens of shops, theaters, banks, government buildings and hotels. They stopped in a few but bought nothing. Occasionally they separated, first Gerber and Morrow walking ahead, and then Fetterman and Morrow. At last Gerber suggested they take one of the buses to visit the other side of the island.

They found a red double-decker bus that would take them into Aberdeen. They were surprised that it was air-conditioned. They had been in the heat and humidity of the streets and found the sudden change in temperature slightly uncomfortable.

When Morrow seemed to be totally engrossed in sight-seeing, Fetterman leaned close to Gerber and said, "I think I've spotted him."

"Where?"

"Six seats back. I believe he's been with us for the past hour, but then there is a tourist couple that I've seen a few times this morning, too."

"I would opt for them," said Gerber, grinning. "Good protective coloration."

"Yes, sir. But I think it's the lone man. He's stuck to us tighter than they have, and it's not that unusual for a tourist to get on this bus at this time of the day."

"Keep an eye on him."

"What do you plan to do?"

"Let's see if we can get him alone somewhere and then question him. He's probably just hired help with no real knowledge, but he might be able to tell us something. Remember, the one thing we don't want to do is cause an incident. We have to be discreet."

"Yes, sir. Discreet."

They settled back to watch the scenery with the rest of the tourists, but as they passed the turnoff for Waterfall Bay, they noticed a car stalled across the road. Gerber shot a glance back at the lone man, but he seemed unconcerned.

Gerber felt a hand on his arm and looked at Fetterman, who sat with his other hand under his shirt as if reaching for a pistol.

Suddenly, two men dressed in three-piece suits, their coattails rippling in the breeze off Telegraph Bay, appeared at the side of the road holding AK-47s. Before the bus had time to come to a halt, they opened fire.

Gerber grabbed Morrow and shoved her to the floor, falling on her as he wrapped his arms around his head for protection. The glass in the windows disintegrated, showering the passengers.

The bus began rocking from side to side as the bullets drummed into it. Bits of metal flew as slugs ricocheted off the frame of the backrests. The relentless rounds chewed up the fabric and stuffing of the seats, creating a snowstorm of foam bits. There were loud bangs as the tires blew. Women and children screamed under the onsaught. One man lay on his side, blood staining his shirt, screaming over and over, "What the fuck?"

Fetterman rolled into the aisle and saw the lone man lying on the floor aiming a small pistol at him. Before the man could shoot, Fetterman drew his own hidden weapon and fired twice, putting one bullet in the man's right eye and the other through his throat. There was a spray of blood as he flipped onto his back, one hand clawing weakly at the wound in his neck. He shuddered briefly, then was still. As dead fingers released the weapon, Fetterman crawled toward him and claimed the gun.

"Mack. Hey, Mack," he called, and when Gerber looked up, he showed him the captured pistol. Gerber nodded once, and Fetterman tossed it to him.

The firing from the outside died, and there was a moment of unnatural quiet before a moan came from one of the wounded.

That was answered by another, and there was a final burst of automatic weapons fire.

Fetterman then took cover behind a seat where he could get a good shot at the door if he needed it. He nodded to Gerber, who was on the other side of the bus, trying to protect Morrow and still cover the emergency exit, as well as providing backup for Fetterman.

Nothing happened right away. It was as if the men outside were waiting for word from their accomplice on the bus. When he failed to appear, one of the men came forward and kicked open the door, shattering the glass that remained in one of the bottom panels. He stepped up into the bus, his AK held loosely in both hands. He leaped to the center aisle, his feet spread wide, daring someone to do something.

Fetterman fired twice. The man spun to the right, throwing his weapon toward the driver's seat. The gunner collapsed to the floor as if his bones had suddenly turned to rubber. There was a splatter of blood on the window caused by one of Fetterman's bullets punching through the man's head.

That was answered by a burst from outside the bus, the sound of running feet and a car engine starting. Seconds later the sounds receded in the distance.

Gerber reached around to help Morrow up. "Are you all right?" he asked. "Were you hit? Are you all right?"

"I'm fine," she said shakily. "What in the hell was that all about?"

"I don't know," said Gerber. "Some kind of bus hijacking, I guess."

She turned her full attention on him, her eyes searching his. "You've been in Hong Kong little more than twenty-four hours, and already someone has tried to mug you and then hijack a bus with you on it. I'm not stupid. What the fuck is going on?"

Before Gerber could reply, Fetterman was kneeling near him. "We'd better get out of here."

"Get out?" asked Morrow, astonished. "What about the people who are hurt? We've got to do something for them."

"Yes, ma'am," he said. "The best thing we can do for them is get out of here and find help fast. There isn't much we can do without medical supplies."

Suddenly there was shouting all over the bus as if most of the passengers realized that the attack was over.

Fetterman got to his feet and leaped to the front where he made sure that the attacker there was dead. He grabbed the AK from the floor, stripped the magazine from it and ejected the round that was chambered. He put the weapon in the front seat but kept the magazine.

Cars were beginning to pull up, and the bus passengers were coming out of their shock. The vehicle rocked as people struggled to their feet and fought one another to get out. Others stopped to help the wounded who were lying on the floor or slumped in seats. A few were crying for help. Others were just crying hysterically.

Fetterman saw the bus driver. He had gotten out of his seat but had been shot three times in the chest and was crumpled behind his seat, nearly hidden. A woman was next to him, holding her leg in both hands and watching as the blood oozed from a wound in her thigh. She was grinning as if she had never seen anything funnier. Her face was turning waxy, and Gerber knew that she was in shock and dying from blood loss.

Gerber and Morrow, both on their feet, worked their way to the front door. Fetterman stepped to the ground to help them out. He then waited to assist the others as they straggled from the bus.

Gerber noticed that some of the occupants in the stopped cars and trucks were rubberneckers, while others seemed genuinely concerned, shouting in Chinese and English, trying to learn what had happened, asking if they could offer any assistance. In the distance there was the wail of a siren.

"Help is on the way," said Fetterman.

"Tony," said Gerber quietly. "You'd better get rid of that weapon."

"Why? I picked it up on the bus."

"Can you prove that?" asked Gerber, meaning he wanted to know if it could be traced to Fetterman.

"Can you prove I didn't?" replied Fetterman.

As the police approached, both Gerber and Fetterman dropped the pistols they held. Gerber didn't like doing that because he didn't know if the Hong Kong police could be trusted, but he had to take the chance. If they held on to the weapons, with so many dead and wounded around, the police might be inclined to shoot first.

"I'm afraid we're going to be busy the rest of the day, Robin," said Gerber. "I guess lunch is out."

"As soon as the police are through with us," she said, her voice low and steady, "you are going to tell me exactly what is happening, and I mean all of it."

"Yes," he said. "I suppose we owe you that much."

IT TOOK A LONG TIME for the threesome to free themselves from the clutches of the Hong Kong police, and even then they had help from the American Embassy, followed by a call from Morrow's paper before they were released. It was nearly dusk, and neither Fetterman nor Gerber wanted to be on the streets after nightfall a second time. They headed straight for the Star Ferry, with Morrow in tow, and returned to Kowloon Peninsula and the hotel.

As they entered the suite but before any of them could either pour a drink or call room service for dinner, Morrow demanded, "What the hell is going on?"

"Why don't you sit down," said Gerber reasonably, "and we'll tell you everything."

She stared at him for an instant, not moving. She then looked at her clothes, still splattered with the blood of the people killed or wounded during the attack, and felt her stomach turn over in her anger. She didn't understand how Gerber and Fetterman could stand there so calmly. But then, she had seen the same reaction from them after they had almost casually disposed of the three muggers the night before.

She paced along the couch, spun and headed back. She stopped and was going to shout something at them but thought better of it. She sat down and repeated, as calmly as she could, "What the hell is going on?"

Fetterman had stepped to the bar and had poured a large drink. He handed it to Gerber, who gave it to Morrow. He told her, "You'd better have some of this before we start."

Again she was going to shout at him but took a deep drink and breathed out the liquid fire of the Beam's as it nearly set her insides ablaze. "Stop stalling."

Gerber took another glass from Fetterman, swallowed nearly half the alcohol in it and said, "It started a long time ago, after we first built our camp."

For the next hour he explained about running into an enemy officer, who, it turned out, was Chinese. The man may have planned the first attacks on the camp, may have led the NVA while Gerber and the stripped-down team were working in North Vietnam.

Fetterman mentioned the times he had seen him during raids into Cambodia, or working in villages near the border. Gerber took over again, reminding her about the attempt to assassinate the Chinese officer, which was the case that she had helped them with. The story that she had withheld from publication to save Fetterman and Tyme from court-martial by General Crinshaw, who had pressed charges of murdering a foreign national in a neutral country. Gerber told her that he believed it was the same guy, and Fetterman nodded his agreement.

"And we think," said Gerber, "that it was this same officer who engineered the plan to capture us and then held Fetterman, Tyme and Washington in the POW camp. Since we beat him at that game, we think he is trying to kill us."

Morrow sat there quietly, staring at her feet, her breath coming in rapid gulps. She was remembering everything that she had seen in the past few months. She was remembering the deaths of Vietnamese strikers and Sergeant McMillan.

"How long have you known he is here?"

"We suspected it last night after the mugging. Tony and I discussed it. Finding us here wouldn't have been that hard since we didn't try to hide our plans. We just never assumed that the enemy would chase us into neutral territory. It was—"

"Why didn't you tell me? Don't you trust me yet?"

"Trust has nothing to do with it. We just didn't think it was time to tell you." Gerber shook his head. "We thought we might be followed during the day, but we didn't expect them to attack a busload of innocent people to get us."

"We have to tell the police," she said.

"Oh, no," said Fetterman from the other side of the room. "That's the last thing we have to do. We tell the police, and the Chinese bastard escapes across the border into Red China. No, we've got to keep him in Hong Kong where we can get at him."

Gerber waited for her horrified reaction, but it never came. She might have been thinking about all the death that had come about because of the Chinese officer, or she might have been thinking about fighting a war. In a war people died, and if you could keep those who died limited to the combatants, it made the war a little less horrible. Maybe she thought that by killing the Chinese guy in Hong Kong, they could limit the war in Vietnam slightly, and a smaller number of innocents would be killed.

When nothing was said for a while, Fetterman put his glass down. "Do we eat now?"

Morrow stood and smoothed down her wrinkled and dirty dress. "I think I'll just go to my room and take a bath. I'm not very hungry now."

"Would you like some company?" asked Gerber.

To his surprise, she said, "No. I would like to be alone for a while. I have a lot to think about." She moved to the connecting door and opened it. "I think I'll just spend the rest of the evening by myself."

"Sure," said Gerber. "If you need anything, let me know."

She left without another word.

As soon as the door was closed, Fetterman said, "From what you just said, Captain, I take it that we are going after the Chinese bastard."

"Of course."

"How are we going to accomplish this? We don't have any weapons, and we're alone here."

"Right. That's why, after we eat dinner, you're going to get on the phone and see how many members of the team you can find and convince to come to Hong Kong. I'm going to send a telegram to Bromhead and have him request leave. Then we go hunting."

12

HOTEL REGENCY,
HONG KONG

Fetterman glanced at his watch. He was sitting in a chair, staring at the phone as if willing it to ring. He said unnecessarily, "I make it about six in the morning in the World."

Gerber stood, unable to tolerate the quiet or the room any longer. He looked at the door that connected the room with Morrow's. "I think I'll go out and find a telegrapher's office and see if I can get word to Johnny."

"You can use the phone for that," said Fetterman.

"I know. I just need to get out for a while."

"You think that's wise, given all that's happened in the last couple of days?"

Gerber thought about that and said, "I was going to say I didn't think they'd try anything again so soon. And I didn't think they would attack if there were innocents in the way."

"That doesn't answer the question."

"No, Tony, it doesn't."

"So are you still going out?"

"Yeah. I can't stand it around here. I have to get out and do something."

Fetterman stole yet another glance at his watch and then put his feet up on the table as if he wanted to relax. He stretched and yawned. "You should learn how to relax, Captain. Sometimes you have to lie in wait for days before you have a chance to act, and if you expend all your energy trying to make something happen, you may find yourself short when the time comes."

"Thank you, Master Sergeant," said Gerber. "And no, you don't have to look at your watch again because only two minutes have passed since you looked at it the last time."

"Touché, Captain."

"I won't go far, Mom." Gerber smiled. "I just have to get out for a few minutes, even if it's only down to the lobby."

"I'll stay here and start the calls as soon as it's late enough in the World."

GERBER HAD BEEN GONE for more than an hour, but Fetterman wasn't worried about him. After all, Gerber was a Special Forces officer and was supposed to be able to take care of himself. Finally, when Fetterman figured it was about eight o'clock in the morning in Austin, Texax, where Tyme had said he was going to spend his leave, the sergeant picked up the phone and asked for the overseas operator. He gave Tyme's phone number, having memorized it before Tyme went on leave.

On the other side of the world, Fetterman heard the phone ring twice, three times, until someone finally answered it with a simple hello. He was a little surprised by that, used to having people answer with their rank, name and unit of assignment, but there was no mistaking the voice. Fetterman nearly shouted into the handset, "It's about time you answered."

There was a pause and then, "Sergeant Fetterman? Is that you?"

"It's me, Boom-Boom, calling you to find out what kind of trouble you've gotten yourself into without the old master sergeant around to keep you straight."

"You sound so far away. Are you in town?"

"Of course not. I'm in Hong Kong with the captain, trying to keep the world safe for democracy. Or maybe that's safe *from* democracy."

"Hong Kong? I'll be damned."

"Listen, Boom-Boom, this is costing me more than I care to think about. I've got a problem and I need some help. How soon can you get here?"

"Get there? To Hong Kong? Why?"

"Remember when we were in Bangkok and the captain told us that the wrong body had been shipped for burial? Well, the right one is here, only it's not a body yet."

There was a pause before Tyme spoke again. "You mean . . ."

"He's here. In Hong Kong."

"I don't know how fast I can get the arrangements made, Tony. I can probably get out to the West Coast this afternoon, but I don't know how soon I can get a flight west from there."

"Once you know that, send me a telegram, and we'll arrange transport for you from the airport." Fetterman went on to give him the name of the hotel and the room number. "I'll expect to see you in a few hours."

"Any special equipment you'd like me to bring? Anything that you might not have there?" asked Tyme.

"Just yourself. That's all we need."

"I'll let you know when I'll arrive. See you then."

As soon as Fetterman completed the call to Tyme, he asked the overseas operator to dial the number he had for Galvin Bocker. He went through the same ritual, trying to convince Bocker that they needed him in Hong Kong as soon as he could get there. Bocker, too, wanted to know if he should bring a weapon, and again Fetterman discouraged the idea. He told Bocker that they could find weapons in Hong Kong, that Special Forces NCOs were supposed to be resourceful and that they would have to make their weapons if they couldn't buy them.

Next Fetterman tried to locate Sam Anderson but had no luck. Instead, he spoke with Sam's father, who said he'd give the message to Sam that Fetterman had called. Then he asked the operator to connect him with Sully Smith. A woman answered the phone, and Fetterman asked for Sully. A moment later he came on the line, and Fetterman told him what he wanted. Sully said he would catch a plane as soon as he could.

Fetterman tried a couple of other team members after speaking with Sully. Either they weren't home, or no one wanted to answer the phone. T. J. Washington, the medic, had taken off on a car trip. No one was sure when he would be back or exactly where he had gone. Fetterman left his name and number in case Washington checked in soon.

It was the same with Derek Kepler. The Intelligence NCO could have been a real asset to them, but he was off doing something else and no one at his home knew exactly what it was. Fetterman mumbled something about stealing an aircraft carrier for the camp and then thanked Kepler's father.

JUSTIN TYME SLOWLY CRADLED the phone and turned to look at the blond woman who sat at the small, round kitchen table, which needed to be stained and was surrounded by three mismatched chairs. She was wearing a frayed, blue robe, which she hadn't bothered to fasten so it hung open. She wore nothing underneath. She was drinking orange juice and staring at him.

"What was that?" she asked.

"I have to go to Hong Kong."

Carefully, precisely, she set the glass on the table and said quietly, "Just like that? You get a phone call and have to go to Hong Kong. After I've waited nearly a year for you to come home, you calmly announce that you have to go to Hong Kong?"

Tyme sat down and picked up his fork. He was thinking about the call and what Fetterman had said. The Chinese officer was in Hong Kong. Out in the open where they could get at him. Slowly he became aware that the woman was talking to him.

"I'm sorry, Linda. I've got to go." He hadn't heard her and was trying to fill the gap in the conversation.

She stood, throwing her napkin onto the table. "Got to go. Just like that. No discussion. No explanations. You just have to go."

"Linda, you haven't given me a chance to explain. No chance at all."

But Linda wasn't interested in listening at that moment. She left the kitchen and ran to the bedroom to find her clothes. That did it, she decided. She wasn't going to spend another minute with him. She just couldn't believe that he was actually going to leave her after having been home for less than a week.

She heard footsteps near the doorway and looked up to see Justin watching her as she picked up the jeans she'd worn the day before. Wearing only panties and a bra, she turned to face him.

"How can you consider going back?"

"Linda, listen to me." He moved forward and sat on the edge of the bed. "I'm not going back right now. I'm only going to Hong Kong for a couple of days. If Sergeant Fetterman called, then there must be something wrong. He wouldn't have called otherwise."

"If you go, then we're finished. I've waited a year for you to come home. It hasn't been easy on me. A lot of people—men—have called, but I've tried to be loyal. And what for? So that you can run off the first time the phone rings. To make it even worse, you've volunteered to stay there killing innocent women and children for an extra six months. You didn't even have the courtesy to ask me about it."

Tyme pushed a hand through his hair. He reached out for her, but she pulled away. "Where the hell did you get that crap about killing women and children?"

"The news. I saw it on the news. A man burned himself to death in front of the Pentagon to prove that what we're doing in Vietnam is wrong. To let us know that we're killing innocent women and children."

Tyme's temper finally snapped. "Bullshit," he shouted. "There has been nothing on the news about us killing women and children. Maybe the VC, but not us. We haven't done anything like that."

"You drop bombs indiscriminately and that kills the—"

"What the hell are you talking about? I haven't dropped a bomb on anyone. I'm doing a necessary job that—"

"Supports a dictator who oppresses the innocent," she finished for him. "And they're using B-52s to drop the bombs. I saw pictures on the news. I saw it all."

Tyme jumped up and stormed to the door. He stopped and looked back, taking in the scene because he believed it would be the last time he would see it: Linda, still in her panties and bra, standing in front of the tiny closet with its sliding, wooden doors; the lavender bedspread that had mostly fallen on the floor; the little black-and-white TV on the nightstand; Linda's clothes on a chair.

"Where in the hell are you getting all this?" he asked again, his voice subdued now.

"I've been around. I've seen the reports. I've been to lectures on the campus."

"Oh!" he said. "Lectures on the campus. Impartial discussions of our imperialist advances on the oppressed people of South Vietnam. Pinkos who think that everything the VC does is all right and everything we do is wrong. Well, let me tell you about the lives we've saved with our medical assistance. Or the farmers who show us where all the enemy's booby traps are hidden so that we won't step on them. Does that sound like they don't want our help?''

Tyme turned to go, then stopped and looked back. "Can we talk about this seriously? I mean, what the politicians and the protestors say shouldn't come between us. You know me better than that.''

She held up a blouse in front of herself as if suddenly embarrassed by her semi-nudity. "I know you can't sleep well at night.''

Tyme felt he was gaining control again. "That's easy, Linda. Hell, one day I'm in Vietnam, where Charlie might drop a mortar round on me or begin an assault on the camp, and the next I'm in downtown Austin. Of course I can't sleep.''

"It's more than that," she said quietly. "It's what you do and what I do and how I feel. Maybe it *would* be better if you just go.''

"Maybe it would," he said. He turned and retraced his steps to the kitchen so that he could phone the airlines.

WHEN HE HUNG UP Galvin Bocker went back to the living room and sat down. His wife turned her attention from the new color TV that dominated one side of the tiny room in their quarters on the Army base. There were two chairs on either side of it and a couch, frayed from the kids jumping on it, faced the set. A worn, thin carpet of light gray covered the floor. She asked, "Who was that, dear?''

Bocker sat watching the TV for a moment. "One of the men from the team. Had some information for me.''

"Oh, is he in town?''

Bocker looked at his wife and said, "No. He's in Hong Kong. He wants me to go there.''

The woman looked from him to their two young daughters, who sat together on the floor coloring. They didn't like to color all that much and the weather outside was beautiful, but it had been so long since their father had been home that they just wanted to be near him, to reassure themselves that he was real, that he was home. They sensed the distress in their mother's voice but didn't understand it. Both turned to watch, the coloring books forgotten.

"When?" she asked quietly.

Now Bocker stood and said, "I'm sorry, Sara. As soon as I can. There is some kind of trouble, and they need my help.''

There were tears in her eyes as she said, "But what if we need your help? We do need it. We need you." There was nothing in her voice that was accusing; there was only hurt because he would be leaving again so soon after arriving. A single phone call, and he had to go.

She had been the wife of a Special Forces NCO long enough to understand the unwanted calls. She knew her husband would have to respond to the call for help. She just didn't think it was fair because so many of the other service wives had husbands who didn't have to go. Other wives had husbands who worked regular hours in the motor pool or supply and who never had to go overseas.

"If you needed my help, I would stay," he told her. "I'll be back as soon as I can. I still have over three weeks left of my leave, and I can take some extra time if I want it. I have some extra leave time I can use."

"Let me help you pack." She moved over to him and reached out and took his hand. "The girls will be all right for a few minutes," she whispered.

Bocker smiled his understanding. "A few minutes?" he asked.

As they entered the bedroom, Sara closed the door and locked it behind her. She began to unbutton her blouse and said seductively, "Well, maybe more than a few minutes."

SAM ANDERSON SR. told his wife he had to go to the airport. She asked if there was something wrong. "I don't think so," he answered. "It didn't sound like it, but the sergeant who called said that he would appreciate it if I would tell Sam to call him."

The elder Anderson walked out to the garage and got into his car. He headed toward the airport, which was only ten minutes away. As he drove, he wondered if there was something more to the phone call, even though Fetterman had told him not to worry. Why would he call all the way from Hong Kong if there wasn't trouble?

At the small private airfield, Anderson Sr. pulled his car up next to his son's, which was parked in front of a light blue metal building. On the taxiway he could see a Cessna with the door on the passenger's side removed. As he watched, it took off and climbed, circling the field until it was a barely visible speck thousands of feet above him, weaving among the puffy white clouds.

Mr. Anderson turned off the engine and opened the door to let the early-morning breeze blow through. With his hand he shielded his eyes from the sun and watched as a tiny shape tumbled from the aircraft. It was followed by another and another until there was a string of six people falling.

As they plummeted to earth, Anderson Sr. wasn't worried. Then, as he could see shapes beginning to look vaguely human, he wondered if they weren't getting too close to the ground. He sat forward, waiting, silently praying for the chutes to open. He saw the deep colors of the jumpsuits and began to distinguish the arms and legs of the people.

"Where are the chutes?" he asked silently and then out loud again, "Where are the chutes?"

He started to get out of the car as the first chute blossomed, followed quickly by others until there was only one person freefalling. Anderson was sure he could recognize his son.

"Sammy," he yelled. "Pull your rip cord!"

And then he saw the parachute stream out of its pack, a tiny white blob trailing black cords and slowly, agonizingly slowly, open up, retarding the younger Anderson's descent.

Moments later all the sky divers were on the ground, gathering their chutes and then trotting across the airfield toward the buildings that housed the airport offices and training rooms.

Sam saw his father and waved once before disappearing into the building. A moment later he reappeared, escorting a tall, slender woman with long brown hair that hung to the middle of her back. She was dressed in a jumpsuit and had a baseball cap on her head. The skin of her oval face was nearly perfect, and when she smiled, she had deep dimples. The only flaw was a nose that was flattened slightly as if it had been broken sometime in the past.

"Hi, Dad," the demolitions expert said as he approached. "Do you know Brandi?"

"I don't think so," his father replied. "Hello, Brandi."

"Something you need, Dad? I'm sure you didn't come all the way out here just to watch me jump."

"No. Especially the way you do it. Scared me to death. Why do you have to wait so long before opening your chute? You were the last one."

"It wasn't all that long. I've made jumps where we couldn't open them until we were within five hundred feet of the ground. I popped it while at a thousand."

Anderson Sr. clapped both palms against his ears. "I don't want to hear it."

Grinning, Anderson Jr. took the woman's hand and said, "Okay, Dad. Won't tell you about it. Now what did you want?"

"You got a call from a Sergeant, ah, Fetterman? Yeah, Fetterman. Gave me a number and told me to have you call him when it was convenient."

"He tell you what he wanted?"

"No, just that he's in Hong Kong."

Anderson laughed. "Hong Kong. I wonder what he's doing there."

"Didn't say."

"Okay, Dad. Let me take care of my equipment and I'll be right home. Be about thirty minutes or so."

The elder Anderson smiled at the young woman. "Brandi, I'm sure that Mrs. Anderson would be delighted if you could join us this morning for a late breakfast, if you haven't eaten already. Or maybe I should say an early lunch."

The younger Anderson laughed and said, "Brandi, would you like some breakfast with my folks? My mom is an excellent cook."

"Hey, since I invited you," said Anderson Sr., "I figured I'd do the cooking."

"Okay, Dad," he said, turning to look at Brandi. "You want to eat at my house, even if my dad cooks?"

"Sure, Sam," she said. "Might be fun to eat with civilized people again. That is, if you promise to be on your best behavior."

"Thank you, Brandi. Make my Dad think I'm a slob."

"We'll see you in a little while, Sam. Brandi, it was nice meeting you." Mr. Anderson got into his car and started the engine.

SULLY SMITH REPLACED the receiver, then walked to the door and out to the garage where his 1957 two-tone Chevy was parked. The hood was up, there was a cloth over one of the red fenders and parts of the engine were scattered over the floor and a workbench. Rather than go back to work on the car, he opened the door on the driver's side and got in. He put his hands on the wheel as if he were going to back out of the garage. He just sat there.

Thirty minutes later his sister, a thin woman with long black hair, brown eyes and an olive complexion, entered the garage. She was wearing shorts and a blouse. For a moment she stood staring at her brother, wondering what had been said on the phone to upset him. Finally she asked, "Frank, what's wrong?"

He had been called Sully for so long that he momentarily forgot that his sister still called him Frank. He looked at the mess he had made of his car. "I won't be able to finish this."

"So?" she said. "You can leave it here. Tom won't mind."

"Right. He'll be thrilled to have your brother's car spread all over his garage with no prospect of getting it fixed in the next six months or a year."

"If he doesn't like it, he'll just have to put it back together himself."

Smith turned and looked at his sister carefully. "What does the family think of the war, sis? Or your friends?"

"What do you mean?"

"I mean, do they support us? Do they think we should get out? I see on the news that some people don't like what we're doing. I just wondered how everyone felt. Hell, I saw the antiwar rallies staged in Washington. I didn't know it was so widespread."

She pondered the question for a while, picking at a small scab on her bare knee. "I don't think they really give it much thought. They see it on the news, just like you did, but it's so far away, and if they don't really know anyone who is over there, they just sort of ignore it. They don't care. We stay in Vietnam or we leave it. This is the first time anyone has really protested the war. Ever since that guy burned himself to death in front of the Pentagon."

"Maybe they don't say anything because they know your brother is there."

"No, Frank. I think they just don't care. It doesn't affect them. Maybe there are some jobs at King Radio because of the war, but it doesn't affect them in any way they can touch. It's somebody else's problem. They don't think about it."

Smith got out of the car and let his eyes roam the inside of the garage. There were bikes that hadn't been used in a while. Boxes with labels telling him that they held old clothes or books or toys that the children had outgrown. There was a rack of garden tools and a red lawn mower in one corner. He could see outside, to the bright green lawn, which didn't seem to be as green as the vegetation in Vietnam, and the small garden, which didn't seem to be surviving the late fall too well. Middle-class America at its best. Things simple and easy. No hard choices and no chance to really live. Go to work, come home, then go to work again.

Suddenly Sully wished he could change places with his brother-in-law because, even if it wasn't an exciting life, it was one worth living. At the end of ten years, what would he have to show? Service stripes on the sleeve of his uniform, ribbons above the pocket showing bravery or service and tours of duty. Smith smiled. Or the memories of dozens, hundreds, of things that he had been allowed to blow up. Encouraged to blow up.

"I'm glad most of the people don't know about Vietnam," said Smith. Then, as an afterthought, he said, "I have to go to Hong Kong soon."

"We'll have your car here when you get back," she said.

He walked over to her and kissed her on the cheek. "I think that means more to me than anything you could have said."

IN THE HOTEL IN HONG KONG, Fetterman stood up and walked to the bar to pour himself a drink. He looked at his list and came to the conclusion that all in all he didn't have very good luck in finding the team. He wasn't sure exactly what Gerber had in mind but thought he might have gotten through to enough of them to complete the task. He wished he'd found T.J. because they might need the services of a medic. No matter.

He walked to the connecting door and put his ear against it, wondering what Morrow was doing. He could hear nothing on her side. She might still be in the tub, although she had left them a couple of hours earlier. She was probably in bed asleep, like a normal person.

Fetterman went back to the bar and topped off his drink again as he thought about Morrow. Her reactions during the shooting on the bus and its aftermath certainly hadn't been those of the average American female. She hadn't gotten hysterical; she had been thinking about survival and what had to be done. Maybe it was because she had seen so much blood and gore while in Vietnam, or maybe it was a result of some of the training she had taken prior to arriving in the war zone. Whatever the reason, her reactions had been very good. She was sensible, cool and quiet. She was an outstanding lady, intelligent, beautiful, and Fetterman decided he would be proud to have her on his team if it was allowed.

He went back to the chair, the one he had turned so that he could watch the lights of the city and the boats in the harbour. He reached over and turned off the lamp in order to see better and wondered what had happened to the captain.

Fetterman wasn't worried; it was just that the captain should have been back by now. As he had thought earlier, the captain was certainly able to take care of himself, but Fetterman didn't like the way the forces had been divided. Team members scattered all over the World, or world, he thought ironically, because Bromhead was still in Vietnam, the captain out somewhere and Morrow apparently asleep behind a locked door. Fetterman didn't like it. Any of it.

13

THE STREETS OF
HONG KONG

Gerber moved to one of the phones in the hotel lobby. He called a telegrapher's office to send the telegram. Then, feeling as if he hadn't spent enough time out of the room, he decided to take a walk around the block, at the very least. He exited the hotel, turned right and crossed the street so that he walked past the Peninsula Hotel as one of the green Rolls-Royces deposited a wealthy couple at the door. He looked at the woman carefully, his eyes focusing on the diamonds around her neck, figuring that she was wearing, at minimum, his whole year's salary.

He rounded the corner and looked back, but the couple was gone, waved inside by the uniformed doorman and aided by three bellhops. But, as he turned to continue his walk, he caught a flash as if someone was breaking for cover. Before he moved too far, he stopped again, wondering if he had picked up a tail already. Then up the street from him he saw a man in a soiled suit, sitting on the curb and holding his head in both hands. He was staring at the street dejectedly. Gerber walked rapidly over to him because he looked like an American.

Gerber approached and said, "Hey, you need a hand?"

The man looked up at him and tried to smile. "Sure."

The guy reeked of liquor, and it was only then Gerber realized that he was drunk. He had probably spent the last several hours in one of the better clubs, sucking down a lot of his military pay. That's what Gerber assumed because the man had short black hair and a very neat mustache. Both marked him as a military man. Not to mention the civilian suit that looked new.

"Name's Gerber. Want me to help you to your hotel?"

"Larko," said the man. "Dennis Larko. You American?"

"Uh-huh. Now would you like a hand finding your way back to your hotel?"

Larko smiled and then began to giggle. He rubbed a hand over his oval face, smearing the dirt that was on it. His dark eyes were a bit glazed. He looked like a tall, burly man, but it was hard to tell since he was sitting. "It's around here somewhere. I know it is. I just can't seem to find it."

Gerber helped Larko to his feet and stood back while the other man swayed back and forth, trying to maintain his balance. The captain asked for the third time, "Where's your hotel?"

Finally Larko said, "It sounds like an island or something. I forget the exact name."

"You mean the Peninsula?"

"Yeah! That's it. Air Force gave us TDY for the couple of days we're here so we thought we'd try the best."

"Well, it's not that far. Come on." Gerber half pushed, half guided Larko down the street until they arrived at the Peninsula. He kept his eyes open but didn't see a sign of the man he thought had been following him earlier. Maybe he had run off when Gerber stopped to help the drunk.

The doorman gave them a dirty look but didn't try to stop them as they entered the hotel. He even opened the door for them, but then stood away from them as if afraid he would be contaminated somehow. They made their way to a bank of elevators hidden away from the front desk and waited for one going up. Larko wasn't sure of the floor or the room number but gave one to Gerber anyway. Gerber suggested that they look at the key, but Larko claimed he'd lost it.

After two misses they found the right room. Another man opened the door and was surprised to see Larko accompanied by a stranger because he had left earlier with an Oriental woman. That could explain what had happened to his room key, Gerber thought.

He guided the man to the bed and tried to sit him down, but Larko collapsed on his side, drew his feet up, coughed once and then emitted a ragged snore.

The other man introduced himself as Loechner and thanked Gerber for helping his friend. Gerber noticed a couple of flight suits hanging behind the door. "You guys pilots?"

"No, flight crew. Have a C-130 parked out at the airport and we've got an RON here. Maybe be here a couple of days if we don't get a mechanical problem fixed."

"Well, have fun and don't get too drunk." Gerber left, thinking he had missed something but not sure what it was.

He returned to their suite at the Regency and found Fetterman sitting in the dark with his chair facing the window. He didn't turn on the lights and made his way to the bar. After pouring himself a drink, he asked, "You see anything more of Robin? She say anything to you?"

"Went to sleep a while ago. Never reappeared."

"How do you know she's asleep?" asked Gerber.

Although Gerber couldn't see it, Fetterman grinned at the window. "When you're a master sergeant, you have to know these things. Besides, I went in and checked on her."

"She didn't lock the door?"

"Of course she locked the door, but since when has a locked door stopped any of us? Don't worry, I relocked it on my way out so she won't know."

"Have any luck getting hold of the team?"

"Some of them." Fetterman stood and closed the curtains before turning on the light. "Probably begin arriving sometime late today or early tomorrow, depending on flight connections."

Gerber sat on the couch and said, "Got the telegram off to Johnny so he might be here soon."

"Okay, Captain, what's the plan now? We haven't really thought about that."

"Same thing, I imagine. He's going to be looking for us and knows where we are. We let him come to us. We'll just have to be ready."

"I don't suppose you have a weapon," said Fetterman. "I had to throw away the only one I had."

"Shit," said Gerber, slapping his knee. "That's what I forgot."

"Sir?"

"While I was out, I ran into a drunk airman. Helped him to his hotel and then didn't think to ask them if they could get us some weapons. They're a C-130 crew and might be able to do it."

"That could solve one problem."

"You have another?"

"I'm a little concerned about Robin," said Fetterman. "She's a very strong lady, but I don't think she responded to today's activities with enough emotion. She's got it bottled up in her, and I don't like that. She didn't rant at us for not telling her about the Chinese guy, and she didn't seem to be too upset by the number of innocent people killed or hurt today."

"It might be," said Gerber, "that she has seen enough death and destruction with us that she is slightly immune. She won't go to pieces at the first sight of blood."

"I thought of that," answered Fetterman, "but I decided that we are dealing with a woman who is basically a middle-class American and who has been shielded from some of the realities of the world. I'm afraid that we should get more emotion out of her, if only outrage at the way people treat other people."

"So what do you want to do about it, Tony?"

"I was thinking that maybe you should talk to her, Captain. Tomorrow, alone. Find out what she's thinking and feeling. I'm worried about her."

Gerber felt his chest go cold and his head spin as Fetterman made his suggestion. The last thing he wanted was to be thrown into a situation where he would be alone with her, talking about feelings and emotions. It was a minefield strewn with all sorts of extra booby traps.

"You think it's necessary?"

"Yes, sir, I do. The sooner the better."

"All right. Tomorrow, as soon as we finish breakfast, I'll have a talk with her." Gerber didn't relish the idea.

BEFORE GERBER HAD A CHANCE to talk to Morrow the next morning, they got a call from the Hong Kong police. There were a number of questions that needed to be answered again. The three of them left for the police station on Hong Kong Island just after nine o'clock. Gerber was studying Morrow, trying to see if there was something wrong with her, but after a good night's sleep she seemed to have shaken off the effects of the day before.

At the police station they were questioned individually. Gerber watched as Morrow was led away, two policemen flanking her and a female officer following. He stood there until they entered one of the interrogation rooms that lined the narrow hallway.

One of the two officers accompanying Gerber opened a door next to them and gestured to the American to go through it. There were two chairs, one on either side of a small, rectangular table shoved against a wall. A green glass ashtray rested in the middle of the table, and on the far wall there was a two-way mirror. Gerber sat in one of the chairs, wondering if they were going to play good cop-bad cop with him or if the interrogation technique would be less subtle.

One of the police officers took the other chair. He was a small man wearing a three-piece suit. He had straight black hair, large oval eyes, a small nose and very even white teeth. He grinned to show them and then stroked the pencil-line mustache over his wide mouth. For a moment he didn't say anything. He just smiled. Finally he pulled a pack of American Salem cigarettes from a side pocket and held them out, offering Gerber one.

Gerber smiled and shook his head. "No, thank you."

"Okay." The man had an English accent. "I am Detective Lo. We've invited you back because our interviews with the other surviving passengers suggest that you and your friend were armed. Would you care to explain that?"

"Well—" Gerber rubbed his chin "—actually, we were able to take the weapons away from the men who started shooting at us."

"Three or four heavily armed men and you were able to take their pistols away from them?" The detective rocked back in his chair and lit one of his cigarettes, blowing the smoke at Gerber.

"Of course, it wasn't quite that easy," said Gerber, "but that is correct. Sergeant Fetterman spotted one of them on the bus and was able to take his weapon."

"Sergeant Fetterman?" asked Lo, raising his eyebrows in surprise. "Sergeant of what?"

"Now don't be naive," said Gerber. "You know perfectly well that Sergeant Fetterman is in the United States Army. And so am I."

"Then you are familiar with weapons. You might say at home with them," said the police officer.

Gerber laughed out loud. "Listen, you're not going to get me to admit that I smuggled a pistol into Hong Kong. Do I have access to weapons? Yes. Hundreds of them, up to and including 8 mm mortars. If you'd like something larger, I think I could get it. Oh, and machine guns, too. But smuggle one into Hong Kong. No. I didn't do that. The weapons we used we took away from the men who attacked."

"Then you admit you shot them?"

Gerber took a deep breath and sighed. "I went over all this yesterday with your uniformed officers. They have the pistols. They have our statements."

"Yes, I read over those. Most interesting. I find there are questions I can't answer."

"Such as?"

The uniformed officer suddenly jumped so that he was standing next to the table. He pounded a fist on it, the sound ricocheting in the tiny room like a rifle shot. "Enough of this," he screamed. "Just enough. We know you're lying to us. Come clean and we'll forget about the smuggling. You did us a favor, but we don't like the way you lie to us."

Slowly Gerber turned to face the other police officer. He was dressed in a tailored uniform with a black Sam Browne belt. He held a high peaked cap under his arm. His eyes were wild, and his hair hung in his face. He had bad breath.

"I'm sorry," said Gerber, "but I'm sure you've checked my background by now. The American Embassy is sure to have helped you. You should know that I am an expert in unarmed combat. Sergeant Fetterman took the man by surprise. We used his own weapons on him. We used them on his friend."

The uniformed man began to chatter in rapid Chinese. His voice became louder as if he were losing his temper. He slapped the table twice and then stood erect, his hands on his hips.

The other man answered him slowly, calmly, smoking his cigarette. He crushed it out and lit a second one. He gestured with it and then knocked the ash into the tray.

The conversation continued like that until the plainclothesman put out his third cigarette. The uniform glared at him for a moment and then stormed out of the room, slamming the door behind him.

"He's not happy with me," said Lo. "He thinks you're lying and that we should get to the bottom of those lies."

"And you?" asked Gerber.

"I'm not sure. I'm not worried about it enough to pursue it. You did us a favor by breaking up the hijacking. I wish you could have done something about it sooner, but I'm glad you were there."

"Well, then, what's the problem?"

"The problem," said the detective, shaking another cigarette from his pack, "is that damned pistol. The big .45 that's standard U.S. Army issue. A punk like that shouldn't have had it."

"But we shouldn't have had it, either," responded Gerber.

"No," agreed Lo, "but you have a better chance of finding one." He hesitated and added, "Unless something new comes up about the weapons, I'm happy with your story. You won't be hearing from us again."

"Is there anything else? I'd like to get out of here."

"No, that's all for now," said Lo. "But please, if you find it necessary to leave Hong Kong, let the American Embassy know where you go in the event we need to speak with you again."

Gerber got to his feet and stepped to the door. "I'll be in town for another several days," he said.

The man escorted Gerber back to the entrance of the police station where Fetterman sat on a hard wooden bench waiting. He was sitting beside an Oriental woman who had one wrist handcuffed to the arm of the bench. The wall behind him was splattered with dried spit, vomit and blood. There was a large desk where the booking sergeant sat, elevated so he looked down on those brought in. There was constant traffic through the room, doors slamming and people screaming. Eyes closed, Fetterman looked as if he didn't have a care in the world or any idea where he was. Gerber stopped in front of Fetterman and asked, "Where's Robin?"

Fetterman opened his eyes. "Gone. Left about half an hour ago. Before I got out here."

"You didn't follow her?"

"I've only been out here about three minutes myself." Fetterman got up, smiled at the woman on the bench, then said to Gerber, "She said she'd meet us for lunch."

As they left the police station, Gerber said, "I don't like this. They separated us too easily, and now Robin has gone on without us."

"You think that might be a problem?"

They reached Jackson Road and began walking north toward the berth of the Star Ferry. As they passed the Hong Kong Club Building, a large, formidable structure, Gerber said, "Can't you see it as such? We haven't had control of anything since we got here. We've been letting the opposition have the initiative from the word go."

"We haven't had much choice."

"And we still don't, but we've got to keep everyone else from interfering with us. I should've told Robin to stay right there until we were finished, but I didn't expect things to break the way they did."

"You have a reason for feeling this way, Captain?" asked Fetterman. "Or are you just borrowing trouble?"

"Probably borrowing trouble. I'm just uneasy after all that's happened."

Back at the hotel they stopped at the front desk to see if there were any messages. They learned that Anderson thought he would be in about midnight. There was nothing from any of the other team members. They rode the elevator up and let themselves into the living room of the suite. Morrow was not there, and there was no evidence that she had been.

Gerber shrugged off his jacket and dropped it on the couch. He moved to the control knob of the air conditioner and turned it up, then wandered around the room, wondering if Robin had ordered lunch for them or if she had gone out shopping. He didn't think she would venture too far until they returned, but there was no telling. He went to the connecting door, knocked twice and called, "Robin! Robin? You in there?"

"I can open it, if you would like, Captain."

"Robin?" yelled Gerber, "we're coming in."

Fetterman moved to the door and took out a tiny kit, selecting two slender metal picks, one with a slight hook on the end. He slipped the hooked piece into the lock, twisted it and slowly inserted the second piece as he felt the tumblers fall. A second later he twisted the knob and pushed the door open.

Immediately Gerber was alert. The little of the other room that he could see was a shambles. Fetterman noticed it, too, and jumped back so that he was no longer in a line of fire from the other room.

They held their positions for a couple of minutes, but there were no movements or sounds in the room. Gerber glanced at Fetterman. He shrugged and pointed to the left, indicating he wanted to take that position. He would be going through the door at an angle, toward the bathroom. If anyone was hidden there, Fetterman would be in a position to see him.

Gerber nodded and pointed to the left, telling Fetterman that he would follow him but dive into the main part of the room. He held up one hand, counting down silently using his fingers.

When he reached zero, Fetterman leaped, rolled on his shoulder and came up facing the bathroom. He kicked the door open and let it slam against the wall, but there was no one hidden there or in the tiny closet opposite him.

When Fetterman moved, so did Gerber. He followed Fetterman but dived at the bed, rolled across the mattress and came to his feet with his back to the wall, facing the room. It, too, was empty.

"Clear here," said Gerber.

Fetterman appeared around the corner. "Nothing in there. Her clothes are in the closet and her other stuff still in the bathroom. None of it has been touched."

The sheets and blankets were off the bed. One of the chairs was overturned, the table lay on its side and two of the lamps were broken. Papers and books were scattered on the floor, and there was shattered glass everywhere. The phone had been ripped from the wall. Gerber was surprised that the hotel management hadn't been up to find out about the phone.

"I guess this means they have escalated the war," said Fetterman.

"She's still alive, though," said Gerber. "There's no blood anywhere, so they didn't shoot her or stab her. If they'd killed her, they would have left the body because there would be no reason to take it with them. Not to mention the problem of carrying it out."

"They would have had a similar problem taking her out alive."

"They could have walked her out," said Gerber. "Held a knife at her back and told her that, if she squawked, she would die, a would her rescuers. That would have kept her quiet."

Fetterman sat on the bed. "Okay. I think you're right abou that. But why keep her alive?"

"Obviously because she allows them to control us. As long a she's alive, they know we'll obey their orders. They hold the trump card."

"Do they?"

"To a point, I suppose. We can't do anything reckless tha would endanger her, but there'll be a point where that handle wil break right off," said Gerber.

"And now?"

"Let's search through here carefully and see if we can find any clues. I doubt that it'll do us any good, but we can't afford to overlook anything."

"And if we don't find anything?"

"Then we order up some lunch," said Gerber somewhat callously, "and wait for them to make contact. They will."

14

HOTEL REGENCY,
HONG KONG

Although Gerber had talked about eating and not worrying, he was not eating and he was worrying. He sat with a large steak in front of him. He had cut into it once but only took the single bite. He drained his wine in one healthy gulp, then poured himself a cup of coffee. He just sat while the meal got cold.

The knock at the door came as no real surprise. They suspected that someone would be contacting them. They just didn't know what form the contact would take. Fetterman leaped to the door, waited until Gerber was in position, then whipped it open. No one was there, only an envelope that fell to the floor. Fetterman looked up and down the hallway, but it was empty except for an Oriental woman pushing a maid's cart slowly toward the elevator.

Without a word Fetterman picked up the envelope and handed it to Gerber, who thought about fingerprints and booby traps and then ripped it open. The talent being used was probably imported from Red China, and the fingerprints, if there were any, probably would be no good. No way to trace them. And they wouldn't booby-trap the envelope because it made no sense.

He held it up by the opposite end and shook out the contents. There was one piece of paper and one Polaroid-type photograph that landed facedown. Gerber ignored the photo, fearing the worst. Fearing it would be a picture of Morrow's body.

Gerber read the note.

The woman dies if you do anything to annoy us. We want to see you alone, tomorrow. Be ready. We will call. If you disobey, the woman dies.

Gerber reached down and picked up the photo. He turned it over and studied it slowly. There was no change in his expression. Fetterman had been watching closely. When Gerber didn't speak, he reached over and took the snapshot out of his captain's hand.

It showed Morrow, stripped of all her clothing, lying on her side, her hands bound behind her. She had been badly beaten. There were dark bruises on her stomach, chest, thighs and face. One of her eyes was nearly puffed closed, and there was blood on her chin and shoulder and splattered on her legs.

Fetterman turned the photo facedown on the table. "Captain?"

"Yes, Tony."

"What do we do?"

"Right now, we wait. There is nothing else we *can* do. Wait until the team gets here and hope they make it before we need them tomorrow."

"We can't meet them at the airport," said Fetterman. "The opposition will have someone there looking for us. Or in the lobby to follow us. If they find out the team is arriving, they'll kill her."

"Right, but if we're lucky, they won't know what they look like. We'll have someone else meet them and tell them to assemble here at the hotel."

"And then?"

"And then we see what happens. I'll call those Air Force guys and see if I can get them to help. Or maybe you can call the homes of the team members who are coming and find out what airline they're using. Maybe we can get a message to them that way."

"Yes, sir. Anything else?"

"Not right now." Gerber reached over, picked up the picture and looked at it one more time. He wondered what she must be thinking, how she must be feeling. He had promised himself to protect her and failed. She had followed them to Hong Kong, only to be kidnapped and beaten. He knew that the beating was done only to make him lose his temper. But the plan had backfired because it only made him stop and think. It had made him slow down and methodically think through each step. He knew what he would do. Still, he wondered about Morrow and her feelings.

MORROW TRIED TO OPEN HER EYES behind the blindfold but couldn't because it was tied so tight. Her mouth was filled by a gag, and she could feel saliva gathering and dripping out because she couldn't swallow easily. Her jaw ached from being held wide open by the gag.

Her body felt like one huge angry bruise from the beating. She tried to shift her position, but she was so tightly bound she could hardly breathe. She could only lie on her side, her knees drawn up and held in position by the ropes. She closed her eyes and tried to relax, hoping that Gerber would come to her rescue. She remembered the lengths to which he had gone to free his men from Crinshaw when the general had arrested them, and later from the POW camp when they had been captured. She was sure that he wouldn't forget about her.

In her mind she ran down the events after the police had questioned her. She had left the station after waiting for only ten minutes and being told that it would be an hour or more before the police finished with Gerber and Fetterman. There was nothing that she needed to worry about, they had told her, so she decided to meet them at the hotel. She asked the desk sergeant to tell them and left the station alone. She walked to the Star Ferry with no trouble, crossed the harbour and went to the hotel.

In her room she started to undress but changed her mind. Instead, she went into the living room and poured herself a drink. It was a bit early to be drinking, but she didn't think Gerber or Fetterman would care; besides, they weren't around.

A sharp knock sounded on the door to the suite, and she went to answer it. As she opened the door, it was shoved against her hand, and an Oriental man rushed in. Before she could say a word, the man hit her in the stomach. She felt the air flee her lungs, and she fell to her knees, her head spinning, as she rolled to her side. She tried to breathe, but it seemed as if her lungs were paralyzed.

A second Oriental, shorter than the first, entered the room and stepped over her, moving toward the window. The one who had hit her grabbed her by the arms and lifted her to her feet. She leaned against the wall, using it to support her as she struggled to catch her breath.

The men talked to one another in rapid Chinese. The first man pushed her through the doorway into her room, and she tripped, sprawling to the floor near the foot of the bed. Both men began laughing then, and one of them kicked her lightly on the bottom.

They both then began to search the room, throwing Robin's papers and books onto the floor. They jerked the blankets and sheets from the bed and knocked the phone onto the floor. It landed close to where she lay, and when they turned their backs to search through her suitcases and the dresser drawers, she grabbed the phone. She spun the dial, trying to get the operator, but one of the men saw her. He leaped toward her and jerked the wires from the wall.

They continued their search, ignoring her. They threw glasses at the walls, knocked one of the framed paintings onto the floor and kicked over one of the chairs. When they had done enough damage to the room, they jerked Morrow to her feet.

"We go now. You go with us. You make noise, we kill you. You understand?"

Morrow didn't want to talk to either of the men. She wanted them to leave her alone. She had hoped they were just there to rob her and prayed that they would leave when they had what they wanted. But they took nothing, and now they were telling her that she had to go with them.

One of them grabbed a handful of her hair, jerking her head back so that she was staring at the ceiling. The other demanded, "Do you understand?"

She tried to nod but couldn't with the man pulling on her hair. She gasped and said, "Yes. Yes! I understand."

She felt the pressure on her head relax slightly, then she was hit in the stomach again. She dropped to her knees and clutched her middle, trying to breathe, unable to move at all. There was a curtain of black descending over her eyes, but she finally gulped in a mouthful of air.

The man laughed and kicked her in the chest, sending pain through her. She felt as if she were going to throw up.

Again she was lifted to her feet, and one man pinned her arms behind her while the other stood in front of her and pretended he was going to hit her. Each time Robin flinched, they laughed uproariously, as if they had never seen anything funnier.

Then, before they left, he hit her a final time, aiming the blow at her crotch. She hadn't thought that a woman could be hurt like that but found out she was wrong. She wanted to reach down, to hold herself, but the man wouldn't let her. She tried to squeeze her legs together, but her knees were shaking, and she seemed to have no control over them.

She remembered little of the trip through the hotel lobby. No one seemed to pay any attention to her, although one of the men was helping her walk. She was dumped into the back seat of a car, and as they pulled away from the curb, she was pushed to the floor. When she tried to look up, the man shoved her head down. For a moment everything stayed like that. Then her captor grabbed her arms, forced her face to the floor and bound her hands behind her.

The trip seemed to last forever. The man wouldn't let her move at all. She had to stay on her knees, her nose pressed to the floor mat of the car. Each time she tried to turn her head, the man pulled her hair.

When the car finally stopped, she could smell the country air around her. The back door opened and she was dragged out. She had enough time to see that she was not in the city anymore before being pushed into a building. There were other Oriental men there waiting for her.

Everyone stood watching and then one of them moved forward, grabbed her blouse and tried to rip it from her shoulders. The cloth proved to be a little too tough, and someone handed him a knife. Carefully he cut all her clothes from her until she was standing in front of them completely nude.

Wordlessly they began beating her. Before they had been afraid to touch her face because she had to walk through the hotel lobby, but now they didn't care. Each time she fell down, they lifted her up and waited until she stopped swaying before hitting her again.

Finally she fell to her side, and they left her like that. They tied her more tightly, wrapping ropes around her knees and ankles, and then took a couple of pictures. That done, they gagged her, blindfolded her, and then left her where she was.

Now all she could do was wait. She knew what they were doing and knew that she wasn't in danger of dying soon. They wouldn't kill her because they still needed her, as a lure, to pull in Gerber and Fetterman. All she had to do was hang on until they came to rescue her. The beating, while painful, had really been only superficial. She could wait patiently, trying to remember what Fetterman had told her about patience.

GERBER SPENT THE REST of the day sitting in the hotel room, sipping Beam's Choice and trying to concentrate on the TV. There wasn't anything that he wanted to watch, but he tried to keep his mind occupied. He watched an English language broadcast of the news that announced the American First Air Cav had completed a sweep through the Ia Drang valley, claiming to have killed 1,771 VC and NVA. It was the first use of the airmobile concept and the first use of B-52s in the Vietnam War.

Occasionally he would glance away from the TV at the photo lying facedown on the table. He was tempted to reach over and look at it again but denied himself.

He wondered if he wasn't letting the enemy get to him with the psychological warfare they were waging but realized there was really nothing he could do at that moment. He couldn't go out to buy weapons because he was sure that he would be followed and the purchase reported. Anything he did would be reported—not that it mattered, if all he was doing was sight-seeing.

Fetterman had been strangely quiet. He sat in the corner, his chair positioned so that he could watch the harbour. He held a knife in his hand and was using a leather belt to strop the blade. Not that the blade was dull. It was just something to do while he waited for the captain to pull himself together. He knew it would happen sooner or later and that the captain had to do it himself.

Gerber finally got up and walked over to the TV and slammed a hand against the control knob to turn it off. He shot a glance at Fetterman. "No, Tony, I am not stewing in my own juices. I was just trying to get my mind set and decide what we need to do."

Putting down his knife, Fetterman asked, "And you've decided?"

"It strikes me that they'll have people watching all our movements. They may expect us to go to the police, though I doubt that. They may expect us to try to find weapons. To do that would let them know we don't have many. They may think we'll go to the various clubs and try to recruit American help. Or they may want us to stick to the room and brood about this."

"Yes, sir."

"So the last thing they will expect is for us to go sight-seeing."

Fetterman thought about it and then laughed. "It has possibilities."

"Sure it does. They think they hold all the cards, and in essence they do. What we have to do is something they don't expect. I would think that sight-seeing would be it. How in the hell can we go out and look at the sights without Morrow? Knowing that Morrow is being held captive? It's bound to shake them up."

"You don't think it might backfire, do you?"

"What do you mean?"

"They went to a lot of trouble to kidnap Robin. Now we have the picture and the demand that you meet them alone, but rather than sit around waiting for instructions, we take off for some sight-seeing. They might just kill her then."

Gerber rubbed his chin and said slowly, "No, I don't think so. They'll keep her alive until they've got us. If they kill her, they've played their trump card."

Fetterman clapped his hands together. "All right, then. Let's do it. Shake the bastards up."

"In just a minute. Let me see if I can get in touch with those Air Force boys once. They might be able to help us quite a bit."

"Give them a call while I change my clothes," said Fetterman.

As Fetterman left the room, Gerber picked up the phone and called the Peninsula Hotel, asking for Dennis Larko. He answered the phone on the second ring and said that he remembered Gerber.

"Got a favor to ask," said Gerber.

"Be glad if I can do it," he said.

"I know you're in Hong Kong for only a short time and the last thing you want to do is hang around the airport, but I've got some of my people coming in, and I won't be able to meet them. Wondered if you could do it?"

"Sure. What flight are they coming in on?"

Gerber switched the phone from his right ear to his left. "That's the problem. I don't know. And they won't be coming in together. I'll have to give you a description and let you try to find them."

"You mean I've got to stay out there and meet all the planes?"

"I would suspect that once you've found one of them, you can tell him to find the others. After all, he'd be able to recognize the men. Puts him one up on you."

"All right, I'll do it."

"Good. Thanks. Now the first flight should be arriving about midnight. That doesn't mean one of our guys will be on it, it only means that one could be."

Gerber went on to tell Larko how he wanted the guys to contact Gerber. That done, he thanked Larko for his help and told him that if he ever found himself in South Vietnam, he should look up Gerber, who would find some way to repay him.

As he hung up, Fetterman reappeared, dressed in a clean set of civilian clothes. "Let's go have some fun."

"Not fun, Tony," said Gerber, "but let's go throw out a smoke screen."

"Exactly what I meant."

15

KAI TAK AIRPORT,
HONG KONG

Larko sat outside the glassed-in customs area at the airport, studying the passengers as they disembarked from the planes that had just arrived from the World. He had the descriptions of four men dancing through his head, descriptions that Gerber had given him several times. When a big, blond American passed through Customs, Larko knew immediately that it had to be Sam Anderson.

Larko leaped to his feet, dodged two Asian stewardesses who were dragging their suitcases behind them, ran forward and yelled, "Hey, Sam. That you, Sam?"

The blond man halted in midstride and turned to look. He saw the dark-haired man running toward him waving, but didn't recognize him at all. "Are you talking to me?"

"You remember me, don't you?" asked Larko, seizing Anderson's hand and pumping it furiously. Under his breath he said, "For God's sake, pretend you know me. Call me Dennis."

Still bewildered, Anderson did as he was told. "Is it really you, Dennis? I didn't recognize you. Have you lost weight?"

Larko pulled Anderson to one side, near a bank of telephones and a group of coin lockers, away from the flow of traffic, and whispered, "Your man Gerber gave me a message for you. You're to wait here until Bocker, Tyme and, ah, one other, Smith, arrive. Then you are to go separately to the Hotel Regency and check in under your own names. You are to call Gerber when you are settled."

"Anything else?"

"That's all I was told."

"Thanks for the message, Dennis."

"No problem. Gerber said to be careful because someone might be looking for you that you won't want to meet. See you in the funny papers."

GERBER AND FETTERMAN had crossed Victoria Harbour again and were walking through the Suzie Wong district, window-shopping and killing time. They kept the pace slow as they looked into dozens of shops that displayed jade, pearls or gold, or tailor shops filled with new suits and dresses or just bolts of cloth.

Although Hong Kong was noticeably cooler than Vietnam, the humidity was high, and they had begun to sweat within a block of the hotel. A welcome breeze from the harbour sprang up as they neared the berth of the Star Ferry. A fishy odor drifted toward them from the dock. They turned around then, walking back along Chater Road. At sunset they noticed more women on the street, dressed in short skirts and low-cut tops, walking alone or in pairs. As they were about to enter a restaurant, an Oriental woman with long, white hair boldly walked up to them.

"I go eat, too," she said. "I go eat with you."

Gerber's first reaction was to send her on her way, but Fetterman jumped right in. "Of course you will, my dear. What's your name?"

"You may call me Muffin. Everyone call me Muffin." She waited for Gerber to open the door for her and then led them into the restaurant as if she owned it. She nodded and smiled at the man behind a bar of dark wood and deep red, and ignored the hostess who wanted to seat them at a table that had a snowy cloth and red napkins. Instead, Muffin headed for a booth in the rear of the room.

"What can I say?" asked Fetterman. "I'm intrigued by her white hair. I want to know if it's real or just an imaginative dye job."

"There is only one surefire method I can think of to find out, Tony. What about Mrs. Fetterman and the kids?"

"I think they would like to know, too, Captain," he said with a smile. "You will have noticed that her eyebrows are also white. Besides, she has a cute figure."

"A little small for me," said Gerber, "but I'll admit she has pretty legs. Well, it's up to you, Master Sergeant."

"Thank you, sir. I shall try to live up to the standards set by the great Master Sergeant Protective Association."

They sat down and waited, and when a waitress arrived, they ordered drinks. Fetterman kept up a running conversation while Gerber tried to spot a tail. He was sure there had to be one. He had decided to stay out until fairly late, hoping that the tail would be with them and no one would be left to watch the hotel. It might mean that his team members could get in without anyone seeing them.

"So," said Fetterman after Muffin had ordered the most expensive entrée on the menu, "do you have a last name?"

"Yes. I am called after my father, who was an Englishman serving in Hong Kong. I am Muffin Hill."

"An interesting name," said Fetterman. He smiled again. "I understand that, when one of you finds a friend, you telephone all your friends and invite them for a party."

"I am alone."

"Yes. I see that." Fetterman was surprised when he noticed that she had green eyes. It was very strange to see an Oriental with anything but brown eyes, but then, they all had black hair, and Fetterman could see no sign of black roots. Either the dye job was so new that the hair hadn't grown out at all, or it was the natural color.

Gerber broke into the conversation. "You have your protective coloration. How do you know it's not a plant?"

Muffin looked from one man to the other but didn't understand what was being said.

"Does it make any difference?" answered Fetterman. "Either way, we are one up."

From that point they ate their dinner slowly. Sometimes, as he swallowed something that was particularly tasty or during one of the many outbursts of laughter, Gerber would remember the picture of Morrow bound and gagged. There would be a twinge in his gut, and he would find himself almost short of breath, but then he would force it from his mind, knowing that he was doing the only thing he could. He was fucking with the opposition in the only way he could.

From the restaurant they went dancing, with Fetterman and Gerber spending a great deal of money, buying expensive drinks in the clubs and discos that Muffin suggested. They were filled with young American men with short hair dancing with long-haired Oriental women. Strobe lights flashed in time to the beat of rock music sung in heavily accented English. In some of the clubs, seminude women danced alone in cages suspended from the ceiling or on the bar, while in others the women were naked and swayed in time to music that only they heard. Gerber gently but firmly rebuffed most of the overtures made by other women, sometimes dancing with them, sometimes buying them a drink, but always sending them away.

Muffin steered their course for them, taking them deeper into the Suzie Wong District but never mentioning money. They both assumed that she was getting a kickback from all the places they visited. Neither man cared. If the situation had been different, Gerber would have laughed about the probable reaction of the opposition. You don't grab someone's girlfriend and make death threats and expect the victim's friends to go out on the town, picking up prostitutes, dining and dancing.

Finally about two, having spotted no one following them, they decided to head back to the hotel. Fetterman was now holding hands with Muffin and talking to her as if she was his long-lost love. Gerber was amazed at the change in the man. He had seen the sergeant slit the throats of enemy soldiers, use a flamethrower to break up a human wave assault and fight in hand-to-hand death struggles. Fetterman was not someone who would be described as gentle, and yet he was treating Muffin with the greatest kindness. He was treating her as if she were the most important person in his life right at that moment, asking her questions about herself, about how she lived. But even the questions showed a gentleness because they weren't the typical "how-did-a-nice-girl-like-you" or "why-do-you-do-it" kind. They were about her family or her schooling or what she really liked.

Gerber sat back and watched the master, or rather, the master sergeant, at work. He was dancing with her, displaying a knowledge of the new steps that went with the driving rock music that surprised and amused Gerber. He wished he could do it himself.

As they walked back toward the Star Ferry, the evening having turned chilly under the bright stars overhead, it was assumed that Muffin would accompany them, although no one had said anything. At the gate Fetterman paid her penny fare and then carefully handed her enough money for the return trip. She smiled at him and then wrinkled her nose as the sea breeze brought the odor of dead fish to them.

They entered the hotel, and the bell captain nearly ran across the lobby toward them. He halted only a foot or so away and stared at Muffin with hate-filled eyes. He was trying to silently tell her to get out of his hotel because she didn't belong. She had not, or did not, pay him a kickback for his services.

Fetterman stepped forward. "Is there a problem here?"

"This woman . . ." he said. "This woman—"

"Is with us," said Fetterman. He patted the man on the shoulder and slipped a large bill to him. He winked at the bell captain and asked again, "Is there a problem?"

"No, sir. None at all." He stepped to the bank of elevators and pushed the Up button.

"Thank you," said Gerber.

Upstairs, as they entered the middle room of the suite, Gerber saw that the message light on the phone was blinking. He nodded toward it, and Fetterman indicated he understood. He held open the door to their bedroom and said to Muffin, "Would you care to freshen up?"

As soon as she was through the door, Gerber was on the phone for his message. He listened and held a thumb up to tell Fetterman it was good news. Into the receiver he said, "We're in room 802. You and Sully come on up. If there's anyone in the hallway, walk on by, you got that?"

He hung up and said to Fetterman, "That was Justin. He and Sully have made it. Saw Sam Anderson at the airport. We've got a couple of people here now."

"Good. Good."

Before anyone could say any more, the door to the other room opened to reveal Muffin. She had taken off her dress and had put on a garter and stockings. She had a light silk robe that hung to her hips wrapped around her shoulders. She moved directly to Fetterman and took his hand.

"Ah, Tony . . ." said Gerber.

"No. You misunderstand. We have a couple of visitors coming."

She grabbed the front of her robe and held it tightly clasped in front of her. "No way," she said. "I here for you, not for friends."

There was a knock at the door, and Gerber said, "Tony, take her into the other room, and tell her that we have to talk to our friends but that we have no big plans."

Twenty minutes later all the Green Berets that Fetterman had been able to phone were gathered in the room. They wore a variety of civilian clothes, from Tyme's navy-blue, three-piece suit to Sully's tan trousers and short-sleeved shirt. They looked like a convention of hit men. Anderson had arrived with Bocker after both Smith and Tyme had finished their first drink. At that point Fetterman joined them so that they could discuss the problem.

"I'm afraid," said Fetterman, "but I think Muffin believes we're all going to join her, one at a time, and she is going to get very rich. Right now she's enjoying the idea. At first she didn't like it, but when I didn't pursue the topic, she talked herself into it." He grinned at that.

"Okay, Captain," said Tyme, "why don't you let us in on what's going on." He waved a hand to indicate the others. "I think we all left some fairly pissed-off people in the World when we dropped everything to fly to Hong Kong. I know my girlfriend will probably never speak to me again."

"Justin, I'm sorry about that, I really am, but you know I wouldn't have let Tony call if it hadn't been important."

"Yes, sir, I know. If I didn't think it was, I would've stayed in the World. Besides, if she was that uptight about my coming here, I doubt things would have lasted much longer anyway. Especially with her attending the antiwar rallies in Austin."

Gerber nodded. "Any of the rest of you have a problem with leaving?"

There was a chorus of no's and not really's. Gerber said, "Fine. With luck we'll have this thing resolved in a day or two, and you all can head back home for the rest of your leave. If you want to take a couple of extra days, I'll make sure that it gets approved in Saigon."

Then he outlined everything that had happened right up until the time that Fetterman and he had walked back into the hotel. He told them everything in great detail. He told them that he wanted to try to find the Chinese man the next day and what he planned to do when they found him.

"You threw away your weapons?" asked Tyme sarcastically when Gerber finished the narration.

"I'm afraid so, Justin. Had no choice," Gerber told him.

"Even Tony?" he asked as if amazed that Fetterman would casually dispose of a weapon, even a .45.

"Yes, Boom-Boom," answered the master sergeant.

"Then you're lucky I came." Grinning, the team's light weapons specialist hauled a .45 from the inside of his shirt and laid it on the table. "I have a couple of others secreted in my suitcase. They're broken into small parts so that I could get them through Customs, but I can put them back together in an hour."

"Ammunition, Boom-Boom?" queried Fetterman.

"Probably not more than a hundred rounds. I have a false bottom in my case for extra mags and ammo. A very thin false bottom so that it's not obvious and holds very little."

"And you waltzed through Customs just like that?" asked Smith incredulously.

"The trick is to not look like you have anything you're not supposed to have. Besides, I figured that, as a member of the United States Army, if I got caught, they would tell me I was a very bad boy, confiscate the weapons and let me go. No big deal."

"The next item is to find a way to wire me up so you can all keep track of my whereabouts," said Gerber. "I respect everyone's tracking ability in the jungle, but this is the city, and I won't be leaving much in the way of footprints and broken branches and bent grass. I wondered if there was something we could get to make the task a little easier."

"How much time will we have, Captain?" asked Bocker.

"I don't really know. I figure they'll call sometime about noon."

"I'll have to wait until some of the electronics stores open, but I might be able to rig something up for us," said the common sergeant. "Be a little crude, but it should work."

Gerber clapped his hands and rocked back on the couch. He looked at the men in the room with him and nodded at them. For the first time since Morrow had been abducted, he felt really good. It was all going to come together. He was sure of that. Each of these men had a talent that would allow him to beat the Chinese bastard and get Morrow back. By nightfall the next day he was sure that the situation would be resolved. They might have to stay up all night working out the details, but he was positive they could be worked out.

He pulled out the orientation map that they had picked up in the hotel lobby and spread it out on the table. Looking at it, he realized that there was a lot more to Hong Kong than he thought. Lots of islands and lots of open country and still no clue about where to look. But that didn't matter because he had part of the team with him and they would be able to work their way through the problem quickly.

He had forgotten that on the other side of the door was a woman of Chinese and British descent who might not be the best friend of the Occidental men. He had forgotten that she could be standing with her ear to the door overhearing every word that was said.

16

IOTEL REGENCY,
HONG KONG

Tyme and Smith went into Morrow's room for some privacy while they assembled the weapons that Tyme had smuggled. Some of the mess in the room had been cleaned up by Fetterman while he waited for Gerber to come out of his trance during the afternoon. Tyme and Smith finished straightening it up, made the bed and then called the front desk to have the lamps replaced. Although he wasn't responsible for the breakage, Tyme assured the clerk that they would pay for the damage.

In the living room of the suite, Fetterman sat alone, staring into Victoria Harbour, fascinated by all that he could see out there. The buildings of Hong Kong Island seemed to grow out of the blackness of the harbour. The red, green and white lights shimmered on the water, reflecting back at him. And the lights of the buildings on the island, streaking in the water and shifting in the swells, flashed and flickered and melted like watercolors in the rain.

Bocker sat at the table, making a list of the components he would need to construct the radios early the next morning. He sketched a simple radio, looked at it and added a couple of things to it.

Gerber wandered around the room, as if he couldn't think of anything to do, while Anderson sat in front of the television, trying to find an English language program. The Hong Kong film industry seemed to be stuck in the feudal period with hundreds of men in bizarre costumes engaging in martial arts combat. There was no plot to any of the movies.

The sudden trill of the phone startled each of them. Only Fetterman seemed to remain relaxed. Gerber nearly leaped over a chair to get to it and snatched the receiver from the hook.

"Yeah," he demanded. "I mean, hello."

"Hello, Captain. This is Captain Bromhead."

"Johnny! Where the hell are you?" Gerber covered the mouthpiece with a hand and announced to everyone as if they hadn't heard, "It's Captain Bromhead." On the phone, he repeated, "Where the hell are you?"

"I'm here."

"In Hong Kong?"

"No, sir. Here in the hotel. I'm in the lobby and figured that I would come up, if you would be kind enough to give me the room number. Your return address on the telegram didn't have a room number."

Gerber told him and then cautioned him, "We think we might be watched. Come on up, but if you see anyone in the hallway, walk on by."

"See you in a few minutes." He hung up.

"Forgot about Johnny," said Gerber. "I guess I didn't really expect him to be able to shake himself loose from Crinshaw or the brass hats."

Anderson turned off the TV in disgust. "I'll hit the head, if there are no objections."

"You don't need to announce it, Sam," said Gerber. "You can just go."

Anderson opened the door, saw movement and jumped back. He looked in. "Hey, there's a lady in here."

"Oh, my God," said Fetterman, nearly exploding out of his chair. "I forgot all about her." He rushed to the door and reached in. "Muffin, I'm sorry. Please come out and join us. I just don't know what I was thinking."

Muffin had changed back to her street clothes, and there was no evidence that she had carried anything else with her. Her silk robe, garter and stockings were well concealed beneath her street clothes or in her tiny purse. She entered the room as if she were angry about being left alone for so long. She glanced significantly at the bar.

"Would you care for a drink?" asked Anderson.

"I take a banana daiquiri," she said.

"Fine, except that we have no bananas."

"Then I take whatever it is you have." She studied Anderson, impressed by his size.

While Anderson kept her occupied with the drink, Fetterman pulled Gerber to one side and said, "We can't let her go now. We don't know what she might have overheard."

"Damn, Tony, that was stupid."

"I know, Captain. I'm sorry about it. I thought the protective coloration would help us."

"I didn't mean to imply that it was your mistake. I should have remembered she was in there, too. Damned poor judgment on my part."

"Yes, sir."

"Okay, now we'll have to keep her with us at all times and not give her a chance to signal her friends, if she has any who would care."

"Let Anderson do it, sir," said Fetterman. "He seems to be getting along with her quite well."

"We'll see how things break in the morning and then decide who will have to remain behind. Damn, thought our force had been increased by one and now we've lost that again."

"Sir, if I might suggest . . ."

"Don't go getting formal on me all of a sudden, Tony. If you have an idea, let me have it. I haven't exactly been dazzling up to this point."

"Why don't you call your Air Force buddy again? I doubt he would be upset about having to baby-sit Muffin. All he has to do is make sure she doesn't have a chance to call anyone. If she is legit, then we pay for her time and she is happy. If she isn't, she can't squawk about it because we still hold her."

"I'll call him in the morning."

There was a knock on the door. Anderson, without waiting to be told, opened it and saw Bromhead standing there. "Captain Bromhead," he said.

"What happened to Johnny?" Bromhead asked.

"You're a captain now, sir, and I have to be polite to you. It's the code of the West and the law of the jungle and the way the cookie crumbles," he said with a grin.

"Fine. Then grab one of these suitcases and help me in with them. They weigh a ton apiece."

Gerber came forward to shake hands with his former executive officer. "How are things going at the Triple Nickel?"

Bromhead noticed the Oriental woman. With her white hair it was hard not to. He said, "I'll brief you in a moment."

"Well, get your ass in here, and let me buy you a drink," said Gerber. "Damn, I'm glad you made it."

An hour later, while Anderson and Muffin sat together in the other room discussing life histories, the rest of the team was in Morrow's bedroom with Tyme and Smith. Bromhead hauled his suitcases into the room, and when he saw Tyme and Smith working on the old .45s that they had stripped and cleaned, he smiled.

"I knew you incompetents wouldn't bring any real weapons." The new captain opened up one of his cases, unhooked a flap and started taking out pieces of metal. Then he looked up and saw the look on Gerber's face. "Oh, by the way, everything was under control at the camp before I left." He continued, "I went into the captured arms locker and found a couple of the better-looking AKs. I figured that if something was going on that was important enough for the captain to send me a telegram, then it was important enough for me to try to bring some real weapons." He shot a glance at Fetterman and added, "I couldn't get your flame-thrower in here, Tony. The tanks are just too big to fit. Sorry."

Fetterman smiled. "That's all right, sir. The AKs are fine. Just fine."

"Jesus, sir!" said Tyme. "You sure took them apart."

"Didn't want them to look like anything resembling a weapon," he said. "They break into smaller parts than the M-14 or the M-16. Afraid I had to leave the stocks behind because they looked just like stocks. Might have provided a clue for the customs guys."

"You bring any spare magazines?" asked Tyme.

"Of course. Took all the rounds out of them. Put about a dozen into my other suitcase. They really don't look much of anything else, except magazines for a weapon, but the customs guys just waved me through without really looking into the bags. Guess it was too late at night."

Tyme already had one nearly assembled. He said, "We'll just use them like grease guns. I suppose if we really need a stock, we can fashion one from some scrap lumber."

"You brought two?" asked Gerber.

"Sure did."

"Okay, with the weapons that Justin brought in, we're going to be fairly well armed. Coordination may be a problem, but we'll just have to work our way around that. First thing in the morning we'll go get the stuff that Galvin needs."

Fetterman spent most of the night sitting in his chair and staring at the lights of Victoria Harbour and Hong Kong Island. The lights began to fade slowly as the sun came up and the sky first paled, tinted to red and then started to brighten. As the outlines of the buildings and boats on the water seemed to materialize out of the gloom, Fetterman pushed himself out of his chair and found Gerber sleeping on the couch. He touched the captain's shoulder and told him it was time to get up.

Gerber, looking the worse for wear, his beard discoloring his face, rubbed his eyes and sat up. "Okay, let's get this show on the road."

"Yes, sir. Boom-Boom and Sully have the weapons ready. We don't have much in the way of ammo, so we can't go shooting indiscriminately, but we should have enough."

"Bocker?"

"Has his list and his plans and is going out in a couple of hours. He'll eat breakfast then. We don't want to order too much up here from room service, or the dining room might get suspicious, and that could tip our hand."

"We can order for four because there should be three of us and the bell captain knows about Muffin."

"Maybe we should only order three. That keeps the numbers right if someone wants to check. Besides, Boom-Boom and Sully have a room, so they can order all they want."

"You forgot about Morrow," said Gerber. "As far as anyone in the hotel knows, she's still up here."

"But the opposition knows that she's not, and if they start counting meals, they're going to get funny numbers."

"All right," said Gerber grumpily, "let's not get bogged down in trivia. Have the troops scatter, and we'll meet back here about ten. That'll give everyone a chance to do anything they need to and will probably give us some time before the call comes in.''

"I'll have Sully come back as soon as he's eaten. He can help Galvin put the radios together.''

"Anyone think about having Sully cook up some explosives for us?''

"I thought about that, but he said anything he makes would be fairly unstable, and it wouldn't be a good idea to blow up the room. Besides, he claimed it wouldn't give us that much of an advantage.''

Gerber clapped his hands together a couple of times as if to rally a slumping ball team. ''I'm tired of all this. Let's get going. We've been screwing around long enough. It's payday.''

The morning slipped away quickly. Bocker went out and bought nearly a hundred dollars' worth of radio parts and rushed back to make his transmitters and receivers. He was proud of himself because he didn't think he had been followed. Still, he stopped two floors above Gerber's, then walked back down, figuring that any tails in the lobby would see that the elevator didn't stop on the right floor.

Tyme and Sully took Bromhead to their room and ordered a giant breakfast. Afterward, they all decided to catch a little sleep. When the phone rang, they all got up and took the stairs to the floor above them. There was no one in the hallway as they entered Gerber's room again.

As soon as it was late enough, Gerber called Larko and told him what he wanted. Larko was hesitant, pointing out that he had already returned the favor once and that he didn't have much time left in Hong Kong. It was only when Gerber mentioned that Larko would have to baby-sit a woman of questionable virtue for a couple of hours that Larko said he thought he could handle it.

At ten they were all back in the room, including Larko. Muffin was more than a little upset when she learned that Larko would be looking after her because she had thought she would have had an opportunity to earn some big money with all the Americans present. But so far only Anderson had touched her, and that had been on the knee as they sat together talking. She was also concerned because she hadn't had a chance to call the man who had asked her to count the number of Americans in the room.

Because they were waiting for the phone call, Gerber did not want to compromise the security of the mission, so he took the opportunity to get rid of Muffin and Larko. The look on Larko's face told Gerber that the flight engineer was only too happy to comply. Then Gerber carefully searched Morrow's room and found the keys to the rental car. He took the team members to the garage, telling them that he, Fetterman and Morrow hadn't used the car that much because there was no place to park in Hong Kong, but now, with two assault rifles, they could use the trunk. Since it had spent most of its time in the garage, Gerber doubted the enemy would know they had it.

Using the map once more, Gerber said, "I have to assume we'll end up in the New Territories because they are the closest to the Red Chinese border and there is a lot of empty space out there. Lots of hills and forests for them to lose themselves in. If we get on a boat for one of the other islands, we could be in trouble."

"We'll work around it somehow, Captain," said Fetterman.

Gerber rubbed his sweaty palms on his trousers. "Sorry. I'm more than a little nervous about this one. We're way out of our depth in the urban environment."

"Take it easy, Captain," said Tyme. "We all grew up in the city and know how to act. That's natural for us. Becoming jungle fighters was the unnatural act, and we've already accomplished that. So things might work out."

"I'm not sure I like that." Gerber smiled. He pointed at the equipment that Bocker had assembled on the table. "You want to show me this stuff?"

Quickly Bocker explained his radios. They were fixed frequency, and the one that Gerber carried would have a hot mike. It would transmit anything said near Gerber or by Gerber so that, if he was unable to press a button, he could still give clues as to his whereabouts. If that failed for whatever reason, they could always triangulate. That would get them into the right area.

With that, there really was nothing else for them to do. They were trained to react to the situation, and all the planning in the world wouldn't help now. Fetterman had even reminded them of the old military saying: "When the shooting starts, the plan goes out the window."

At ten minutes to twelve, the phone rang. Gerber leaped for it, stopped his hand inches from it and took a deep breath. It rang a

second time and he said, "Here we go, gentlemen. Let's be cool."
He then picked up the receiver and said, as casually as he could,
"Hello."

"We have the woman. You come. Alone."

"Fine. Where?"

"We tell you. Now you go along Nathan Road to the park. You
stop on the northeast corner outside the fence. You be told where
to go then. We see anyone, we kill the woman." The phone went
dead.

"That's it," said Gerber as he hung up. He quickly relayed to
the team members the brief message he'd been given. "Time to
move."

Before anyone could stand, Fetterman said, "Captain, I don't
like this one little bit. If they wanted to assassinate us, they could
do it anytime. This Mickey Mouse game they have designed
makes no sense to me."

"It could be that they want to capture a Special Forces officer
and take him into Red China for interrogation," said Tyme.

"Gentlemen, we don't know the motivations. Maybe the
Chinese bastard wants to watch each of us die for some demented
reason. Makes no difference now. Or maybe he threw this together because of the opportunity he found. Tony and me in Hong
Kong, just a couple of miles from Red China. The cards have been
dealt, and it's time to ante in. No choice in the matter, unless we
want to let Morrow die."

"You didn't ask to speak to her," criticized Fetterman. "You
should have asked to speak with her."

"Makes no difference now. She is either alive or she isn't, but
now we get near the Chinese bastard."

17

NATHAN ROAD,
HONG KONG

Before Gerber could reach the door, Bromhead asked, "Shouldn't we try to rent another car or two?"

Gerber stopped with his hand on the knob, wondering if that was something he should have thought of, and then decided it wasn't. They had the one car, and Fetterman held the keys to it. Finally Gerber said, "Let's just play this one as it has been dealt now. We can sit here and try to think of everything, but when all is said and done, we could still be sitting here trying to think. We'd be like the team that trained so hard for the big game that we couldn't play when it happened."

"Still," said Bromhead, "we don't want to overlook something by rushing forward without thinking the whole thing through carefully."

"Everyone knows his assignment," said Gerber, ignoring that. "If you get separated, come on back here. We'll check in if we need to do anything." Gerber opened the door and stepped into the hallway. Before he moved, he checked his watch, and then began to walk toward the elevators.

When the door closed, Fetterman immediately said, "This is what the captain doesn't need to know. I'm not *that* interested in getting Miss Morrow back. That doesn't mean we should ignore the threats to her, but the major concern has got to be to protect the captain. He's going to be trying to protect her."

"Which means?" asked Tyme.

"Our priorities," said Fetterman. "First is to protect the captain whether he likes it or not. Second is to kill the Chinese son of a bitch because he deserves it. Third, we get Miss Morrow out of there. That is the way it has got to be."

"So what do we do?" asked Smith.

Fetterman glanced at Bromhead, who said, "This is your show, Master Sergeant. You've been in on it a lot longer than I have."

"Thank you, Captain. First, I want everyone to put on two or three extra shirts. As we move through the streets and rotate the tails, we can peel a shirt so that we don't become recognizable by our clothes.

"Second, I think the two guys in the car—" he looked at Tyme and Smith "—why don't you take it and proceed up Kowloon Park Drive to Austin Road, and then drive along it so that you'll pass the captain as he waits for his contact."

"And then?"

"We play it by ear just as the captain said, but I don't want him to be more than thirty seconds from help the moment he hits that corner of the park."

"Then we'd better get going," said Smith.

"We wait until he leaves the hotel," said Fetterman. "We know where he's going, and we have to assume that the bad guys have someone in the lobby watching for a big exodus of Americans. We have a few minutes."

Bromhead was going to take charge then, to give them some kind of a pep talk, but couldn't think of anything that needed to be said. Each of them knew what to do, and each would do it. All he had to do was let them do their jobs.

GERBER DIDN'T WANT to tip his hand so he didn't look back as he left the hotel lobby. He walked out the main entrance, stopped at the top of the steps and let the breeze from the sea wash over him. There was a faint odor of fish and salt in it, but he was becoming used to it. He put his hand to his eyes to shade them from the afternoon glare, then descended the steps, turned to his left and made his way to Nathan Road. Once there, he took a few seconds to look around, then headed north, almost as if he were window-shopping, but he kept his pace steady, figuring that anyone following would become suspicious if he moved too slowly.

The corner of the park where he was supposed to receive his next set of instructions was just under a klick from the hotel doors. He didn't like the way the meeting was set up, but he could do nothing about it.

As he walked past tailors, jewelry dealers, rug merchants and a multitude of bars, nightclubs and restaurants, he began to wonder about the whole setup because that was exactly what it was. A setup. One of the men, he forgot which one, had said it the night before. The whole thing made no sense. The Chinese bastard should have killed Morrow as soon as he got her picture taken. Keeping her alive made no difference one way or the other. She was a loose end that should be taken care of as soon as possible. In fact, she probably was already dead, and the whole exercise was ridiculous.

It was then that Gerber realized the only way he would not have begun the exercise was if her dead body had been found. At that point he would have packed up his marbles and gone home. The only way the Chinese officer could be sure that Gerber would come was to keep Morrow alive until he caught Gerber. If he balked at the meeting, the officer had to have some way to persuade him to come, and that was a living Morrow. Another picture or a phone call. They had to be sure he would be willing to risk his life.

At that moment Gerber felt Morrow was still alive. He didn't understand the rationale behind the plan, but he knew she would not die until he was safely in the hands of the enemy. For an instant he thought about turning around and letting one of the other team members walk the point. But he knew he couldn't do that. It was his job. His responsibility and he had to do it, although the other way was more logical.

Not far away he could see the corner of the park where he was supposed to wait. The area nearby was fairly open, making it hard for anyone to lie in ambush. There was a black wrought-iron fence around the park, a couple of broadleafed bushes with bright flowers on them a hundred meters from the street and several tall palm trees. But no real cover for anyone. Maybe that was the thought the opposition had. Keep it out in the open so no one could grab the messenger.

Over the transmitter, he said, "I'm about to enter the park. Johnny, don't grab the messenger. Let him go because he won't know anything anyway."

He had just set foot in the park when a young Chinese woman wearing a yellow silk dress accidentally bumped his arm. Gerber felt her try to slip him a piece of paper, and he grasped it without really looking at her. He took a couple of steps and mumbled, "I've got a note. Young woman gave it to me. Watch her, but don't touch her."

He stopped and unfolded the paper, then turned and looked but could not see any sign of the messenger. Over his radio, he said, "I'm going to the ferry pier just off Jordan Road. I'll take my time getting there. Johnny, get them positioned."

BROMHEAD, WHO WAS WALKING DOWN the street with Fetterman, looked at him and said, "We could grab a cab."

"I don't know. The driver will undoubtedly be Chinese."

"And the odds that he'll be working for our man are extremely remote. We're moving too slow as it is. . . ."

Fetterman stopped walking and crouched so that he could carefully examine his map, aware that the crowds around him were watching him closely. He could feel the comfortable weight of the .45 on his hip and touched it with his wrist as if to reassure himself that it was still there.

Finally figuring out what he wanted, he stood and told Bromhead where to place the others. "Have Tyme and Smith stationed on the north side. If this is the break, they'll be in the best position to follow."

GERBER PRETENDED that he was momentarily lost, killing nearly ten minutes getting himself back on the right track, although it was nearly a straight shot from the corner of the park to the pier. He stayed in the center of the sidewalk, avoiding the approach of hucksters and hookers. Finally he announced, "I'm going in. I hope you're ready."

Just as he said that, he spotted Bocker and Anderson arguing with a Chinese man who obviously thought he had made a sale. Gerber was on the side of the street opposite them, and neither looked up as he walked by. Then, from behind him, he heard the squealing of tires and turned in time to see a yellow car screech to a stop next to him.

"It's a yellow Volkswagen Beetle," he said quickly before he was grabbed by a small man. His abductor didn't speak, and Gerber's first reaction was to kick him in the crotch, but he resisted the temptation. Instead, he allowed himself to be forced into the back seat of the tiny car. Another guy sat there, making it a tight squeeze in the confines of the small German car.

As the door closed and they sped off, Gerber said, "Where are you taking me?"

There was no answer, and Gerber was about to say something to give his team directions, just in case, when he caught a flash of blue out of the corner of his eyes. He was sure it was the Mustang. He wanted to turn his head to look but was afraid of giving away the location of the chase car. Instead, he demanded once again to know where they were taking him.

In response, the man who had grabbed him reached over and began searching him for weapons. Gerber grasped the thug's hand as it touched him and held it in an ironlike grip so the man couldn't move. A click near his ear told Gerber that the second man had just cocked a pistol. The searcher grinned as Gerber relaxed the tension and let himself be frisked. All they found was a pocket knife with a razor-sharp blade, which Fetterman had insisted Gerber take as a cover. No one would believe he would leave the hotel without some kind of weapon, even one that was hardly lethal. They found his radio but didn't realize it because Bocker had disguised it in a cigarette package. They ignored it, tossing it to the floor of the car. Casually Gerber retrieved it and stuffed it into his pocket.

They rolled north out of the city, following the main road, picking up speed as the buildings and traffic began to thin. Gerber knew that, if he was being followed by his team, they would have to drop way back or be spotted. He stared out of the car windows, looking for some marker that he could alert his people to the moment he got the chance. They crossed some water and entered a smaller, built-up area that he thought was Tsuen Wan. He asked about it, but no one replied, as if they didn't speak any English, which Gerber didn't believe. Anyone brought in on this would speak English.

Before they left the city, they took the north fork of the road and began climbing into a mountainous region. Gerber remembered from the map that the road forked again, and although it eventually rejoined the main road, it would waste too much time if his boys went the wrong way. He took a chance and said, "I didn't know there were mountains in Hong Kong."

"You talk too much," said the man who had searched him.

Gerber grinned to himself. He now knew two things. He was right. They could speak English, and they didn't realize what he was doing. He relaxed, waiting for the turn that he would have to signal to his men.

IT WAS SMITH who spotted the yellow car as it flashed by. He pointed it out to Tyme. He floored the gas pedal, and they wove into the line of traffic, barely missing two other cars. Then Tyme slowed down until they were four or five vehicles behind the yellow VW. They could hear the static from the captain's radio and knew that it hadn't been found as they had left the city.

Tyme was afraid of the open area, but the traffic didn't drop off and they could maintain a loose tail without worrying about being seen. They felt sure they were right behind him when the captain asked if they were in Tsuen Wan.

Smith slapped the dash of the car with his hand and yelled over the noise of the wind, "That's right, Captain! Give us an itinerary. Fucking beautiful!"

In the city Tyme wanted to remain a safe enough distance away without getting too close. The traffic was heavy, and somehow the yellow car got farther ahead until they lost sight of it. Smith stood in the seat, trying to see over the vehicles just in front of them but had no luck. With one hand gripping the top of the windshield, he cupped the other at the side of his mouth and yelled, "I don't see him. I don't see him."

Tyme didn't even glance up. "We'll get them as soon as the traffic thins."

Then over the radio they heard Gerber say something about mountains, and Tyme knew immediately that he had taken the wrong turn. He slammed on the brakes, nearly pitching Smith over the top of the windshield. Behind him, there was a cacophony of car horns and squealing brakes as a dozen other cars swerved to avoid each other. A couple of cars grazed one another, but there was no major damage.

Tyme spun the wheel as he backed up rapidly, causing the Mustang to swing around abruptly. When they were facing the way they had come, he floored the accelerator and took off in a cloud of blue smoke as the tires fought to grip the pavement.

They came to the road that headed north, and Tyme took the corner without slowing, the car drifting to the other side. Tyme pulled in the direction of the skid until he corrected it, then hit the gas again. They flew forward, rocketing up the hill in pursuit of the yellow car. He didn't slow again until he caught a glimpse of it in the distance.

WHEN THEY TURNED onto a dirt side road, Gerber was tempted to say something, but there was no way to clue the rest of the team without alerting his captors. He rode on in silence, hoping that the Mustang had kept them in sight.

They kept going, eating up the distance, came to another side road and pulled into it. They stopped then, as if waiting to see if anyone were following them. Gerber held his breath, but the Mustang seemed to have lost them.

When they started moving again, Gerber asked, "Are we getting close?"

The man who had spoken earlier just grinned, displaying broken yellow teeth. He didn't answer the question and gave no indication that he had understood it.

Moments later they slowed for a gate, and a man appeared out of a bush to unlock it. His job was to guard the approach to the hideout and report anyone who came near. If the trespassers appeared too persistent, he would probably shoot them.

They continued down the road, went around a bend and stopped near an old frame house that showed obvious Victorian influences. The three-story house had lots of windows and two large, round spires. It couldn't have looked more out of place if it had been an Arab tent.

As they exited the car, Gerber could see a body of water nearby that appeared to be a reservoir. He had no idea what the name of it might be because he hadn't studied the map that closely. He hoped Tyme and Smith had been close enough to see which way the VW had turned because there was no way he could give that clue. But he could ask about the water.

"Is that a reservoir?" he asked innocently.

Feeling safe, the Oriental slapped Gerber and demanded that he shut up.

Gerber didn't respond to that. He rubbed his face as if the blow had been more painful than it was and said, "Sorry. Just asking. I guess this means we've arrived." He hoped his men would get the idea that they were no longer moving and he would have to ditch the radio. He prayed he wasn't premature with the decision.

As they moved to the house, Gerber worked the cigarette package containing the radio out of his pocket so that it lay concealed in his hand. When no one was looking, he dropped it and tried to kick it out of sight. The last thing he wanted was for the enemy to find it and know that his men could be closing in. Of course, they didn't know that he had any men other than Fetterman.

Gerber was escorted up the steps to the large, pillared porch. One of the men opened the door, and while they waited, he went inside. Then he was back and waved them all in.

The entrance foyer looked just as Gerber figured it would. A staircase led to the second floor, and doors concealed the rooms on either side. At the end of the hallway was another closed door.

Gerber was taken to the right after one of the men opened the double doors. The room there was a large, well-furnished library with a desk set near a bay window overlooking the lake. Bookshelves dominated three walls from floor to ceiling, and they contained hundreds of leather-bound volumes. Two wing chairs were positioned near a fireplace. Between them was a table that held a diorama depicting some ancient battle with hundreds of miniature figures locked in combat.

The men all filed out. The last one said, "You will wait right here. Do not try to escape because there are armed men all over the estate." The man had a pronounced British accent, which reminded Gerber of Minh. But then Hong Kong was a British possession.

"I have no plans for escape," said Gerber.

Left to his own, Gerber wandered around the room, trying to get a feel for it. The Orientals who left had seemed out of place.

He decided that the house and the furnishings must have belonged to an Englishman who had been forced, persuaded or just plain wanted to sell it as it was. Everything about it, with the exception of the model battle, suggested the Occidental mind.

Gerber was studying the battle, trying to place it, although he didn't know that much about Chinese history, when the doors opened again. The two men standing there moved aside, and a third man entered.

Gerber had never gotten a good look at the man. Fetterman had seen him a couple of times, once through binoculars and once through the bars of a cage. Still, Gerber knew instantly who it was. The Chinese officer they had been chasing for almost a year. The one who had marked them for death more than once. The man who had failed every time he had run into Gerber's team.

He was shorter than Gerber had expected. In his mind the officer had taken on gigantic proportions. Looking at him now, Gerber thought he was smaller than Fetterman.

The man stepped into the room and pointed his pistol at Gerber's head. "If I had any sense at all, Captain," he said, "I would shoot you dead this minute."

18

THE STREETS OF
HONG KONG

Fetterman didn't like the enforced inactivity as he stood outside
the car rental shop. When the men in the VW had grabbed the
captain, his first reaction had been to run after them. Bromhead
had jerked on his arm, dragging him in the opposite direction and
shouting that they needed a car. Bromhead assured him that Tyme
and Smith could keep up with the yellow car while they sought
more transportation.

They had run back along Nathan Road until they found a car
rental agency. While Fetterman stood outside watching the
crowds, Bromhead hurried in to rent something.

Within minutes Bromhead reappeared driving a new green
Chevy. He leaned out the window and said casually, "Care to join
me for a ride?"

As Fetterman got into the car, Bromhead said, "Anything new?
Still heading toward the north?"

"Yes, sir."

Bromhead spun the wheel and touched the gas pedal. The car
responded as if he had floored the accelerator, and they shot back
up Nathan Road, dodging the crowds, double-decker buses and
rickshaws. Fetterman found a map in the glove box and used it
to trace a path to Tsuen Wan. He looked at the street signs and
discovered they were on the right path.

"Punch it, sir. We're doing fine."

They flashed up to Boundary Road, and Fetterman suddenly pointed. "There's Anderson."

Bromhead glanced through the windshield. There was no mistaking the hulking white man, but he couldn't see Bocker, who was supposed to be working with Anderson. The captain jerked the wheel to the right, crossed over the traffic coming from the other direction and swerved to the curb. He blew the horn twice, trying to get Anderson's attention.

Fetterman leaped out so that Anderson and Bocker, who materialized from the crowd, could climb into the tiny backseat. Almost before everyone could get into the car, Bromhead slammed the stick into Drive and shot forward again.

As they reached Tsuen Wan, they heard Smith's voice on the radio. "We think they have turned from the main road. We're going to drop back quite a ways so that we don't run up on them."

Seven minutes later Bromhead and his companions caught up with Tyme and Smith. They had pulled to the side of the highway and were standing there, looking along a dirt road. Bromhead turned in behind them, and everyone in the Chevy got out.

"I think they turned off here," said Tyme, pointing to the east along a dirt road. He spread the map he was holding out on the trunk. He laid an arm along one side of it to hold it down and pointed.

"The last thing we heard the captain say was something about a reservoir. There are two along this road, if the road goes through. There is the one here back the other way, but we should have seen it if that was the right one."

"You didn't follow?" asked Bromhead.

"No, sir. We were afraid they might turn off and wait to see if they were followed. We could get away with passing them on this road because it's a main one, but that dirt track would be a dead giveaway."

"Okay," said Fetterman, looking at Bromhead to see if he was going to object. "We have to press on. There is no way around it. I guess we take it slowly and stop at the top of each rise to explore the area around us before heading down."

"One other thing," said Tyme. "We haven't heard a word out of them since then."

"You lose the signal?" asked Bocker.

''No. We've got the carrier wave, but we haven't heard anything.''

''We can't worry about that now,'' said Bromhead, studying the map. ''We've got to find the captain.''

''Let's split up,'' said Fetterman, noticing there were two roads that could lead them to the reservoir, if they had the right one spotted. ''We don't have all day to debate this. Boom-Boom, you take Sully and Galvin and take the northern road. You find something, you give us a shout.''

''All right.''

Fetterman looked over his shoulder at Bromhead. ''Sir, we follow the southern road and see if we can spot anything.''

''Let's move it,'' said Bromhead.

FOR A MOMENT everything seemed to stand still. Gerber was almost afraid to move. He felt closer to death at that moment than he ever had before because he knew the Chinese officer was right. The quickest, smartest thing to do was shoot Gerber. If the situation was reversed, Gerber doubted he would hesitate.

Instead of shooting him, the officer walked toward the desk. He sat behind it, then placed his pistol on the top. Indicating the chairs opposite, he spoke again. ''Sit down, Captain Gerber, and let us talk about Vietnam, the war and your death.''

As Gerber started to speak, the Chinese man held up a hand to prevent it. He said, ''You will not be helped. I know that your Sergeant Fetterman is still in your suite.''

''How do you know that?'' asked Gerber.

''I have my ways. I will say that a certain party would report to me if he had gone out.''

Gerber took a deep breath and let his eyes roam around the room again. The two men still stood next to the door. He asked, ''What is this all about?''

''I think you know, Captain. You have made me look bad many times. You have foiled plan after plan.'' His voice rose slightly, as if the memories were causing him to lose his temper. ''You sent people out to kill me. You sent your men out to shoot me.''

Gerber couldn't help himself. He smiled and said, ''It was nothing personal.''

The man stood and leaned his hands on the desk so that he had one on each side of the pistol. He glanced down at it, as if becoming aware of it for the first time, but he didn't touch it. He said, "You will not be laughing much longer." He nodded to the guards, and both of them disappeared.

"This is getting a little melodramatic," said Gerber. He was getting lost in the ridiculousness of the situation. It was only in the movies that people were kidnapped off the streets of Hong Kong and held prisoner. It all smacked of a poor movie plot, and he was having trouble taking any of it seriously. He was tempted to stand and walk out.

The doors reopened and Morrow, naked, her hands bound behind her, was pushed into the room. The blindfold still covered her eyes, and she tripped and tried to catch her balance. She fell heavily to her side with a grunt of pain, but she didn't move.

Gerber was on his feet. "Enough of this!" He started toward her, but someone grabbed him from behind. He felt a pistol pressed against the back of his neck and stopped moving.

Morrow turned her head as she heard his voice and nearly wailed, "Kirk? Is that you?"

"Gag her!" ordered the Chinese man.

Before Morrow could speak again, a rag was forced into her mouth and tied in place. All she could do was make sounds deep in her throat.

"Now," said the Chinese officer, "you will finally understand the error of your ways. You will see how the Oriental mind works. This is something that you, as a Western man, would never think of."

He gestured again, and Morrow was lifted to her feet. She stood there, afraid to move, while one of the other men brought an old wooden chair to the center of the room. She was forced to sit on it and then was bound to it.

In a calm voice, as if lecturing to a class of students about ancient civilizations, the Chinese man said, "You are going to have the pleasure of watching Miss Morrow tortured to death."

Gerber nearly jumped out of his chair, but several hands held him fast. When he stopped struggling and fell back, the man said, "If he moves like that again, shoot him in the knee." He pointed at Gerber. "And you will still have to watch, but it will no longer be too comfortable."

There were no more words spoken in the room for several minutes. Gerber stared at the Chinese man for a while, trying to see if he was bluffing in some kind of bizzare, sadistic game. Gerber then turned his attention to Morrow, who was sitting so rigid that her muscles stood out as if etched on her skin.

Gerber wanted to reach out and let her know that the situation was not nearly as bleak as it seemed. He couldn't tell her that their captor may have left men waiting for Fetterman to leave their hotel room, but the Oriental officer didn't know that Gerber had half a dozen men who should be out looking for them at that moment. Men who had a good idea of where Gerber was. He had faith in his men and knew they would arrive sometime. He hoped that Morrow would not have to suffer too much before they did.

She was sitting with her head erect, making sobbing noises deep in her throat. It was the only sound in the room except for the loud ticking of a clock.

IT WAS INCREDIBLY EASY to find the house, although they hadn't known they were looking for a house. Bromhead stopped on a hill. Fetterman took out a pair of Zeiss binoculars and scanned the countryside spread out in front of them. The yellow car sat partially concealed behind a large bush, but there was no mistaking it. As soon as they saw it, Anderson was on the radio, giving the details to the other team members, letting them know where the house was and which reservoir it was near.

While Anderson spoke on the radio, Bromhead pulled their car out of sight, then consulted his map. To Bromhead, he said, "I make it little more than a klick down there. Not a whole lot of good cover."

"How many guards do you think they'll have?"

"Christ, sir, I can't guess."

They moved back to the crest and got down on their bellies so that they wouldn't be silhouetted against the skyline. Fetterman studied the valley below him. It wasn't much of a valley, more of a shallow depression in the terrain, like a huge saucer. The house sat at the bottom of the saucer but on a slight rise so that it was ten or twelve feet above the surrounding ground. A thin brown ribbon that was the access road wound its way along the depression floor, away from the reservoir and to the main road about three or four hundred yards away. Through the binoculars, Fetterman could see a metallic gate across the access road and the outline of a small guard hut hidden in a bush.

For five full minutes he studied the grounds around the house. When he looked up, he said, "To do this right will take nearly an hour. We have to approach all the guard positions carefully, several of them at the same time."

"How many guards?" asked Bromhead again.

"At least eight," answered Fetterman, "but I can see spots for another half dozen. We'll have to hit each of those because we can't assume they'll be unmanned."

He pointed across the dip in the terrain. "You see the giant tree near that finger of the reservoir? Well, if they put a guy there, he can watch four other positions. We'll have to take all five at once so that none of them will see us taking any of the others."

"Can we do that?" asked Anderson.

"We're going to have to. Now the guy at the gate we can ignore until the end because he can't really see any of the others. There are one or two other blind spots like that, and we'll hit them last."

"Okay," said Bromhead, taking over. "I see where you're going with this. We slip down the hillside from six different positions and hit six different guards at once. Then move on and take out some more, until we have the area cleared. One guy then goes for the gate guard while the rest of us slip into the house."

"Yes, sir. The coordination is going to have to be almost perfect for it to work."

They crawled back and retrieved the rest of their equipment from the car. Bromhead and Fetterman studied the maps, found the best place for the other car and radioed the position to Tyme, Smith and Bocker. Then Fetterman described the areas they should leave from, each man taking one of the positions that Fetterman was describing. As the last thing, he told them that he now had five minutes to one. At one o'clock they would jump off, and each of them would have to be in position no later than one-thirty. They couldn't afford to waste any more time than that. If they didn't hurry, they could assume that the captain would be killed, as would Miss Morrow. Bromhead nodded his approval of the plan, and Fetterman told them to begin.

As they reached the crest of the hill again, Bromhead said, "It wasn't much of a plan."

"No, sir. But we're stuck way out here without the benefit of artillery, air support or good prior recon. All we can do is try to approach the house without being seen, then enter it."

"I know," answered Bromhead, "but that doesn't mean I have to like it."

When they were in position, Bromhead took his pistol and stuck it in his pocket. He figured it would be hard to draw quickly, but he wasn't as likely to lose it as if he had it stuck in the waistband of his pants. Then he pulled his knife with its razor-sharp blade. He used some mud to dull the shine so that he wouldn't inadvertently alert the enemy. He noticed that Fetterman was ready, then looked far to the right. He could just see Anderson's back as the big man, hidden from the house by the hill, was running along, trying to get to his place nearly five hundred yards away.

When the second hand on his watch touched the twelve, letting him know that the five minutes had passed, Bromhead began to crawl down the hill, staying in the high grass, following the natural contour of the ground as it sloped downward. Occasionally he would look up over the grass, sighting his target. He wasn't hurrying but moving slowly, using the noise of the wind through the grass to mask the sounds of his movement. He stopped once to look at his watch, saw that he had plenty of time and slowed down. He didn't want to get too close to his man too soon. Although he didn't believe in ESP, he knew that the presence of another human could be detected on some subliminal level by some people. He couldn't see any reason to give his man a chance to play that game.

He was fifteen yards from the guard when he thought he heard a high-pitched scream from the house. It sounded like a woman's voice, and the sound was quickly cut off. The man in front of him snickered at the sound of pain.

Bromhead looked at his watch and realized that the laughing man now had less than five minutes to live.

As time began to run out for the guard, Bromhead started his slow, soundless crawl forward. The man was facing the house now, his attention drawn by the scream. It made Bromhead's job that much easier because the guard should have been studying the hillside around him. Any threat would come from the countryside, not from the house.

At that moment Bromhead heard something to his right and then, through the tall grass, saw it. Anderson had grabbed his man a little early, and in the struggle the two had stood. Bromhead's target heard the noise and turned to look, raising his AK-47 as he did. Bromhead leaped the last few feet, hitting the sentry in the back with his shoulder and sending him to the ground. Before he could recover, Bromhead plunged the knife into the guard's back to the hilt. There was a bubbling of blood around the wound as the knife pierced the man's lung. Bromhead twisted the blade, jerking it to the right as he held the man's face pressed to the soft earth.

Underneath him the lookout spasmed once, kicked his leg and then bucked as if trying to dislodge Bromhead. He kicked again and made a strange, gagging sound in his throat as he died. Bromhead jerked his knife clear, watching the blood drip from the blade.

Anderson, never realizing that he had been almost shot from behind, grabbed the guard he had stalked and stood him up. They faced each other for an instant, then Anderson seized the man's ears and twisted as sharply and quickly as he could. He snapped the man's neck easily and let the body drop to the ground. He went to one knee then, crouching near a tree and waited to see what the others were going to do. He couldn't see or hear anything. He just waited for the five minutes he was supposed to, then started off toward his second target.

Fetterman dispatched his mark quickly and professionally. He came up behind him quietly, slipped a hand over the nose and chin holding the mouth shut, and cut the man's throat with a clean swipe of his knife. With the guard dead, Fetterman laid the body down in the grass, checked it and found a ring of keys, a radio and, most important, a weapon with spare ammo. Fetterman was tempted to take the keys but was afraid they would jingle at the wrong moment so he left them. He made sure that the radio would not work again without major repair and then took the weapon and ammo. He checked the load and the spare magazines. That finished, he moved off toward the next guard.

Bromhead had no trouble with his second target. He could see evidence that a guard sometimes used that position but hadn't in the last few days. He crawled to the middle of it and stopped where he could watch the house. There were more screams coming from it, and although he couldn't really recognize the voice, he was sure it was Morrow's.

The drawn-out shriek seemed to hang in the air, then lose some of its human quality, and Bromhead wanted to rush forward, burst through the front door and save her. He knew it was a stupid plan and would result in them all dying, but the sound of the pain in the house was almost enough to make him forget rational thought. Under his breath he damned Fetterman and Gerber for getting Morrow into the trouble she was in even as he realized it wasn't their fault. It was her own. He just didn't want to think about what was happening to her.

Fetterman's luck with his second target was not as good as Bromhead's. But his man was not moving and was not looking around. He was sitting, a rifle across his knees. It looked as if he had gone to sleep in the warm sunlight of the lazy afternoon, but Fetterman didn't believe it. Slowly he got to his feet, keeping his head and shoulders low so that he couldn't be seen from the house. Taking a step toward the man, he measured the distance and then leaped. He jammed his knee into the man's back as he seized him by the chin, jerking his head up so that he could use the knife again. The master sergeant sliced at the throat with such strength that he nearly severed the head from the body. He let the man slump to his side and began checking him for other weapons. Fetterman added a pistol to his collection and then broke open the rifle, taking the bolt and the trigger housing so that the weapon was useless.

Anderson made short work of the second sentry that he found. He came up behind the man who was urinating on a small bush. Without a word or a sound, Anderson kicked the man's feet from under him so that he fell to his back, and as he did, Anderson stomped on his throat, crushing it. The man's face went pale, then bright red and purple. He clawed at his neck, ripping the skin and leaving long, bloody gouges as his eyes bulged. The guard's feet began drumming on the ground as he slowly strangled.

To stop the noise, Anderson used his knife. He plunged it into the man's chest and drew it out. The wound was traumatic, and the shock killed the guard.

Like the other team members, Anderson searched him, picking up an extra weapon and ammo but leaving the radio alone. He then began moving toward the house as he had been instructed to do. He tried to come up on it slowly, carefully, so that anyone inside would not notice his approach.

He reached the rendezvous before everyone except Fetterman, who was crouched behind a large bush, watching the house. There were still screams coming from it, but they had lost some of the intensity. Fetterman suspected that the enemy in there, savoring their power, were giving their victim a chance to recover so that the show would be that much better for them. He knew from the screams that Morrow wasn't in danger of dying soon because she had too much energy. With luck they would have her and the captain freed in less than fifteen minutes.

When the rest of the team arrived, they took an inventory of the weapons and found that each now had two pistols, ammo for both and nearly everyone had either a rifle or an AK. Fetterman nodded, figuring they had more than enough to take the house and kill every enemy soldier in it. He had thought to kill only every Chinese in it but decided that the North Vietnamese might have supplied some of the men for the venture.

Quietly, almost without speaking, they made the final plans, mapping the doors and windows they would hit and how they would do it. Bocker was detailed to move a hundred yards down the road and ambush anyone who came up that way. Fetterman said he thought there should only be one man coming from that direction but wasn't certain. They didn't need a bunch of people showing up behind them. Bocker nodded his understanding.

Bromhead then looked at his watch, as if they were going to synchronize again, but said, "Everyone straight on what we're going to do?"

"We take any prisoners?" asked Anderson half seriously.

Bromhead looked at Fetterman, knowing how he felt about the Chinese officer. They had discussed it at length at the camp when they were both still in Vietnam, and he suspected that Fetterman would want to try.

But Fetterman, said, "You see him, you kill him. You don't give him a chance because if you do, he'll eat you alive. If he's standing in front of you with his hands up, he dies anyway. We take no more chances with that son of a bitch. He's too dangerous to live."

"Sarge—" Tyme started to say.

"Boom-Boom, kill him. Just remember that he is the one who planned the assassination of Ian. He was the one who planned our capture in Vietnam, and he is indirectly responsible for the deaths of every member of our team since we arrived in Vietnam. He knows the rules of the game and has elected to play."

Bromhead nodded at Bocker and said, "We'll go in three minutes. That's all the time you get."

"I'll be ready." He got to his feet, glanced at the house as if to check the position of the windows and began to move up the road using all the cover available, dodging from cars to bushes to the trunks of trees.

When he was out of sight, Bromhead said, "Let's do it."

IN THE HOUSE, the Chinese officer started slowly, figuring he had all the time he wanted. At first he made sure that Morrow and Gerber understood the nature of her helplessness. One of the others fondled her, watching her squirm as his hands rubbed her and pinched her. Each time Gerber so much as shifted his weight, one of his guards would point a weapon or cock a pistol until he relaxed.

Finally they tired of that because they were getting no real reactions from it. One of the men left the room and returned, carrying a small box with electrical cords on both ends. He set it on the desk in front of his superior and bowed his way back to his position.

"This," said the Chinese man, "is exactly what you think. A variation on the old field phone trick. I attach the electrical leads to sensitive portions of Miss Morrow's body, and with this rheostat, I can increase the voltage from a very mild, somewhat sexually arousing current to something that is quite painful. In fact, we can increase the power to such an extent that our victim will snap her own bones with her muscular contractions. Interesting, don't you think?"

Gerber couldn't think of anything that he found less interesting. But he wasn't concerned about that. He was more worried about the rest of the team because if they didn't arrive soon, it would be too late for them to be of any help. He wondered if they had somehow lost him and couldn't find him.

While he worried about that, the Chinese man watched as the electrodes were taped to Morrow's body. He then stood, walked to her and repositioned one of them so that it would be in a more sensitive location on her thigh. He checked the ropes to make sure she was securely fastened to the chair. That done, he smiled at her and patted her cheek.

"Now we shall see what you are made of, Captain," he told Gerber. "How much will you let her suffer before you have to try to stop it? Oh, you'll fail, but how long can you watch?"

He spun the rheostat, and Morrow's body contracted as the electricity coursed through it. With the gag in her mouth, she couldn't scream. When the pain stopped, she collapsed against the chair and felt the sweat bead on her body. She tried to cry out but didn't have the energy.

After several minutes of that, with Morrow becoming numb, the leader said, "I think that gag is inhibiting her. Please remove it." He then issued the order in Chinese so that there would be no mistake. "Now," he said, "let's see how long she can hold out."

He used the rheostat again and was very pleased with the piercing scream from Morrow. He nodded his approval. "I should have thought of that sooner. She didn't need the gag. It is much better this way." He looked at Gerber. "Don't you think so?"

IT TOOK THE TEAM only two minutes to get into attack position. After they had the house surrounded, they all moved to it so that each was standing beside the window or door he was supposed to use. Since they didn't want to give anyone a chance, they were all going to try to move at the same second. The first shot, however, would signal the assault if the time hadn't come yet.

As they all touched the house, there came a bloodcurdling shriek from inside, and that told Fetterman which room he wanted to hit.

Inside the house one of the men approached the Chinese man and whispered something to him. He gave the rheostat a sadistic twist that sent Morrow into a spasm of pain, then shut it off rapidly. He stepped across the room to where one of the guards stood at the door and said, "You say that the outside men have not reported in? Any of them?"

"None."

He assumed immediately that something had happened to the radio and started to the radio room to check it out. He didn't hear the Special Forces men step onto the porch or position themselves around the house.

It had taken them nearly three hours to get to that point from the time of the phone call. A lot had happened and more was about to. Fetterman studied the second hand of his watch as it crept around until it struck the zero minute. Without hesitation he turned and leaped through the window, shattering the glass and splintering the wood of the frame as he rolled into the house. He landed on his shoulder and came up with a pistol in each hand. He saw a flash of movement to his right and turned to meet it. He fired once, and the bullet took the man in the head, exploding out the back in a fountain of crimson. He died before he even knew that the house had been invaded.

Bromhead came through the other window and nearly landed on top of one of the Oriental guards. Both tumbled to the floor, but Bromhead had his pistols out. He pulled the triggers of the two he held. One bullet missed completely, burying itself in the floor, but the other went through his adversary's side, working its way into his leg and severing the femoral artery. He had a few seconds to realize that he had been killed before his blood jetted out of his body, staining the hardwood floor and the carpeting, pooling under him.

As the windows shattered, Gerber kicked out, striking the crotch of one of the men standing near him. The man went down with a high-pitched shriek. Gerber grabbed the man's hand, wrenching the gun from it. He turned it on the other guard and shot him four times in the chest. The slugs printed such a tight pattern it could have been covered by a quarter, and each would have been fatal. He spun then and kicked the screaming man in the head, trying to punt it into the lake outside the house.

With all the guards in the room either dead or out of commission and stripped of their weapons, Fetterman shouted, "Where is the son of a bitch?"

"Through there," gestured Gerber. "Just seconds in front of you."

Fetterman waved at Bromhead, and together they ran for the door. Bromhead wanted to stop to see how Morrow was, but Gerber was there, and he would have to take care of her. Bromhead needed to support Fetterman.

As the two of them ran from the room, Gerber went to Morrow, crouching in front of her. He untied the blindfold but held it in front of her eyes to protect them from the sudden light. He whispered to her, "I'm going to remove the blindfold."

When she nodded, he let the cloth drop away, and for the first time in a long time, he could see her whole face. He didn't like what he saw. There were pain lines etched among the bruises and dried blood. He looked deep into her emerald eyes and saw something dancing back there but wasn't sure if it was an accusation or relief.

From somewhere in the house, he could hear shooting. Single shots from pistols and maybe some from a rifle or two, but none from AKs. There were flurries of firing and then silence, followed by more as his men began to clear the house room by room.

Gerber was kneeling in front of Morrow, unsure of what to do next. He reached around her, felt the ropes that bound her wrists but couldn't get at the knots. They were pulled too tight. He glanced over her shoulder and saw that her hands were discolored, an ugly purple from where the rope bit into her flesh. He didn't want to move from in front of her but had to if he was going to free her from the ropes. A knife lay next to the dead man by the door. Gerber picked it up and slit the ropes. Morrow didn't react. Her arms swung forward and hung at her sides, devoid of muscular control.

Using the knife, Gerber cut away the rest of the ropes. Although free at last, Morrow didn't move. Gently Gerber reached out and lifted her. She staggered to her feet, trying to maintain her balance, like a child about to take its first steps. Then with some effort she lifted her arms, slipping them around his neck as if she were afraid that he would get away. Or maybe afraid that if she let go, she would discover that she was still being held captive and the rescue was just a dream.

Gerber's soldier instincts were to help his men, but he figured they could take care of the rest. He was needed right where he was. He carefully disengaged himself from Morrow so that he could look for some type of apparel for her. He almost didn't do it when he saw the look on her face, as if she thought he were deserting her.

In a hall closet he found a short silk robe. He took it from the hanger and draped it around Morrow's shoulders. She stood stiffly, as if afraid to move now that the blood was beginning to circulate freely in her hands and feet. She clenched her teeth as the pain, much more severe than the normal tingling from a limb that had gone to sleep, hit her. She moaned softly, and tears trickled down her cheeks as she struggled to keep from crying out.

Gerber took her in his arms and held her against his chest. She lapsed into a paroxysm of uncontrollable shivering, which seemed to match the chatter of automatic weapons fire echoing through the house.

19

As soon as he saw that the captain was all right, Fetterman ran for the open door opposite where he was standing. He stopped for a moment next to the doorjamb, his back against the wall, listening for sounds beyond the opening. He glanced at Bromhead, who was on the other side of the entranceway, facing him. When he nodded, they burst through, but the hallway was empty except for the body of an Oriental. In the room across the hall, there were two more bodies but no sign of the other Americans who had broken through the windows there.

From upstairs Fetterman heard the sound of running feet, and he pointed upward. He leaped the first few steps, then started moving slowly toward the landing, keeping to the side, almost leaning on the dark, wooden rail so that there was less chance of the risers squeaking.

Bromhead followed a few feet behind him and on the opposite side of the staircase, keeping his back to the wall. He still held two pistols, one pointed upstairs and one down.

As they gained the landing, Fetterman halted because he was in a bad position. Bromhead could work his way across it, keeping his back against the wall and get a view of part of the second floor without having to expose himself too much.

When Bromhead was across and had a foot on the next step, he waved to Fetterman, who nearly leaped forward. Just as he did, Bromhead heard something above him, stepped up and saw the foot and shin of someone. He held up a hand to tell Fetterman to stop and then took careful aim. He pulled the trigger and was rewarded by a scream as a man fell to his side, grabbing at his shattered shin. As soon as he fell into view, Bromhead fired twice more. The bullets hit the man in the chest, rolling him to his back as he died.

Together they rushed up the stairs, figuring that anyone who had been in the upstairs hallway or watching would have ducked back into the rooms there. They would have a couple of seconds when no one would be watching.

Just as they thought, the hallway was empty, the hardwood floor bare. Now, below them, they heard a few shots and realized that one of the other team members had found something. Both men resisted the temptation to run back to see what was happening.

Instead, Fetterman turned to his right and kicked at the door there, hitting it near the knob. The wood splintered but did not give way. Rather than kick it again, Fetterman dived to the left as someone inside opened fire, putting four rounds through it.

Bromhead turned his back to that situation, watching the hallway. Someone poked a head out, and Bromhead snapped off a shot, smashing the doorframe near the face.

At that moment Fetterman kicked the door again, and as it swung open, he dived through it, landing on his stomach. He saw a shadow slide by him, rolled as someone fired, the bullets chewing up the floor where Fetterman had been.

Fetterman fired five times without aiming, tracking his weapon when he saw the shadow move. Two of the bullets struck the enemy in the shoulder, one in the chest and one in the stomach. The last one ripped through the man's pants, burning his leg but not doing any real damage. Not that it mattered. The man was dead as he hit the floor, his blood staining his clothes and the carpet.

Bromhead leaped through the door. "You all right?"

"No problem. This isn't the right guy, either."

"I think there's only one more guy up here. I took a shot at him but missed."

Fetterman got to his feet, checked the loads in his weapon and then picked up the pistol dropped by the enemy. He stuffed it into his back pocket. Then he moved to the door and peeked through it.

Quickly they went down the hall, peering into open doorways. There were places to hide but nothing obvious, and there was no good cover. Nothing that would really stop a bullet. But they had to hurry because they had yet to find the Chinese officer, and Fetterman was sure that the guy would have an escape hatch.

They took positions on either side of the only closed door left and waited for an instant. Fetterman nodded that he was ready. Bromhead's foot lashed out, impacting on the wood near the lock. The door crashed inward, slamming against the wall. Bromhead only had time to leap clear before someone opened fire with an AK-47 on full auto.

But the man was apparently watching Bromhead so intently that he never saw Fetterman, who jerked off a quick round. The bullet hit the enemy's weapon, cracking some of the wood, forcing the barrel away from Bromhead. The man pulled the trigger, stitching the floor with a short burst.

Fetterman fired again, and the man's head seemed to disintegrate into a cloud of crimson. He flopped backward, one shoulder landing against an antique table, knocking it over. A lamp crashed to the floor, shards of glass spraying across it.

From downstairs they heard a single shot, and Fetterman knew instinctively that it was the Chinese guy. He looked at Bromhead as if to confirm his belief and then ran from the room, racing downstairs.

IN THE LIBRARY, Gerber knelt near Morrow, who was now sitting in one of the wing chairs. Her eyes were closed, and her hands rested in her lap, the angry red welts from the ropes evident around them. Her breathing was slow and regular, almost as if she were asleep.

Gerber had kept his eye on the man he had kicked, and as he rolled over, trying to reach a weapon, Gerber had kicked him again, this time in the chin. The man lost consciousness then, and Gerber bound his wrists with the rope that he had cut from Morrow's body.

At the sounds of gunfire, Gerber would look at the wall or the ceiling, as if he could see through to the battle. There were sounds of bodies hitting the floor, and Gerber ached to run from the room, but he felt he had an obligation to Morrow. He felt somehow responsible for the ordeal she had had to face during the past few hours and it was his duty to stay with her.

As one battle erupted upstairs, Morrow opened her eyes and caught Gerber looking. She knew that the horror and trauma of the past few hours was so close that she was in a state of shock. But she knew that Gerber wanted to help his men.

She reached out, touched his shoulder and said simply, "Go on, Kirk. Do what you have to."

Gerber started at the sound of her voice and then reached up to pat her hand. "You're sure? You'll be okay?"

"Go. Please."

Gerber stepped to the door, stopped and looked out. He saw Fetterman running down the stairs followed by Bromhead. "Tony, what's the situation?"

"Think we've got the upstairs cleared. Going to check on the guys in the back now. Haven't found him yet."

"You got an extra pistol?"

Fetterman jerked the one in his rear pocket clear and handed it to Gerber, who immediately checked the clip. There were only five rounds in it, but he didn't think he would need more than that.

There was another shot, and the three of them ran toward the back of the house. There was a door leading into the kitchen, but they didn't hesitate at it. They all burst through, Gerber going one way, Bromhead the other and Fetterman straight ahead.

Tyme was sitting slumped on the floor, a pistol held in one hand. His fingers were stained with blood. He smiled up at them. "He missed me, almost. It was close, but it doesn't mean much."

"Where are the others?" asked Gerber.

"Downstairs. It's a whopping huge cellar down there."

Gerber frowned. Houses in Hong Kong didn't have cellars. Then he remembered the previous owner, probably some eccentric Englishman who needed to be reminded of home.

"Where are the stairs?"

Tyme nodded. "Through there. There's some kind of mudroom or pantry and a door to the left. Big window on the right. Stairs are in there."

There was a shout then, bubbling up through the floor, and they couldn't tell whether it was an American or Chinese. Then there were running steps on the wooden stairs as two shots were fired from below. Through the kitchen door they saw the cellar door fly open, and all three of them fired at once as a figure flashed by them and leaped headfirst toward the window.

Fetterman was the first to react because he had recognized the Chinese bastard. It was a brief glimpse, but he saw enough to know.

He crossed the floor in two giant jumps and reached the window. Outside, he could see the man fleeing across the grass, down the slope toward the reservoir. Fetterman dropped one of his pistols and used his other hand to steady his aim. For a moment everything that he knew about shooting came to mind, but his brain was moving too slowly so he forced the thoughts out and let his instincts take over. Carefully, cautiously, he squeezed the trigger, letting the weapon fire itself when it was ready.

It seemed to take the bullet forever to reach its target. He thought he had missed because the man kept running, but he staggered once, began running again and fell forward. Fetterman climbed through the window, keeping his eyes on the spot where his target had fallen, knowing instinctively that he wasn't dead.

It was like something from a horror movie. Just as everyone thought the monster was dead, it came back again, stronger than ever. The Chinese guy didn't just get to his feet, he exploded to them, running hard for the reservoir, as if there were some kind of sanctuary there.

Fetterman dropped to the ground and aimed again. His shot missed.

But the man seemed to be running slower, as if the life, the energy, was seeping from him. He stumbled slightly, regained his balance and then began a second sprint.

Fetterman took off after him, trying to reduce the range between the two of them. The master sergeant was stronger and seemed to be gaining strength as he moved. Fetterman felt he would catch the man soon before he got much farther away.

Suddenly the fugitive swerved to the right and ran out on a small pier that Fetterman had never seen. It looked as if he were walking on water.

Fetterman skidded to a halt, believing that there was no way he could catch the man if there was a boat hidden there. He had never considered the landlocked reservoir as an escape route, but if the man had a boat, he could lose the Special Forces men before they could find a way around the lake. He could lose himself in the New Territories and make his way back to Red China before any of them could get to a car and drive around the lake.

He raised his pistol, aimed and pulled the trigger. There was no reaction by the enemy. Fetterman fired again and again and kept firing until the slide locked back and the trigger jammed tight. He dropped his hand to his side and watched as the Chinese guy suddenly jerked upright, took one step forward and toppled into the water.

"Got you, you fucking bastard," said Fetterman. "Finally got you."

As he stood watching the shoreline, waiting for the man to reappear, he was joined by Bromhead and Gerber, neither sure what to say or if they should say anything at all.

"I'll check it out," said Fetterman. "I saw him go into the lake."

Bromhead started to speak, but Gerber stopped him. He said, "We'll go back up to the house and get ready to move out. Meet you there in twenty minutes or so."

They split up. Gerber and Bromhead found Smith and Anderson helping Tyme to his feet. He was laughing at them, trying to convince them that his wound was not very serious.

"Hell," he said, "I've hurt myself worse sliding into third base. This is nothing."

"You see anything or anyone else downstairs?" asked Gerber.

"No, sir. It's a maze down there—that's how he got behind us."

"Don't worry about it," said Gerber. "Let's just get everyone together and get the hell out. We don't need to find anyone else."

They hurried back through the house. Only Gerber entered the room where Morrow sat. She hadn't moved during the final action. Gerber had no idea how long it had taken. He moved to her and took her hand, squeezing it gently to let her know that he was there.

"We're getting out, Robin," he said.

She turned her head, staring at him, and said one word, "Good."

They all moved outside. Bromhead whistled once and then shouted, "Galvin! Let's get the fuck out of here."

Tyme pointed to the cars and said, "Anyone know how to hot wire those things?"

"Won't have to," said Smith. "There are keys in them."

Gerber said, "You guys go on without me. I'll wait for Fetterman. We'll all meet back at the hotel and then scatter. Back to the World or whatever. Oh, and tell Larko he can let Muffin go. She can't hurt us now. Thank him for his help."

They began to pile into the cars, all but Morrow. She stood her ground and said, "I'll wait with you."

"Robin, you really should get to a doctor. You've had a very rough time."

"I'll wait with you," she repeated dully.

Gerber looked to the others for help, but they offered none. Then Bromhead reached out and took her elbow. "Robin, let us take you to a doctor."

"No," she said quietly. "I'll wait here with Mack. I'm all right now. I want to stay."

Gerber finally said, "Okay. We'll catch up as soon as Fetterman gets here."

They both watched the others climb into two cars and take off. They didn't stop to open the gate but just smashed through it. None of them looked back.

Gerber opened a door of the car that was left there and helped Morrow in. He said, "You sure that you're all right? The last few days have been rough."

She tried to smile. "I ache all over and I think I have a broken rib. I've a couple of cuts on my face, but they'll only leave tiny scars. Those bastards didn't really do any permanent damage." She almost giggled. "They would have, but you showed up in time."

"Robin, I'm really sorry about all this. I—"

"Don't be sorry. It's not your fault. I'm the one who followed you. I'm the one who left you at the police station while I flitted back to the room, and I'm the one who opened the damned door when that bastard knocked on it. It's really my fault."

"Okay, you win. Listen, when we get back to the hotel, you want to make some arrangements?"

"Arrangements to do what?" she asked.

"Arrangements for us to go somewhere to rest and relax. Somewhere on the other side of the world. Maybe Hawaii or Bermuda or something." He held up a hand to ward off the protest that he expected and said all too fast, "I don't mean anything by that. I just thought that we might travel together as friends."

"Jesus," she said, "are all men as stupid as you? Yes, I'll take a trip with you. And I'm not worried about my virtue, especially now."

Before Gerber could respond, Fetterman reappeared. "I hit the guy," he said. "Twice. I know that. I saw him go into the water. I couldn't find the body."

Gerber looked at Morrow and smiled at her for some reason that he didn't fully understand. To Fetterman, he said, "Don't worry about it. It's over now. We can all go back to the hotel, then get out of Hong Kong. We more than made up for Ian's death."

"I couldn't find the body. Found blood on the dock," he said. "Found quite a lot of it, but I couldn't find the body."

Fetterman slid in beside Morrow, and Gerber walked around the front so that he could open the driver's door. "Don't worry about it," repeated Gerber as he started the engine. "You got him. I'm sure you did. He's not supernatural, he was just very good."

"I don't like it, Captain," said Fetterman. "I'm not going to be happy until I can touch his body and make sure there is no pulse."

"As I said, he is not supernatural. He eluded us in Vietnam only because he could use the border as a barrier to protect himself. He just let us catch him off guard here, away from the border. Hell, Tony, he was very good. You were better. That's all there is to it."

"Are you sure?" asked Fetterman, wanting to believe it.

"Of course. Now let's get out of here."

GLOSSARY

AC—Aircraft Commander; pilot in charge of the aircraft.

ACTUAL—Actual unit commander as opposed to the radio telephone operator (RTO) for that unit.

AFVN—Armed Forces radio and television network in Vietnam. Army PFC Pat Sajak was probably the most memorable of AFVN's DJs with his loud and long, "GOOOOOOOOOOOOD MORNing! Vietnam." The Spinning Wheel of Fortune gives no clues about his whereabouts today.

AK-47—Soviet assault rifle normally used by the North Vietnamese and Vietcong.

AO—Area of Operations.

AO DAI—Long dresslike garment, split up the sides and worn over pants.

AP ROUNDS—Armor-piercing ammunition.

ARVN—Army of the Republic of Vietnam; a South Vietnamese soldier. Also known as Marvin Arvin.

ASH AND TRASH—Single ship flights by helicopters taking care of a variety of missions such as flying cargo, supplies, mail and people among the various small camps in Vietnam, for anyone who needed aviation support.

BAR—Browning Automatic Rifle.

BEAUCOUP—Many.

BISCUIT—C-rations; combat rations.

BLOWER—See *Horn*.

BODY COUNT—Number of enemy killed, wounded or captured during an operation. Used by Saigon and Washington as a means of measuring the progress of the war.

BOOM-BOOM—Term used by Vietnamese prostitutes to sell their product.

BOONDOGGLE—Any military operation that hasn't been completely thought out. An operation that is ridiculous.

BOONIE HATS—Soft cap worn by the grunts in the field when they were not wearing steel pots.

BUSHMASTER—Jungle warfare expert or soldier skilled in jungle navigation. Also a large deadly snake not common to Vietnam but mighty tasty.

C-123—Small cargo airplane; Caribou.

C-130—Medium cargo airplane; Hercules.

C AND C—Command and Control aircraft that circles overhead to direct the combined air and ground operations.

CARIBOU—Cargo transport plane; C-123.

CHINOOK—Army Aviation twin engine helicopter; CH-47; shit hook.

CHIEU HOI LEAFLETS—Propaganda leaflets telling the enemy that they would be well treated if they surrendered.

CHURCH KEY—Beer can opener used in the days before pop tops.

CLAYMORE—Antipersonnel mine that fires 750 steel balls with a lethal range of 50 meters.

CLOSE AIR SUPPORT—Use of airplanes and helicopters to fire on enemy units near friendlies.

CO CONG—Term referring to female Vietcong.

DAI UY—Vietnamese Army rank equivalent to Captain.

DCI—Director, Central Intelligence. The director of the Central Intelligence Agency.

DEROS—Date Estimated Return from Overseas.

DONG—A unit of North Vietnamese money about equal to an American penny.

FIIGMO—Fuck It, I've Got My Orders.

FIVE—Radio call sign for the Executive Officer of a unit.

FNG—Fucking New Guy.

FOOGAS—Jellied gas similar to napalm.

FREEDOM BIRD—Name given to any aircraft that took troops out of Vietnam. Usually referred to the commercial jet flights that took men back to the World.

FRENCH FORT—Distinctive, triangular-shaped structure built by the hundreds by the French.

FUBAR—Fucked Up Beyond All Recognition.

GARAND—M-1 rifle, which was replaced by the M-14. Issued to the Vietnamese early in the war.

GO-TO-HELL RAG—Towel or any large cloth worn around the neck by grunts.

GRUNT—Infantryman.

GUARD THE RADIO—Term meaning to stand by in the commo bunker listening for messages.

GUNSHIP—Armed helicopter or cargo plane that carries weapons instead of cargo.

HE—High-explosive ammunition.

HIT THE HEAD—Go to the bathroom. A navy term.

HOOTCH—Almost any shelter, from temporary to long-term.

HORN—Specific kind of radio operations that use satellites to rebroadcast messages.

HORSE—See *Biscuit*.

HOTEL THREE—Helicopter landing area at Saigon's Tan Son Nhut Air Force Base.

HUEY—Bell helicopter. Called a Huey because its original designation was HU, but later changed to UH. Called a Slick.

IN-COUNTRY—Term referring to American troops operating in South Vietnam. They were all in-country.

INTELLIGENCE—Any information about the enemy operations. It can include troop movements, weapons capabilities, biographies of enemy commanders and general information about terrain features. It is any information that would be useful in planning a mission.

KA BAR—Type of military combat knife.

KIA—Killed In Action. (Since the U.S. was not engaged in a declared war, the use of KIA was not authorized. KIA came to mean enemy dead. Americans were KHA or Killed in Hostile Action.)

KLICK—One thousand meters; a kilometer.

LBJ—Long Binh Jail.

LEGS—Derogatory term for regular infantry used by airborne qualified troops.

LIMA LIMA—Land line. Telephone communications between two points on the ground.

LLDB—Luc Luong Dac Biet; South Vietnamese Special Forces. Sometimes referred to as the Look Long, Duck Back.

LP—Listening Post. Position outside the perimeter manned by a couple of soldiers to warn of enemy activity.

LZ—Landing Zone.

M-14—Standard rifle of the U.S. Army, eventually replaced by the M-16. It fires the standard NATO 7.62 mm round.

M-16—Became the standard infantry weapon of the Vietnam War. It fires 5.56 mm ammunition.

M-79—Short-barreled, shoulder-fired weapon that fires a 40 mm grenade. These can be high explosive, white phosphorus or canister.

MACV—Military Assistance Command, Vietnam. Replaced MAAG in 1964.

MEDEVAC—Medical Evacuation; Dustoff. Helicopter used to take wounded to medical facilities.

MIA—Missing In Action.

NCO—Noncommissioned Officer; noncom; sergeant.

NEXT—The man who says he's the next to be rotated home. See *Short-Timer*.

NINETEEN—Average age of the combat soldier in Vietnam, in contrast to age twenty-six in the Second World War.

NOUC-MAM—Foul-smelling (to the Americans, at least) fermented fish sauce used by the Vietnamese as a condiment. GIs nicknamed it "armpit sauce."

NVA—North Vietnamese Army. Also used to designate a soldier from North Vietnam.

OD—Olive drab; standard military color.

OPERATION BOOTSTRAP—Program in the Army to help men on active duty complete their college education. Men in the program were still considered to be on active duty.

P-38—Military designation for the small, one-piece can opener supplied with C-rations.

PCOD—Personnel Coming Off Duty.

PETER PILOT—Co-pilot of a helicopter.

POW—Prisoner Of War.

PRC-10—Portable radio.

PRC-25—Standard infantry radio used in Vietnam. Sometimes called "Prick 25."

PROGUES—Derogatory term describing fat, lazy people who inhabited rear areas, taking all the best supplies for themselves and leaving the rest for the men in the field.

PSP—Perforated Steel Plate. Used instead of pavement for runways and roadways.

PULL PITCH—Term used by helicopter pilots that means they are going to take off.

PUNGI STAKE—Sharpened bamboo hidden to penetrate the foot, sometimes dipped in feces.

QT—Quick Time. It came to mean talking to someone quietly on the side rather than operating in official channels.

R AND R—Rest and Relaxation. The term came to mean a trip outside of Vietnam where the soldier could forget about the war.

RF STRIKERS—Local military forces recruited and employed inside a province. Known as Regional Forces.

RINGKNOCKER—A graduate of military academy. The term refers to the ring worn by all graduates.

RON—Remain Overnight.

RP—Rally Point.

RPD—7.62 mm Soviet light machine gun.

RTO—Radiotelephone Operator; radio man of a unit.

RULES OF ENGAGEMENT—Rules telling American troops when they could fire and when they couldn't. Full Supression meant that they could fire all the way in on a landing. Normal Rules meant that they could return fire for fire received. Negative Suppression meant that they weren't to shoot back.

SAPPER—Enemy soldier used in demolitions. Uses explosives during attacks.

SIX—Radio call sign for the unit commander.

SHIT HOOK—Name applied by troops to the Chinook helicopter because of all the ''shit'' stirred up by the massive rotors.

SHORT—Term used by a GI in Vietnam to tell all who would listen that his tour was almost over.

SHORT-TIMER—GI who had been in Vietnam for nearly a year and who would be rotated back to the World soon. When the DEROS (Date of Estimated Return from Overseas) was the shortest in the unit, the person was said to be ''Next.''

SKS—Simonov 7.62 mm semiautomatic carbine.

SFOB—Special Forces Operations Base.

SMG—Submachine gun.

SOI—Signal Operating Instructions. The booklet that contained the call signs and radio frequencies of the units in Vietnam.

SOP—Standard Operating Procedure.

STEEL POT—Standard U.S. Army helmet. The steel pot was the outer metal cover.

TAI—Vietnamese ethnic group living in the mountainous regions.

TDY—Temporary Duty.

THREE—Radio call sign of the Operations Officer.

THREE CORPS—Military area around Saigon. Vietnam was divided into four corps areas.

THE WORLD—The United States.

TOC—Tactical Operations Center.

TWO—Radio call sign for the Intelligence Officer.

VC—Vietcong. Also called Victor Charlie (phonetic alphabet) or Charlie.

VIETCONG—Contraction of Vietnam Cong San. A guerrilla member of the Vietnamese Communist movement.

VIETCONG SAN—Vietnamese communists. A term used since 1956.

VNAF—South Vietnamese Air Force.

WIA—Wounded In Action.

WILLIE PETE—WP; white phosphorus; smoke rounds. Also used as antipersonnel weapons.

XO—Executive Officer of a unit.

ZAP—To ding, pop caps or shoot. To kill.

TAKE 'EM NOW

FOLDING SUNGLASSES
FROM GOLD EAGLE

Mean up your act with these tough, street-smart shades. Practical, too, because they fold 3 times into a handy, zip-up polyurethane pouch that fits neatly into your pocket. Rugged metal frame. Scratch-resistant acrylic lenses. Best of all, they can be yours for only $6.99. **MAIL ORDER TODAY.**

Send your name, address, and zip code, along with a check or money order for just $6.99 + .75¢ for postage and handling (for a total of $7.74) payable to Gold Eagle Reader Service, a division of Worldwide Library. New York and Arizona residents please add applicable sales tax.

Remove from pouch...

unfold once...

GOLD EAGLE

Gold Eagle Reader Service
901 Fuhrmann Blvd.
P.O. Box 1325
Buffalo, N.Y. 14240-1325

unfold twice...

and they're ready to wear.

GES1–RRR

Offer not available in Canada.

1. How do you rate _____ ?
   (Please print book TITLE)

   1.5 ☐ excellent   .3 ☐ good   .1 ☐ poor
   .4 ☐ very good   .2 ☐ fair

2. How likely are you to purchase another book in this series?
   2.1 ☐ definitely would purchase   .3 ☐ probably would not purchase
   .2 ☐ probably would purchase   .4 ☐ definitely would not purchase

3. How do you compare this book with similar books you usually read?
   3.1 ☐ far better than others   .4 ☐ not as good
   .2 ☐ better than others   .5 ☐ definitely not as good
   .3 ☐ about the same

4. How did you *first* become aware of this book?
   8. ☐ read other books in series   11. ☐ friend's recommendation
   9. ☐ in-store display   12. ☐ ad inside other books
   10. ☐ TV, radio or magazine ad   13. ☐ other _____
   (please specify)

5. What *most* prompted you to buy this book?
   14. ☐ read other books in series   17. ☐ title   20. ☐ story outline on back
   15. ☐ friend's recommendation   18. ☐ author   21. ☐ read a few pages
   16. ☐ picture on cover   19. ☐ advertising   22. ☐ other _____
   (please specify)

6. Please check the statements you feel best describe this book.
   25. ☐ Easy to read
   26. ☐ Realistic conflict
   27. ☐ Original plot
   28. ☐ Story was too short
   29. ☐ Good humor in story
   30. ☐ Liked the subject
   31. ☐ Too predictable
   32. ☐ Not enough description of setting
   33. ☐ Couldn't put the book down
   34. ☐ Slow moving
   35. ☐ Too much violence
   36. ☐ Interesting characters
   37. ☐ Not enough humor
   38. ☐ Didn't like the subject
   39. ☐ Fast paced
   40. ☐ Difficult to read
   41. ☐ Story was too long
   42. ☐ Believable characters
   43. ☐ Not enough suspense
   44. ☐ Unrealistic conflict

7. Have you any additional comments about this book?
   _____
   _____

8. What types of books do you usually like to read?
   47. ☐ Mystery   50. ☐ Espionage/Spy   52. ☐ Action/Adventure
   48. ☐ Horror   51. ☐ Science Fiction   53. ☐ Westerns
   49. ☐ War

9. Have you purchased any books from any of these series in the past 12 months? Approximately how many?

	No. purchased		No. purchased
☐ Mack Bolan	(55) ____	☐ War Dogs	(63) ____
☐ Soldier of Fortune	(56) ____	☐ Able Team	(64) ____
☐ Saigon Commandos	(57) ____	☐ The Destroyer	(65) ____
☐ Death Merchant	(58) ____	☐ The Black Eagles	(66) ____
☐ SOBs	(59) ____	☐ The Assassin	(67) ____
☐ The Survivalist	(60) ____	☐ Vietnam: Ground Zero	(68) ____
☐ Nick Carter	(61) ____	☐ Phoenix Force	(69) ____
☐ TNT	(62) ____	☐ Michael Sheriff: The Shield	(70) ____

10. Please indicate your age group and sex.
    78.1 ☐ Male   79.1 ☐ under 15   .4 ☐ 23-26   .7 ☐ 35-49
    .2 ☐ Female   .2 ☐ 15-18   .5 ☐ 27-30   .8 ☐ 50-64
       .3 ☐ 19-22   .6 ☐ 31-34   .9 ☐ 65 or older

Thank you for completing and returning this questionnaire.

VG9876543

NAME _____
(Please Print)

ADDRESS _____

CITY _____

ZIP CODE _____

BUSINESS REPLY MAIL

FIRST CLASS   PERMIT NO. 717   BUFFALO, NY

POSTAGE WILL BE PAID BY ADDRESSEE

NATIONAL READER SURVEYS

901 Fuhrmann Blvd.
P.O. Box 1395
Buffalo, N.Y. 14240-9961

1. How do you rate _____ ?
   (Please print book TITLE)

   1.5 ☐ excellent   .3 ☐ good   .1 ☐ poor
    .4 ☐ very good   .2 ☐ fair

2. How likely are you to purchase another book in this series?
   2.1 ☐ definitely would purchase   .3 ☐ probably would not purchase
    .2 ☐ probably would purchase   .4 ☐ definitely would not purchase

3. How do you compare this book with similar books you usually read?
   3.1 ☐ far better than others   .4 ☐ not as good
    .2 ☐ better than others   .5 ☐ definitely not as good
    .3 ☐ about the same

4. How did you *first* become aware of this book?
   8. ☐ read other books in series   11. ☐ friend's recommendation
   9. ☐ in-store display   12. ☐ ad inside other books
   10. ☐ TV, radio or magazine ad   13. ☐ other _____
   (please specify)

5. What *most* prompted you to buy this book?
   14. ☐ read other books in series 17. ☐ title 20. ☐ story outline on back
   15. ☐ friend's recommendation 18. ☐ author 21. ☐ read a few pages
   16. ☐ picture on cover 19. ☐ advertising 22. ☐ other _____
   (please specify)

6. Please check the statements you feel best describe this book.
   25. ☐ Easy to read   35. ☐ Too much violence
   26. ☐ Realistic conflict   36. ☐ Interesting characters
   27. ☐ Original plot   37. ☐ Not enough humor
   28. ☐ Story was too short   38. ☐ Didn't like the subject
   29. ☐ Good humor in story   39. ☐ Fast paced
   30. ☐ Liked the subject   40. ☐ Difficult to read
   31. ☐ Too predictable   41. ☐ Story was too long
   32. ☐ Not enough description of setting   42. ☐ Believable characters
   33. ☐ Couldn't put the book down   43. ☐ Not enough suspense
   34. ☐ Slow moving   44. ☐ Unrealistic conflict

7. Have you any additional comments about this book?
   _____
   _____

8. What types of books do you usually like to read?
   47. ☐ Mystery 50. ☐ Espionage/Spy 52. ☐ Action/Adventure
   48. ☐ Horror 51. ☐ Science Fiction 53. ☐ Westerns
   49. ☐ War

9. Have you purchased any books from any of these series in the past 12 months? Approximately how many?

	No. purchased		No. purchased
☐ Mack Bolan	(55) ____	☐ War Dogs	(63) ____
☐ Soldier of Fortune	(56) ____	☐ Able Team	(64) ____
☐ Saigon Commandos	(57) ____	☐ The Destroyer	(65) ____
☐ Death Merchant	(58) ____	☐ The Black Eagles	(66) ____
☐ SOBs	(59) ____	☐ The Assassin	(67) ____
☐ The Survivalist	(60) ____	☐ Vietnam: Ground Zero	(68) ____
☐ Nick Carter	(61) ____	☐ Phoenix Force	(69) ____
☐ TNT	(62) ____	☐ Michael Sheriff: The Shield	(70) ____

10. Please indicate your age group and sex.
    78.1 ☐ Male 79.1 ☐ under 15 .4 ☐ 23-26 .7 ☐ 35-49
     .2 ☐ Female .2 ☐ 15-18 .5 ☐ 27-30 .8 ☐ 50-64
      .3 ☐ 19-22 .6 ☐ 31-34 .9 ☐ 65 or older

Thank you for completing and returning this questionnaire.

PRINTED IN U.S.A.

VG9876543

NAME _____
         (Please Print)

ADDRESS _____

CITY _____

ZIP CODE _____